Ragged Lady

By

William Dean Howells

I

It was their first summer at Middlemount and the Landers did not know the roads. When they came to a place where they had a choice of two, she said that now he must get out of the carry-all and ask at the house standing a little back in the edge of the pine woods, which road they ought to take for South Middlemount. She alleged many cases in which they had met trouble through his perverse reluctance to find out where they were before he pushed rashly forward in their drives. Whilst she urged the facts she reached forward from the back seat where she sat, and held her hand upon the reins to prevent his starting the horse, which was impartially cropping first the sweet fern on one side and then the blueberry bushes on the other side of the narrow wheel-track. She declared at last that if he would not get out and ask she would do it herself, and at this the dry little man jerked the reins in spite of her, and the horse suddenly pulled the carry-all to the right, and seemed about to overset it.

"Oh, what are you doing, Albe't?" Mrs. Lander lamented, falling helpless against the back of her seat. "Haven't I always told you to speak to the hoss fust?"

"He wouldn't have minded my speakin'," said her husband. "I'm goin' to take you up to the dooa so that you can ask for youaself without gettin' out."

This was so well, in view of Mrs. Lander's age and bulk, and the hardship she must have undergone, if she had tried to carry out her threat, that she was obliged to take it in some sort as a favor; and while the vehicle rose and sank over the surface left rough, after building, in front of the house, like a vessel on a chopping sea, she was silent for several seconds.

The house was still in a raw state of unfinished, though it seemed to have been lived in for a year at least. The earth had been banked up at the foundations for warmth in winter, and the sheathing of the walls had been splotched with irregular spaces of weather boarding; there was a good roof over all, but the window-casings had been merely set in their places and the trim left for a future impulse of the builder. A block of wood suggested the intention of steps at the front door, which stood hospitably open, but remained unresponsive for some time after the Landers made their appeal to the house at large by anxious noises in their throats, and by talking loud with each other, and then talking low. They wondered whether there were anybody in the house; and decided that there must be, for there was smoke coming out of the stove pipe piercing the roof of the wing at the rear.

Mr. Lander brought himself under censure by venturing, without his wife's authority, to lean forward and tap on the door-frame with the butt of his whip. At the sound, a shrill voice called instantly from the region of the stove pipe, "Clem! Clementina? Go to the front dooa! The'e's somebody knockin'." The sound of feet, soft and quick, made itself heard within, and in a few moments a slim maid, too large for a little girl, too childlike for a young girl, stood in the open doorway, looking down on the elderly people in the buggy, with a face as glad as a flower's. She had blue eyes, and a smiling mouth, a straight nose, and a pretty chin whose firm jut accented a certain wistfulness of her lips. She had hair of a dull, dark yellow, which sent out from its thick mass light prongs, or tendrils, curving inward again till they delicately touched it. Her tanned face was not very different in color from her hair, and neither were her bare feet, which showed well above her ankles in the calico skirt she wore. At sight of the elders in the buggy she involuntarily stooped a little to lengthen her skirt in effect, and at the same time she pulled it together sidewise, to close a tear in it, but she lost in her anxiety no ray of the joy which the mere presence of the strangers seemed to give her, and she kept smiling sunnily upon them while she waited for them to speak.

"Oh!" Mrs. Lander began with involuntary apology in her tone, "we just wished to know which of these roads went to South Middlemount. We've come from the hotel, and we wa'n't quite ce'tain."

The girl laughed as she said, "Both roads go to South Middlemount'm; they join together again just a little piece farther on."

The girl and the woman in their parlance replaced the letter 'r' by vowel sounds almost too obscure to be represented, except where it came last in a word before a word beginning with a vowel; there it was annexed to the vowel by a strong liaison, according to the custom universal in rural New England.

"Oh, do they?" said Mrs. Lander.

"Yes'm," answered the girl. "It's a kind of tu'nout in the wintatime; or I guess that's what made it in the beginning; sometimes folks take one hand side and sometimes the other, and that keeps them separate; but they're really the same road, 'm."

"Thank you," said Mrs. Lander, and she pushed her husband to make him say something, too, but he remained silently intent upon the child's prettiness, which her blue eyes seemed to illumine with a light of their own. She had got hold of the door, now, and was using it as if it was a piece of drapery, to hide not only the tear in her gown, but somehow both her bare feet. She leaned out beyond the edge of it; and then, at moments she vanished altogether behind it.

Since Mr. Lander would not speak, and made no sign of starting up his horse, Mrs. Lander added, "I presume you must be used to havin' people ask about the road, if it's so puzzlin'."

"O, yes'm," returned the girl, gladly. "Almost every day, in the summatime."

"You have got a pretty place for a home, he'e," said Mrs. Lander.

"Well, it will be when it's finished up." Without leaning forward inconveniently Mrs. Lander could see that the partitions of the house within were lathed, but not plastered, and the girl looked round as if to realize its condition and added, "It isn't quite finished inside."

"We wouldn't, have troubled you," said Mrs. Lander, "if we had seen anybody to inquire of."

"Yes'm," said the girl. "It a'n't any trouble."

"There are not many otha houses about, very nea', but I don't suppose you get lonesome; young folks are plenty of company for themselves, and if you've got any brothas and sistas—"

"Oh," said the girl, with a tender laugh, "I've got eva so many of them!"

There was a stir in the bushes about the carriage, and Mrs. Lander was aware for an instant of children's faces looking through the leaves at her and then flashing out of sight, with gay cries at being seen. A boy, older than the rest, came round in front of the horse and passed out of sight at the corner of the house.

Lander now leaned back and looked over his shoulder at his wife as if he might hopefully suppose she had come to the end of her questions, but she gave no sign of encouraging him to start on their way again.

"That your brotha, too?" she asked the girl.

"Yes'm. He's the oldest of the boys; he's next to me."

"I don't know," said Mrs. Lander thoughtfully, "as I noticed how many boys there were, or how many girls."

"I've got two sistas, and three brothas, 'm," said the girl, always smiling sweetly. She now emerged from the shelter of the door, and Mrs. Lander perceived that the slight movements of such parts of her person as had been evident beyond its edge were the effects of some endeavor at greater presentableness. She had contrived to get about her an overskirt which covered the rent in her frock, and she had got a pair of shoes on her feet. Stockings were still wanting, but by a mutual concession of her shoe-tops and the border of her skirt, they were almost eliminated from the problem. This happened altogether when the girl sat down on the threshold, and got herself into such foreshortening that the eye of Mrs. Lander in looking down upon her could not detect their absence. Her little head then showed in the dark of the doorway like a painted head against its background.

"You haven't been livin' here a great while, by the looks," said Mrs. Lander. "It don't seem to be clea'ed off very much."

"We've got quite a ga'den-patch back of the house," replied the girl, "and we should have had moa, but fatha wasn't very well, this spring; he's eva so much better than when we fust came he'e."

"It has, the name of being a very healthy locality," said Mrs. Lander, somewhat discontentedly, "though I can't see as it's done me so very much good, yit. Both your payrints livin'?"

"Yes's. Oh, yes, indeed!"

"And your mother, is she real rugged? She need to be, with such a flock of little ones!"

"Yes, motha's always well. Fatha was just run down, the doctas said, and ought to keep more in the open air. That's what he's done since he came he'e. He helped a great deal on the house and he planned it all out himself."

"Is he a ca'penta?" asked Mrs. Lander.

"No'm; but he's—I don't know how to express it—he likes to do every kind of thing."

"But he's got some business, ha'n't he?" A shadow of severity crept over Mrs. Lander's tone, in provisional reprehension of possible shiftlessness.

"Yes'm. He was a machinist at the Mills; that's what the doctas thought didn't agree with him. He bought a piece of land he'e, so as to be in the pine woods, and then we built this house."

"When did you say you came?"

"Two yea's ago, this summa."

"Well! What did you do befoa you built this house?"

"We camped the first summa."

"You camped? In a tent?"

"Well, it was pahtly a tent, and pahtly bank."

"I should have thought you would have died."

The girl laughed. "Oh, no, we all kept fast-rate. We slept in the tents we had two—and we cooked in the shanty." She smiled at the notion in adding, "At fast the neighbas thought we we'e Gipsies; and the summa folks thought we were Indians, and wanted to get baskets of us."

Mrs. Lander did not know what to think, and she asked, "But didn't it almost perish you, stayin' through the winter in an unfinished house?"

"Well, it was pretty cold. But it was so dry, the air was, and the woods kept the wind off nicely."

The same shrill voice in the region of the stovepipe which had sent the girl to the Landers now called her from them. "Clem! Come here a minute!"

The girl said to Mrs. Lander, politely, "You'll have to excuse me, now'm. I've got to go to motha."

"So do!" said Mrs. Lander, and she was so taken by the girl's art and grace in getting to her feet and fading into the background of the hallway without visibly casting any detail of her raiment, that she was not aware of her husband's starting up the horse in time to stop him. They were fairly under way again, when she lamented, "What you doin', Albe't? Whe'e you goin'?"

"I'm goin' to South Middlemount. Didn't you want to?"

"Well, of all the men! Drivin' right off without waitin' to say thanked to the child, or take leave, or anything!"

"Seemed to me as if SHE took leave."

"But she was comin' back! And I wanted to ask—"

"I guess you asked enough for one while. Ask the rest to-morra."

Mrs. Lander was a woman who could often be thrown aside from an immediate purpose, by the suggestion of some remoter end, which had already, perhaps, intimated itself to her. She said, "That's true," but by the time her husband had driven down one of the roads beyond the woods into open country, she was a quiver of intolerable curiosity. "Well, all I've got to say is that I sha'n't rest till I know all about 'em."

"Find out when we get back to the hotel, I guess," said her husband.

"No, I can't wait till I get back to the hotel. I want to know now. I want you should stop at the very fust house we come to. Dea'! The'e don't seem to be any houses, any moa." She peered out around the side of the carry-all and scrutinized the landscape. "Hold on! No, yes it is, too! Whoa! Whoa! The'e's a man in that hay-field, now!"

She laid hold of the reins and pulled the horse to a stand. Mr. Lander looked round over his shoulder at her. "Hadn't you betta wait till you get within half a mile of the man?"

"Well, I want you should stop when you do git to him. Will you? I want to speak to him, and ask him all about those folks."

"I didn't suppose you'd let me have much of a chance," said her husband. When he came within easy hail of the man in the hay-field, he pulled up beside the meadow-wall, where the horse began to nibble the blackberry vines that overran it.

Mrs. Lander beckoned and called to the man, who had stopped pitching hay and now stood leaning on the handle of his fork. At the signs and sounds she made, he came actively forward to the road, bringing his fork with him. When he arrived within easy conversational distance, he planted the tines in the ground and braced himself at an opposite incline from the long smooth handle, and waited for Mrs. Lander to begin.

"Will you please tell us who those folks ah', livin' back there in the edge of the woods, in that new unfinished house?"

The man released his fork with one hand to stoop for a head of timothy that had escaped the scythe, and he put the stem of it between his teeth, where it moved up and down, and whipped fantastically about as he talked, before he answered, "You mean the Claxons?"

"I don't know what thei' name is." Mrs. Lander repeated exactly what she had said.

The farmer said, "Long, red-headed man, kind of sickly-lookin'?"

"We didn't see the man—"

"Little woman, skinny-lookin; pootty tonguey?"

"We didn't see her, eitha; but I guess we hea'd her at the back of the house."

"Lot o' children, about as big as pa'tridges, runnin' round in the bushes?"

"Yes! And a very pretty-appearing girl; about thi'teen or fou'teen, I should think."

The farmer pulled his fork out of the ground, and planted it with his person at new slopes in the figure of a letter A, rather more upright than before. "Yes; it's them," he said. "Ha'n't been in the neighbahood a great while, eitha. Up from down Po'tland way, some'res, I guess. Built that house last summer, as far as it's got, but I don't believe it's goin' to git much fa'tha."

"Why, what's the matta?" demanded Mrs. Lander in an anguish of interest.

The man in the hay-field seemed to think it more dignified to include Lander in this inquiry, and he said with a glimmer of the eye for him, "Hea'd of do-nothin' folks?"

"Seen 'em, too," answered Lander, comprehensively.

"Well, that a'n't Claxon's complaint exactly. He a'n't a do-nothin'; he's a do-everything. I guess it's about as bad." Lander glimmered back at the man, but did not speak.

"Kind of a machinist down at the Mills, where he come from," the farmer began again, and Mrs. Lander, eager not to be left out of the affair for a moment, interrupted:

"Yes, Yes! That's what the gul said."

"But he don't seem to think't the i'on agreed with him, and now he's goin' in for wood. Well, he did have a kind of a foot-powa tu'nin' lathe, and tuned all sots o' things; cups, and bowls, and u'ns for fence-posts, and vases, and sleeve-buttons and little knick-knacks; but the place bunt down, here, a while back, and he's been huntin' round for wood, the whole winta long, to make canes out of for the summa-folks. Seems to think that the smell o' the wood, whether it's green or it's dry, is goin' to cure him, and he can't git too much of it."

"Well, I believe it's so, Albe't!" cried Mrs. Lander, as if her husband had disputed the theory with his taciturn back. He made no other sign of controversy, and the man in the hay-field went on.

"I hea' he's goin' to put up a wind mill, back in an open place he's got, and use the powa for tu'nin', if he eva gits it up. But he don't seem to be in any great of a hurry, and they scrape along somehow. Wife takes in sewin' and the girl wo'ked at the Middlemount House last season. Whole fam'ly's got to tu'n in and help s'po't a man that can do everything."

The farmer appealed with another humorous cast of his eye to Lander; but the old man tacitly refused to take any further part in the talk, which began to flourish apace, in question and answer, between his wife and the man in the hay-field. It seemed that the children had all inherited the father's smartness. The oldest boy could beat the nation at figures, and one of the young ones could draw anything you had a mind to. They were all clear up in their classes at school, and yet you might say they almost ran wild, between times. The oldest girl was a pretty-behaved little thing, but the man in the hay-field guessed there was not very much to her, compared with some of the boys. Any rate, she had not the name of being so smart at school. Good little thing, too, and kind of mothered the young ones.

Mrs. Lander, when she had wrung the last drop of information out of him, let him crawl back to his work, mentally flaccid, and let her husband drive on, but under a fire of conjecture and asseveration that was scarcely intermitted till they reached their hotel. That night she talked along time about their afternoon's adventure before she allowed him to go to sleep. She said she must certainly see the child again; that they must drive down there in the morning, and ask her all about herself.

"Albe't," she concluded; "I wish we had her to live with us. Yes, I do! I wonder if we could get her to. You know I always did want to adopt a baby."

"You neva said so," Mr. Lander opened his mouth almost for the first time, since the talk began.

"I didn't suppose you'd like it," said his wife.

"Well, she a'n't a baby. I guess you'd find you had your hands full, takon' a half-grown gul like that to bring up."

"I shouldn't be afraid any," the wife declared. "She has just twined herself round my heat. I can't get her pretty looks out of my eyes. I know she's good."

"We'll see how you feel about it in the morning."

The old man began to wind his watch, and his wife seemed to take this for a sign that the incident was closed, for the present at least. He seldom talked, but there came times when he would not even listen. One of these was the time after he had wound his watch. A minute later he had undressed, with an agility incredible of his years, and was in bed, as effectively blind and deaf to his wife's appeals as if he were already asleep.

II.

When Albert Gallatin Lander (he was named for an early Secretary of the Treasury as a tribute to the statesman's financial policy) went out of business, his wife began to go out of health; and it became the most serious affair of his declining years to provide for her invalid fancies. He would have liked to buy a place in the Boston suburbs (he preferred one of the Newtons) where they could both have had something to do, she inside of the house, and he outside; but she declared that what they both needed was a good long rest, with freedom from care and trouble of every kind. She broke up their establishment in Boston, and stored their furniture, and she would have made him sell the simple old house in which they had always lived, on an unfashionable up-and-down-hill street of the West End, if he had not taken one of his stubborn stands, and let it for a term of years without consulting her. But she had her way about their own movements, and they began that life of hotels, which they had now lived so long that she believed any other impossible. Its luxury and idleness had told upon each of them with diverse effect.

They had both entered upon it in much the same corporal figure, but she had constantly grown in flesh, while he had dwindled away until he was not much more than half the weight of his prime. Their digestion was alike impaired by their joint life, but as they took the same medicines Mrs. Lander was baffled to account for the varying result. She was sure that all the anxiety came upon her, and that logically she was the one who ought to have wasted away. But she had before her the spectacle of a husband who, while he gave his entire attention to her health, did not audibly or visibly worry about it, and yet had lost weight in such measure that upon trying on a pair of his old trousers taken out of storage with some clothes of her own, he found it impossible to use the side pockets which the change in his figure carried so far to the rear when the garment was reduced at the waist. At the same time her own dresses of ten years earlier would not half meet round her; and one of the most corroding cares of a woman who had done everything a woman could to get rid of care, was what to do with those things which they could neither of them ever wear again. She talked the matter over with herself before her husband, till he took the desperate measure of sending them back to storage; and they had been left there in the spring when the Landers came away for the summer.

They always spent the later spring months at a hotel in the suburbs of Boston, where they arrived in May from a fortnight in a hotel at New York, on their way up from hotels in Washington, Ashville, Aiken and St. Augustine. They passed the summer months in the mountains, and early in the autumn they went back to the hotel in the Boston suburbs, where Mrs. Lander considered it essential to make some sojourn before going to a Boston hotel for November and December, and getting ready to go down to Florida in January. She would not on any account have gone directly to the city from the mountains, for people who did that were sure to lose the good of their summer, and to feel the loss all the winter, if they did not actually come down with a fever.

She was by no means aware that she was a selfish or foolish person. She made Mr. Lander subscribe statedly to worthy objects in Boston, which she still regarded as home, because they had not dwelt any where else since they ceased to live there; and she took lavishly of tickets for all the charitable entertainments in the hotels where they stayed. Few if any guests at hotels enjoyed so much honor from porters, bell-boys, waiters, chambermaids and bootblacks as the Landers, for they gave richly in fees for every conceivable service which could be rendered them; they went out of their way to invent debts of gratitude to menials who had done nothing for them. He would make the boy who sold papers at the dining-room door keep the change, when he had been charged a profit of a hundred per cent. already; and she would let no driver who had plundered them according to the carriage tariff escape without something for himself.

A sense of their munificence penetrated the clerks and proprietors with a just esteem for guests who always wanted the best of everything, and questioned no bill for extras. Mrs. Lander, in fact, who ruled these expenditures, had no knowledge of the value of things, and made her husband pay whatever was asked. Yet when they lived under their own roof they had lived simply, and Lander had got his money in an old-fashioned business way, and not in some delirious speculation such as leaves a man reckless of money afterwards. He had been first of all a tailor, and then he had gone into boys' and youths' clothing in a small way, and finally he had mastered this business and come out at the top, with his hands full. He invested his money so prosperously that the income for two elderly people, who had no children, and only a few outlying relations on his side, was far beyond their wants, or even their whims.

She as a woman, who in spite of her bulk and the jellylike majesty with which she shook in her smoothly casing brown silks, as she entered hotel dining-rooms, and the severity with which she frowned over her fan down the length of the hotel drawing-rooms, betrayed more than her husband the commonness of their origin. She could not help talking, and her accent and her diction gave her away for a middle-class New England person of village birth and unfashionable sojourn in Boston. He, on the contrary, lurked about the hotels where they passed their days in a silence so dignified that when his verbs and nominatives seemed not to agree, you accused your own hearing. He was correctly dressed, as an elderly man should be, in the yesterday of the fashions, and he wore with impressiveness a silk hat whenever such a hat could be worn. A pair of drab cloth gaiters did much to identify him with an old school of gentlemen, not very definite in time or place. He had a full gray beard cut close, and he was in the habit of pursing his mouth a great deal. But he meant nothing by it, and his wife meant nothing by her frowning. They had no wish to subdue or overawe any one, or to pass for persons of social distinction. They really did not know what society was, and they were rather afraid of it than otherwise as they caught sight of it in their journeys and sojourns. They led a life of public seclusion, and dwelling forever amidst crowds, they were all in all to each other, and nothing to the rest of the world, just as they had been when they resided (as they would have said) on Pinckney street. In their own house they had never entertained, though they sometimes had company, in the style of the country town where Mrs. Lander grew up. As soon as she was released to the grandeur of hotel life, she expanded to the full measure of its responsibilities and privileges, but still without seeking to make it the basis of approach to society. Among the people who surrounded her, she had not so much acquaintance as her husband even, who talked so little that he needed none. She sometimes envied his ease in getting on with people when he chose; and his boldness in speaking to fellow guests and fellow travellers, if he really wanted anything. She wanted something of them all the time, she wanted their conversation and their companionship; but in her ignorance of the social arts she was thrown mainly upon the compassion of the chambermaids. She kept these talking as long as she could detain them in her rooms; and often fed them candy (which she ate herself with childish greed) to bribe them to further delays. If she was staying some days in a hotel, she sent for the house-keeper, and made all she could of her as a listener, and as soon as she settled herself for a week, she asked who was the best doctor in the place. With doctors she had no reserves, and she poured out upon them the history of her diseases and symptoms in an inexhaustible flow of statement, conjecture and misgiving, which was by no means affected by her profound and inexpugnable ignorance of the principles of health. From time to time she forgot which side her liver was on, but she had been doctored (as she called it) for all her organs, and she was willing to be doctored for any one of them that happened to be in the place where she fancied a present discomfort. She was not insensible to the claims which her husband's disorders had upon science, and she liked to end the tale of her own sufferings with some such appeal as: "I wish you could do something for Mr. Landa, too, docta." She made him take a little of each medicine that was left for her; but in her presence he always denied that there was anything the matter with him, though he was apt to follow the doctor out of the room, and get a prescription from him for some ailment which he professed not to believe in himself, but wanted to quiet Mrs. Lander's mind about.

He rose early, both from long habit, and from the scant sleep of an elderly man; he could not lie in bed; but his wife always had her breakfast there and remained so long that the chambermaid had done up most of the other rooms and had leisure for talk with her. As soon as he was awake, he stole softly out and was the first in the dining-room for breakfast. He owned to casual acquaintance in moments of expansion that breakfast was his best meal, but he did what he could to make it his worst by beginning with oranges and oatmeal, going forward to beefsteak and fried potatoes, and closing with griddle cakes and syrup, washed down with a cup of cocoa, which his wife decided to be wholesomer than coffee. By the time he had finished such a repast, he crept out of the dining-room in a state of tension little short of anguish, which he confided to the sympathy of the bootblack in the washroom.

He always went from having his shoes polished to get a toothpick at the clerk's desk; and at the Middlemount House, the morning after he had been that drive with Mrs. Lander, he lingered a moment with his elbows beside the register. "How about a buckboa'd?" he asked.

"Something you can drive yourself"—the clerk professionally dropped his eye to the register—"Mr. Lander?"

"Well, no, I guess not, this time," the little man returned, after a moment's reflection. "Know anything of a family named Claxon, down the road, here, a piece?" He twisted his head in the direction he meant.

"This is my first season at Middlemount; but I guess Mr. Atwell will know." The clerk called to the landlord, who was smoking in his private room behind the office, and the landlord came out. The clerk repeated Mr. Lander's questions.

"Pootty good kind of folks, I guess," said the landlord provisionally, through his cigar-smoke. "Man's a kind of univussal genius, but he's got a nice family of children; smaht as traps, all of 'em."

"How about that oldest gul?" asked Mr. Lander.

"Well, the'a," said the landlord, taking the cigar out of his mouth. "I think she's about the nicest little thing goin'. We've had her up he'e, to help out in a busy time, last summer, and she's got moo sense than guls twice as old. Takes hold like—lightnin'."

"About how old did you say she was?"

"Well, you've got me the'a, Mr. Landa; I guess I'll ask Mis' Atwell."

"The'e's no hurry," said Lander. "That buckboa'd be round pretty soon?" he asked of the clerk.

"Be right along now, Mr. Lander," said the clerk, soothingly. He stepped out to the platform that the teams drove up to from the stable, and came back to say that it was coming. "I believe you said you wanted something you could drive yourself?"

"No, I didn't, young man," answered the elder sharply. But the next moment he added, "Come to think of it, I guess it's just as well. You needn't get me no driver. I guess I know the way well enough. You put me in a hitchin' strap."

"All right, Mr. Lander," said the clerk, meekly.

The landlord had caught the peremptory note in Lander's voice, and he came out of his room again to see that there was nothing going wrong.

"It's all right," said Lander, and went out and got into his buckboard.

"Same horse you had yesterday," said the young clerk. "You don't need to spare the whip."

"I guess I can look out for myself," said Lander, and he shook the reins and gave the horse a smart cut, as a hint of what he might expect.

The landlord joined the clerk in looking after the brisk start the horse made. "Not the way he set off with the old lady, yesterday," suggested the clerk.

The landlord rolled his cigar round in his tubed lips. "I guess he's used to ridin' after a good hoss." He added gravely to the clerk, "You don't want to make very free with that man, Mr. Pane. He won't stan' it, and he's a class of custom that you want to cata to when it comes in your way. I suspicioned what he was when they came here and took the highest cost rooms without tu'nin' a haia. They're a class of custom that you won't get outside the big hotels in the big reso'ts. Yes, sir," said the landlord taking a fresh start, "they're them kind of folks that live the whole yea' round in hotels; no'th in summa, south in winta, and city hotels between times. They want the best their money can buy, and they got plenty of it. She"—he meant Mrs. Lander—"has been tellin' my wife how they do; she likes to talk a little betta than he doos; and I guess when it comes to society, they're away up, and they won't stun' any nonsense."

III

Lander came into his wife's room between ten and eleven o'clock, and found her still in bed, but with her half-finished breakfast on a tray before her. As soon as he opened the door she said, "I do wish you would take some of that heat-tonic of mine, Albe't, that the docta left for me in Boston. You'll find it in the upper right bureau box, the'a; and I know it'll be the very thing for you. It'll relieve you of that suffocatin' feeling that I always have, comin' up stars. Dea'! I don't see why they don't have an elevata; they make you pay enough; and I wish you'd get me a little more silva, so's't I can give to the chambamaid and the bell-boy; I do hate to be out of it. I guess you been up and out long ago. They did make that polonaise of mine too tight after all I said, and I've been thinkin' how I could get it alt'ed; but I presume there ain't a seamstress to be had around he'e for love or money. Well, now, that's right, Albe't; I'm glad to see you doin' it."

Lander had opened the lid of the bureau box, and uncorked a bottle from it, and tilted this to his lips.

"Don't take too much," she cautioned him, "or you'll lose the effects. When I take too much of a medicine, it's wo'se than nothing, as fah's I can make out. When I had that spell in Thomasville spring before last, I believe I should have been over it twice as quick if I had taken just half the medicine I did. You don't really feel anyways bad about the heat, do you, Albe't?"

"I'm all right," said Lander. He put back the bottle in its place and sat down.

Mrs. Lander lifted herself on her elbow and looked over at him. "Show me on the bottle how much you took."

He got the bottle out again and showed her with his thumb nail a point which he chose at random.

"Well, that was just about the dose for you," she said; and she sank down in bed again with the air of having used a final precaution. "You don't want to slow your heat up too quick."

Lander did not put the bottle back this time. He kept it in his hand, with his thumb on the cork, and rocked it back and forth on his knees as he spoke. "Why don't you get that woman to alter it for you?"

"What woman alta what?"

"Your polonaise. The one whe'e we stopped yestaday."

"Oh! Well, I've been thinkin' about that child, Albe't; I did before I went to sleep; and I don't believe I want to risk anything with her. It would be a ca'e," said Mrs. Lander with a sigh, "and I guess I don't want to take any moa ca'e than what I've got now. What makes you think she could alta my polonaise?"

"Said she done dress-makin'," said Lander, doggedly.

"You ha'n't been the'a?"

He nodded.

"You didn't say anything to her about her daughta?"

"Yes, I did," said Lander.

"Well, you ce'tainly do equal anything," said his wife. She lay still awhile, and then she roused herself with indignant energy. "Well, then, I can tell you what, Albe't Landa: you can go right straight and take back everything you said. I don't want the child, and I won't have her. I've got care enough to worry me now, I should think; and we should have her whole family on our hands, with that shiftless father of hers, and the whole pack of her brothas and sistas. What made you think I wanted you to do such a thing?"

"You wanted me to do it last night. Wouldn't ha'dly let me go to bed."

"Yes! And how many times have I told you nova to go off and do a thing that I wanted you to, unless you asked me if I did? Must I die befo'e you can find out that there is such a thing as talkin', and such anotha thing as doin'? You wouldn't get yourself into half as many scrapes if you talked more and done less, in this wo'ld." Lander rose.

"Wait! Hold on! What are you going to say to the pooa thing? She'll be so disappointed!"

"I don't know as I shall need to say anything myself," answered the little man, at his dryest. "Leave that to you."

"Well, I can tell you," returned his wife, "I'm not goin' nea' them again; and if you think—What did you ask the woman, anyway?"

"I asked her," he said, "if she wanted to let the gul come and see you about some sewing you had to have done, and she said she did."

"And you didn't speak about havin' her come to live with us?"

"No."

"Well, why in the land didn't you say so before, Albe't?"

"You didn't ask me. What do you want I should say to her now?"

"Say to who?"

"The gul. She's down in the pahlor, waitin'."

"Well, of all the men!" cried Mrs. Lander. But she seemed to find herself, upon reflection, less able to cope with Lander personally than with the situation generally. "Will you send her up, Albe't?" she asked, very patiently, as if he might be driven to further excesses, if not delicately handled. As soon as he had gone out of the room she wished that she had told him to give her time to dress and have her room put in order, before he sent the child up; but she could only make the best of herself in bed with a cap and a breakfast jacket, arranged with the help of a handglass. She had to get out of bed to put her other clothes away in the closet and she seized the chance to push the breakfast tray out of the door, and smooth up the bed, while she composed her features and her ideas to receive her visitor. Both, from long habit rather than from any cause or reason, were of a querulous cast, and her ordinary tone was a snuffle expressive of deep-seated affliction. She was at once plaintive and voluable, and in moments of excitement her need of freeing her mind was so great that she took herself into her own confidence, and found a more sympathetic listener than when she talked to her husband. As she now whisked about her room in her bed-gown with an activity not predicable of her age and shape, and finally plunged under the covering and drew it up to her chin with one hand while she pressed it out decorously over her person with the other, she kept up a rapid flow of lamentation and conjecture. "I do suppose he'll be right back with her before I'm half ready; and what the man was thinkin' of to do such a thing anyway, I don't know. I don't know as she'll notice much, comin' out of such a lookin' place as that, and I don't know as I need to care if she did. But if the'e's care anywhe's around, I presume I'm the one to have it. I presume I did take a fancy to her, and I guess I shall be glad to see how I like her now; and if he's only told her I want some sewin' done, I can scrape up something to let her carry home with her. It's well I keep my things where I can put my hand on 'em at a time like this, and I don't believe I shall sca'e the child, as it is. I do hope Albe't won't hang round half the day before he brings her; I like to have a thing ova."

Lander wandered about looking for the girl through the parlors and the piazzas, and then went to the office to ask what had become of her.

The landlord came out of his room at his question to the clerk. "Oh, I guess she's round in my wife's room, Mr. Landa. She always likes to see Clementina, and I guess they all do. She's a so't o' pet amongst 'em."

"No hurry," said Lander, "I guess my wife ain't quite ready for her yet."

"Well, she'll be right out, in a minute or so," said the landlord.

The old man tilted his hat forward over his eyes, and went to sit on the veranda and look at the landscape while he waited. It was one of the loveliest landscapes in the mountains; the river flowed at the foot of an abrupt slope from the road before the hotel, stealing into and out of the valley, and the mountains, gray in the farther distance, were draped with folds of cloud hanging upon their flanks and tops. But Lander was tired of nearly all kinds of views and prospects, though he put' up with them, in his perpetual movement from place to place, in the same resignation that he suffered the limitations of comfort in parlor cars and sleepers, and the unwholesomeness of hotel tables. He was chained to the restless pursuit of an ideal not his own, but doomed to suffer for its impossibility as if he contrived each of his wife's disappointments from it. He did not philosophize his situation, but accepted it as in an order of Providence which it would be useless for him to oppose; though there were moments when he permitted himself to feel a modest doubt of its justice. He was aware that when he had a house of his own he was master in it, after a fashion, and that as long as he was in business he was in some sort of authority. He perceived that now he was a slave to the wishes of a mistress who did not know what she wanted, and that he was never farther from pleasing her than when he tried to do what she asked. He could not have told how all initiative had been taken from him, and he had fallen into the mere follower of a woman guided only by her whims, who had no object in life except to deprive it of all object. He felt no rancor toward her for this; he knew that she had a tender regard for him, and that she believed she was considering him first in her most selfish arrangements. He always hoped that sometime she would get tired of her restlessness, and be willing to settle down again in some stated place; and wherever it was, he meant to get into some kind of business again. Till this should happen he waited with an apathetic patience of which his present abeyance was a detail. He would hardly have thought it anything unfit, and certainly nothing surprising, that the landlady should have taken the young girl away from where he had left her, and then in the pleasure of talking with her, and finding her a centre of interest for the whole domestic force of the hotel, should have forgotten to bring her back.

The Middlemount House had just been organized on the scale of a first class hotel, with prices that had risen a little in anticipation of the other improvements. The landlord had hitherto united in himself the functions of clerk and head waiter, but he had now got a senior, who was working his way through college, to take charge of the dining-room, and had put in the office a youth of a year's experience as under clerk at a city hotel. But he meant to relinquish no more authority than his wife who frankly kept the name as well as duty of house-keeper. It was in making her morning inspection of the dusting that she found Clementina in the parlor where Lander had told her to sit down till he should come for her.

"Why, Clem!" she said, "I didn't know you! You have grown so! Youa folks all well? I decla'e you ah' quite a woman now," she added, as the girl stood up in her slender, graceful height. "You look as pretty as a pink in that hat. Make that dress youaself? Well, you do beat the witch! I want you should come to my room with me."

Mrs. Atwell showered other questions and exclamations on the girl, who explained how she happened to be there, and said that she supposed she must stay where she was for fear Mr. Lander should come back and find her gone; but Mrs. Atwell overruled her with the fact that Mrs. Lander's breakfast had just gone up to her; and she made her come out and see the new features of the enlarged house-keeping. In the dining-room there were some of the waitresses who had been there the summer before, and recognitions of more or less dignity passed between them and Clementina. The place was now shut against guests, and the head-waiter was having it put in order for the one o'clock dinner. As they came near him, Mrs. Atwell introduced him to Clementina, and he behaved deferentially, as if she were some young lady visitor whom Mrs. Atwell was showing the improvements, but he seemed harassed and impatient, as if he were anxious about his duties, and eager to get at them again. He was a handsome little fellow, with hair lighter than Clementina's and a sanguine complexion, and the color coming and going.

"He's smaht," said Mrs. Atwell, when they had left him—he held the dining-room door open for them, and bowed them out. "I don't know but he worries almost too much. That'll wear off when he gets things runnin' to suit him. He's pretty p'tic'la'. Now I'll show you how they've made the office over, and built in a room for Mr. Atwell behind it."

The landlord welcomed Clementina as if she had been some acceptable class of custom, and when the tall young clerk came in to ask him something, and Mrs. Atwell said, "I want to introduce you to Miss Claxon, Mr. Fane," the clerk smiled down upon her from the height of his smooth, acquiline young face, which he held bent encouragingly upon one side.

"Now, I want you should come in and see where I live, a minute," said Mrs. Atwell. She took the girl from the clerk, and led her to the official housekeeper's room which she said had been prepared for her so that folks need not keep running to her in her private room where she wanted to be alone with her children, when she was there. "Why, you a'n't much moa than a child youaself, Clem, and here I be talkin' to you as if you was a mother in Israel. How old ah' you, this summa? Time does go so!"

"I'm sixteen now," said Clementina, smiling.

"You be? Well, I don't see why I say that, eitha! You're full lahge enough for your age, but not seein' you in long dresses before, I didn't realize your age so much. My, but you do all of you know how to do things!"

"I'm about the only one that don't, Mrs. Atwell," said the girl. "If it hadn't been for mother, I don't believe I could have eva finished this dress." She began to laugh at something passing in her mind, and Mrs. Atwell laughed too, in sympathy, though she did not know what at till Clementina said, "Why, Mrs. Atwell, nea'ly the whole family wo'ked on this dress. Jim drew the patte'n of it from the dress of one of the summa boa'das that he took a fancy to at the Centa, and fatha cut it out, and I helped motha make it. I guess every one of the children helped a little."

"Well, it's just as I said, you can all of you do things," said Mrs. Atwell. "But I guess you ah' the one that keeps 'em straight. What did you say Mr. Landa said his wife wanted of you?"

"He said some kind of sewing that motha could do."

"Well, I'll tell you what! Now, if she ha'n't really got anything that your motha'll want you to help with, I wish you'd come here again and help me. I tuned my foot, here, two-three weeks back, and I feel it, times, and I should like some one to do about half my steppin' for me. I don't want to take you away from her, but IF. You sha'n't go int' the dinin'room, or be under anybody's oddas but mine. Now, will you?"

"I'll see, Mrs. Atwell. I don't like to say anything till I know what Mrs. Landa wants."

"Well, that's right. I decla'e, you've got moa judgment! That's what I used to say about you last summa to my husband: she's got judgment. Well, what's wanted?" Mrs. Atwell spoke to her husband, who had opened her door and looked in, and she stopped rocking, while she waited his answer.

"I guess you don't want to keep Clementina from Mr. Landa much longa. He's settin' out there on the front piazza waitin' for her."

"Well, the'a!" cried Mrs. Atwell. "Ain't that just like me? Why didn't you tell me sooner, Alonzo? Don't you forgit what I said, Clem!"

IV.

Mrs. Lander had taken twice of a specific for what she called her nerve-fag before her husband came with Clementina, and had rehearsed aloud many of the things she meant to say to the girl. In spite of her preparation, they were all driven out of her head when Clementina actually appeared, and gave her a bow like a young birch's obeisance in the wind.

"Take a chaia," said Lander, pushing her one, and the girl tilted over toward him, before she sank into it. He went out of the room, and left Mrs. Lander to deal with the problem alone. She apologized for being in bed, but Clementina said so sweetly, "Mr. Landa told me you were not feeling very well, 'm," that she began to be proud of her ailments, and bragged of them at length, and of the different doctors who had treated her for them. While she talked she missed one thing or another, and Clementina seemed to divine what it was she wanted, and got it for her, with a gentle deference which made the elder feel her age cushioned by the girl's youth. When she grew a little heated from the interest she took in her personal annals, and cast off one of the folds of her bed clothing, Clementina got her a fan, and asked her if she should put up one of the windows a little.

"How you do think of things!" said Mrs. Lander. "I guess I will let you. I presume you get used to thinkin' of othas in a lahge family like youas. I don't suppose they could get along without you very well," she suggested.

"I've neva been away except last summa, for a little while."

"And where was you then?"

"I was helping Mrs. Atwell."

"Did you like it?"

"I don't know," said Clementina. "It's pleasant to be whe'e things ah' going on."

"Yes—for young folks," said Mrs. Lander, whom the going on of things had long ceased to bring pleasure.

"It's real nice at home, too," said Clementina. "We have very good times—evenings in the winta; in the summer it's very nice in the woods, around there. It's safe for the children, and they enjoy it, and fatha likes to have them. Motha don't ca'e so much about it. I guess she'd ratha have the house fixed up more, and the place. Fatha's going to do it pretty soon. He thinks the'e's time enough."

"That's the way with men," said Mrs. Lander. "They always think the's time enough; but I like to have things over and done with. What chuhch do you 'tend?"

"Well, there isn't any but the Episcopal," Clementina answered. "I go to that, and some of the children go to the Sunday School. I don't believe fatha ca'es very much for going to chuhch, but he likes Mr. Richling; he's the recta. They take walks in the woods; and they go up the mountains togetha."

"They want," said Mrs. Lander, severely, "to be ca'eful how they drink of them cold brooks when they're heated. Mr. Richling a married man?"

"Oh, yes'm! But they haven't got any family."

"If I could see his wife, I sh'd caution her about lettin' him climb mountains too much. A'n't your father afraid he'll ovado?"

"I don't know. He thinks he can't be too much in the open air on the mountains."

"Well, he may not have the same complaint as Mr. Landa; but I know if I was to climb a mountain,' it would lay me up for a yea'."

The girl did not urge anything against this conviction. She smiled politely and waited patiently for the next turn Mrs. Lander's talk should take, which was oddly enough toward the business Clementina had come upon.

"I declare I most forgot about my polonaise. Mr. Landa said your motha thought she could do something to it for me."

"Yes'm."

"Well, I may as well 'let you see it. If you'll reach into that fuhthest closet, you'll find it on the last uppa hook on the right hand, and if you'll give it to me, I'll show you what I want done. Don't mind the looks of that closet; I've just tossed my things in, till I could get a little time and stren'th to put 'em in odda."

Clementina brought the polonaise to Mrs. Lander, who sat up and spread it before her on the bed, and had a happy half hour in telling the girl where she had bought the material and where she had it made up, and how it came home just as she was going away, and she did not find out that it was all wrong till a week afterwards when she tried it on. By the end of this time the girl had commended herself so much by judicious and sympathetic assent, that Mrs. Lander learned with a shock of disappointment that her mother expected her to bring the garment home with her, where Mrs. Lander was to come and have it fitted over for the alterations she wanted made.

"But I supposed, from what Mr. Landa said, that your motha would come here and fit me!" she lamented.

"I guess he didn't undastand, 'm. Motha doesn't eva go out to do wo'k," said Clementina gently but firmly.

"Well, I might have known Mr. Landa would mix it up, if it could be mixed;" Mrs. Lander's sense of injury was aggravated by her suspicion that he had brought the girl in the hope of pleasing her, and confirming her in the wish to have her with them; she was not a woman who liked to have her way in spite of herself; she wished at every step to realize that she was taking it, and that no one else was taking it for her.

"Well," she said dryly, "I shall have to see about it. I'm a good deal of an invalid, and I don't know as I could go back and fo'th to try on. I'm moa used to havin' the things brought to me."

"Yes'm," said Clementina. She moved a little from the bed, on her way to the door, to be ready for Mrs. Lander in leave-taking.

"I'm real sorry," said Mrs. Lander. "I presume it's a disappointment for you, too."

"Oh, not at all," answered Clementina. "I'm sorry we can't do the wo'k he'a; but I know mocha wouldn't like to. Good-mo'ning,'m!"

"No, no! Don't go yet a minute! Won't you just give me my hand bag off the bureau the'a?" Mrs. Lander entreated, and when the girl gave her the bag she felt about among the bank-notes which she seemed to have loose in it, and drew out a handful of them without regard to their value. "He'a!" she said, and she tried to put the notes into Clementina's hand, "I want you should get yourself something."

The girl shrank back. "Oh, no'm," she said, with an effect of seeming to know that her refusal would hurt, and with the wish to soften it. "I—couldn't; indeed I couldn't."

"Why couldn't you? Now you must! If I can't let you have the wo'k the way you want, I don't think it's fair, and you ought to have the money for it just the same."

Clementina shook her head smiling. "I don't believe motha would like to have me take it."

"Oh, now, pshaw!" said Mrs. Lander, inadequately. "I want you should take this for youaself; and if you don't want to buy anything to wea', you can get something to fix your room up with. Don't you be afraid of robbin' us. Land! We got moa money! Now you take this."

Mrs. Lander reached the money as far toward Clementina as she could and shook it in the vehemence of her desire.

"Thank you, I couldn't take it," Clementina persisted. "I'm afraid I must be going; I guess I must bid you good-mo'ning."

"Why, I believe the child's sca'ed of me! But you needn't be. Don't you suppose I know how you feel? You set down in that chai'a there, and I'll tell you how you feel. I guess we've been pooa, too—I don't mean anything that a'n't exactly right—and I guess I've had the same feelin's. You think it's demeanin' to you to take it. A'n't that it?" Clementina sank provisionally upon the edge of the chair. "Well, it did use to be so consid'ed. But it's all changed, nowadays. We travel pretty nee' the whole while, Mr. Lander and me, and we see folks everywhere, and it a'n't the custom to refuse any moa. Now, a'n't there any little thing for your own room, there in your nice new house? Or something your motha's got her heat set on? Or one of your brothas? My, if you don't have it, some one else will! Do take it!"

The girl kept slipping toward the door. "I shouldn't know what to tell them, when I got home. They would think I must be—out of my senses."

"I guess you mean they'd think I was. Now, listen to me a minute!" Mrs. Lander persisted.

"You just take this money, and when you get home, you tell your mother every word about it, and if she says, you bring it right straight back to me. Now, can't you do that?"

"I don't know but I can," Clementina faltered. "Well, then take it!" Mrs. Lander put the bills into her hand but she did not release her at once. She pulled Clementina down and herself up till she could lay her other arm on her neck. "I want you should let me kiss you. Will you?"

"Why, certainly," said Clementina, and she kissed the old woman.

"You tell your mother I'm comin' to see her before I go; and I guess," said Mrs. Lander in instant expression of the idea that came into her mind, "we shall be goin' pretty soon, now."

"Yes'm," said Clementina.

She went out, and shortly after Lander came in with a sort of hopeful apathy in his face.

Mrs. Lander turned her head on her pillow, and so confronted him. "Albe't, what made you want me to see that child?"

Lander must have perceived that his wife meant business, and he came to it at once. "I thought you might take a fancy to her, and get her to come and live with us."

"Yes?"

"We're both of us gettin' pretty well on, and you'd ought to have somebody to look after you if—I'm not around. You want somebody that can do for you; and keep you company, and read to you, and talk to you—well, moa like a daughta than a suvvant—somebody that you'd get attached to, maybe—"

"And don't you see," Mrs. Lander broke out severely upon him, "what a ca'e that would be? Why, it's got so already that I can't help thinkin' about her the whole while, and if I got attached to her I'd have her on my mind day and night, and the moa she done for me the more I should be tewin' around to do for her. I shouldn't have any peace of my life any moa. Can't you see that?"

"I guess if you see it, I don't need to," said Lander.

"Well, then, I want you shouldn't eva mention her to me again. I've had the greatest escape! But I've got her off home, and I've give her money enough! had a time with her about it—so that they won't feel as if we'd made 'em trouble for nothing, and now I neva want to hear of her again. I don't want we should stay here a great while longer; I shall be frettin' if I'm in reach of her, and I shan't get any good of the ai'a. Will you promise?"

"Yes."

"Well, then!" Mrs. Lander turned her face upon the pillow again in the dramatization of her exhaustion; but she was not so far gone that she was insensible to the possible interest that a light rap at the door suggested. She once more twisted her head in that direction and called, "Come in!"

The door opened and Clementina came in. She advanced to the bedside smiling joyously, and put the money Mrs. Lander had given her down upon the counterpane.

"Why, you haven't been home, child?"

"No'm," said Clementina, breathlessly. "But I couldn't take it. I knew they wouldn't want me to, and I thought you'd like it better if I just brought it back myself. Good-mo'ning." She slipped out of the door. Mrs. Lander swept the bank-notes from the coverlet and pulled it over her head, and sent from beneath it a stifled wail. "Now we got to go! And it's all youa fault, Albe't."

Lander took the money from the floor, and smoothed each bill out, and then laid them in a neat pile on the corner of the bureau. He sighed profoundly but left the room without an effort to justify himself.

V.

The Landers had been gone a week before Clementina's mother decided that she could spare her to Mrs. Atwell for a while. It was established that she was not to serve either in the dining-room or the carving room; she was not to wash dishes or to do any part of the chamber work, but to carry messages and orders for the landlady, and to save her steps, when she wished to see the head-waiter, or the head-cook; or to make an excuse or a promise to some of the lady-boarders; or to send word to Mr. Atwell about the buying, or to communicate with the clerk about rooms taken or left.

She had a good deal of dignity of her own and such a gravity in the discharge of her duties that the chef, who was a middle-aged Yankee with grown girls of his own, liked to pretend that it was Mrs. Atwell herself who was talking with him, and to discover just as she left him that it was Clementina. He called her the Boss when he spoke of her to others in her hearing, and he addressed her as Boss when he feigned to find that it was not Mrs. Atwell. She did not mind that in him, and let the chef have his joke as if it were not one. But one day when the clerk called her Boss she merely looked at him without speaking, and made him feel that he had taken a liberty which he must not repeat. He was a young man who much preferred a state of self-satisfaction to humiliation of any sort, and after he had endured Clementina's gaze as long as he could, he said, "Perhaps you don't allow anybody but the chef to call you that?"

She did not answer, but repeated the message Mrs. Atwell had given her for him, and went away.

It seemed to him undue that a person who exchanged repartees with the young lady boarders across his desk, when they came many times a day to look at the register, or to ask for letters, should remain snubbed by a girl who still wore her hair in a braid; but he was an amiable youth, and he tried to appease her by little favors and services, instead of trying to bully her.

He was great friends with the head-waiter, whom he respected as a college student, though for the time being he ranked the student socially. He had him in behind the frame of letter-boxes, which formed a sort of little private room for him, and talked with him at such hours of the forenoon and the late evening as the student was off duty. He found comfort in the student's fretful strength, which expressed itself in the pugnacious frown of his hot-looking young face, where a bright sorrel mustache was beginning to blaze on a short upper lip.

Fane thought himself a good-looking fellow, and he regarded his figure with pleasure, as it was set off by the suit of fine gray check that he wore habitually; but he thought Gregory's educational advantages told in his face.

His own education had ended at a commercial college, where he acquired a good knowledge of bookkeeping, and the fine business hand he wrote, but where it seemed to him sometimes that the earlier learning of the public school had been hermetically sealed within him by several coats of mathematical varnish. He believed that he had once known a number of things that he no longer knew, and that he had not always been so weak in his double letters as he presently found himself.

One night while Gregory sat on a high stool and rested his elbow on the desk before it, with his chin in his hand, looking down upon Fane, who sprawled sadly in his chair, and listening to the last dance playing in the distant parlor, Fane said. "Now, what'll you bet that they won't every one of 'em come and look for a letter in her box before she goes to bed? I tell you, girls are queer, and there's no place like a hotel to study 'em."

"I don't want to study them," said Gregory, harshly.

"Think Greek's more worth your while, or know 'em well enough already?" Fane suggested.

"No, I don't know them at all," said the student.

"I don't believe," urged the clerk, as if it were relevant, "that there's a girl in the house that you couldn't marry, if you gave your mind to it."

Gregory twitched irascibly. "I don't want to marry them."

"Pretty cheap lot, you mean? Well, I don't know."

"I don't mean that," retorted the student. "But I've got other things to think of."

"Don't you believe," the clerk modestly urged, "that it is natural for a man— well, a young man—to think about girls?"

"I suppose it is."

"And you don't consider it wrong?"

"How, wrong?"

"Well, a waste of time. I don't know as I always think about wanting to marry 'em, or be in love, but I like to let my mind run on 'em. There's something about a girl that, well, you don't know what it is, exactly. Take almost any of 'em," said the clerk, with an air of inductive reasoning. "Take that Claxon girl, now for example, I don't know what it is about her. She's good-looking, I don't deny that; and she's got pretty manners, and she's as graceful as a bird. But it a'n't any one of 'em, and it don't seem to be all of 'em put together that makes you want to keep your eyes on her the whole while. Ever noticed what a nice little foot she's got? Or her hands?"

"No," said the student.

"I don't mean that she ever tries to show them off; though I know some girls that would. But she's not that kind. She ain't much more than a child, and yet you got to treat her just like a woman. Noticed the kind of way she's got?"

"No," said the student, with impatience.

The clerk mused with a plaintive air for a moment before he spoke. "Well, it's something as if she'd been trained to it, so that she knew just the right thing to do, every time, and yet I guess it's nature. You know how the chef always calls her the Boss? That explains it about as well as anything, and I presume that's what my mind was running on, the other day, when I called her Boss. But, my! I can't get anywhere near her since!"

"It serves you right," said Gregory. "You had no business to tease her."

"Now, do you think it was teasing? I did, at first, and then again it seemed to me that I came out with the word because it seemed the right one. I presume I couldn't explain that to her."

"It wouldn't be easy."

"I look upon her," said Fane, with an effect of argument in the sweetness of his smile, "just as I would upon any other young lady in the house. Do you spell apology with one p or two?"

"One," said the student, and the clerk made a minute on a piece of paper.

"I feel badly for the girl. I don't want her to think I was teasing her or taking any sort of liberty with her. Now, would you apologize to her, if you was in my place, and would you write a note, or just wait your chance and speak to her?"

Gregory got down from his stool with a disdainful laugh, and went out of the place. "You make me sick, Fane," he said.

The last dance was over, and the young ladies who had been waltzing with one another, came out of the parlor with gay cries and laughter, like summer girls who had been at a brilliant hop, and began to stray down the piazzas, and storm into the office. Several of them fluttered up to the desk, as the clerk had foretold, and looked for letters in the boxes bearing their initials. They called him out, and asked if he had not forgotten something for them. He denied it with a sad, wise smile, and then they tried to provoke him to a belated flirtation, in lack of other material, but he met their overtures discreetly, and they presently said, Well, they guessed they must go; and went. Fane turned to encounter Gregory, who had come in by a side door.

"Fane, I want to beg your pardon. I was rude to you just now."

"Oh, no! Oh, no!" the clerk protested. "That's all right. Sit down a while, can't you, and talk with a fellow. It's early, yet."

"No, I can't. I just wanted to say I was sorry I spoke in that way. Good-night. Is there anything in particular?"

"No; good-night. I was just wondering about—that girl."

"Oh!"

VI.

Gregory had an habitual severity with his own behavior which did not stop there, but was always passing on to the behavior of others; and his days went by in alternate offence and reparation to those he had to do with. He had to do chiefly with the dining-room girls, whose susceptibilities were such that they kept about their work bathed in tears or suffused with anger much of the time. He was not only good-looking but he was a college student, and their feelings were ready to bud toward him in tender efflorescence, but he kept them cropped and blighted by his curt words and impatient manner. Some of them loved him for the hurts he did them, and some hated him, but all agreed fondly or furiously that he was too cross for anything. They were mostly young school-mistresses, and whether they were of a soft and amorous make, or of a forbidding temper, they knew enough in spite of their hurts to value a young fellow whose thoughts were not running upon girls all the time. Women, even in their spring-time, like men to treat them as if they had souls as well as hearts, and it was a saving grace in Gregory that he treated them all, the silliest of them, as if they had souls. Very likely they responded more with their hearts than with their souls, but they were aware that this was not his fault.

The girls that waited at table saw that he did not distinguish in manner between them and the girls whom they served. The knot between his brows did not dissolve in the smiling gratitude of the young ladies whom he preceded to their places, and pulled out their chairs for, any more than in the blandishments of a waitress who thanked him for some correction.

They owned when he had been harshest that no one could be kinder if he saw a girl really trying, or more patient with well meaning stupidity, but some things fretted him, and he was as apt to correct a girl in her grammar as in her table service. Out of work hours, if he met any of them, he recognized them with deferential politeness; but he shunned occasions of encounter with them as distinctly as he avoided the ladies among the hotel guests. Some of the table girls pitied his loneliness, and once they proposed that he should read to them on the back piazza in the leisure of their mid-afternoons. He said that he had to keep up with his studies in all the time he could get; he treated their request with grave civility, but they felt his refusal to be final.

He was seen very little about the house outside of his own place and function, and he was scarcely known to consort with anyone but Fane, who celebrated his high sense of the honor to the lady-guests; but if any of these would have been willing to show Gregory that they considered his work to get an education as something that redeemed itself from discredit through the nobility of its object, he gave them no chance to do so.

The afternoon following their talk about Clementina, Gregory looked in for Fane behind the letter boxes, but did not find him, and the girl herself came round from the front to say that he was out buying, but would be back now, very soon; it was occasionally the clerk's business to forage among the farmers for the lighter supplies, such as eggs, and butter, and poultry, and this was the buying that Clementina meant. "Very well, I'll wait here for him a little while," Gregory answered.

"So do," said Clementina, in a formula which she thought polite; but she saw the frown with which Gregory took a Greek book from his pocket, and she hurried round in front of the boxes again, wondering how she could have displeased him. She put her face in sight a moment to explain, "I have got to be here and give out the lettas till Mr. Fane gets back," and then withdrew it. He tried to lose himself in his book, but her tender voice spoke from time to time beyond the boxes, and Gregory kept listening for Clementina to say, "No'm, there a'n't. Perhaps, the'e'll be something the next mail," and "Yes'm, he'e's one, and I guess this paper is for some of youa folks, too."

Gregory shut his book with a sudden bang at last and jumped to his feet, to go away.

The girl came running round the corner of the boxes. "Oh! I thought something had happened."

"No, nothing has happened," said Gregory, with a sort of violence; which was heightened by a sense of the rings and tendrils of loose hair springing from the mass that defined her pretty head. "Don't you know that you oughtn't to say 'No'm' and 'Yes'm?'" he demanded, bitterly, and then he expected to see the water come into her eyes, or the fire into her cheeks.

Clementina merely looked interested. "Did I say that? I meant to say Yes, ma'am and No, ma'am; but I keep forgetting."

"You oughtn't to say anything!" Gregory answered savagely, "Just say Yes, and No, and let your voice do the rest."

"Oh!" said the girl, with the gentlest abeyance, as if charmed with the novelty of the idea. "I should be afraid it wasn't polite."

Gregory took an even brutal tone. It seemed to him as if he were forced to hurt her feelings. But his words, in spite of his tone, were not brutal; they might have even been thought flattering. "The politeness is in the manner, and you don't need anything but your manner."

"Do you think so, truly?" asked the girl joyously. "I should like to try it once!"

He frowned again. "I've no business to criticise your way of speaking."

"Oh yes'm—yes, ma'am; sir, I mean; I mean, Oh, yes, indeed! The'a! It does sound just as well, don't it?" Clementina laughed in triumph at the outcome of her efforts, so that a reluctant visional smile came upon Gregory's face, too. "I'm very mach obliged to you, Mr. Gregory—I shall always want to do it, if it's the right way."

"It's the right way," said Gregory coldly.

"And don't they," she urged, "don't they really say Sir and Ma'am, whe'e— whe'e you came from?"

He said gloomily, "Not ladies and gentlemen. Servants do. Waiters—like me." He inflicted this stab to his pride with savage fortitude and he bore with self-scorn the pursuit of her innocent curiosity.

"But I thought—I thought you was a college student."

"Were," Gregory corrected her, involuntarily, and she said, "Were, I mean."

"I'm a student at college, and here I'm a servant! It's all right!" he said with a suppressed gritting of the teeth; and he added, "My Master was the servant of the meanest, and I must—I beg your pardon for meddling with your manner of speaking—"

"Oh, I'm very much obliged to you; indeed I am. And I shall not care if you tell me of anything that's out of the way in my talking," said Clementina, generously.

"Thank you; I think I won't wait any longer for Mr. Fane."

"Why, I'm su'a he'll be back very soon, now. I'll try not to disturb you any moa."

Gregory turned from taking some steps towards the door, and said, "I wish you would tell Mr. Fane something."

"For you? Why, suttainly!"

"No. For you. Tell him that it's all right about his calling you Boss."

The indignant color came into Clementina's face. "He had no business to call me that."

"No; and he doesn't think he had, now. He's truly sorry for it."

"I'll see," said Clementina.

She had not seen by the time Fane got back. She received his apologies for being gone so long coldly, and went away to Mrs. Atwell, whom she told what had passed between Gregory and herself.

"Is he truly so proud?" she asked.

"He's a very good young man," said Mrs. Atwell, "but I guess he's proud. He can't help it, but you can see he fights against it. If I was you, Clem, I wouldn't say anything to the guls about it."

"Oh, no'm—I mean, no, indeed. I shouldn't think of it. But don't you think that was funny, his bringing in Christ, that way?"

"Well, he's going to be a minister, you know."

"Is he really?" Clementina was a while silent. At last she said, "Don't you think Mr. Gregory has a good many freckles?"

"Well, them red-complected kind is liable to freckle," said Mrs. Atwell, judicially.

After rather a long pause for both of them, Clementina asked, "Do you think it would be nice for me to ask Mr. Gregory about things, when I wasn't suttain?"

"Like what?"

"Oh-wo'ds, and pronunciation; and books to read."

"Why, I presume he'd love to have you. He's always correctin' the guls; I see him take up a book one day, that one of 'em was readin', and when she as't him about it, he said it was rubbage. I guess you couldn't have a betta guide."

"Well, that was what I was thinking. I guess I sha'n't do it, though. I sh'd neva have the courage." Clementina laughed and then fell rather seriously silent again.

VII.

One day the shoeman stopped his wagon at the door of the helps' house, and called up at its windows, "Well, guls, any of you want to git a numba foua foot into a rumba two shoe, to-day? Now's youa chance, but you got to be quick abort it. The'e ha'r't but just so many numba two shoes made, and the wohld's full o' rumba foua feet."

The windows filled with laughing faces at the first sound of the shoeman's ironical voice; and at sight of his neat wagon, with its drawers at the rear and sides, and its buggy-hood over the seat where the shoeman lounged lazily holding the reins, the girls flocked down the stairs, and out upon the piazza where the shoe man had handily ranged his vehicle.

They began to ask him if he had not this thing and that, but he said with firmness, "Nothin' but shoes, guls. I did carry a gen'l line, one while, of what you may call ankle-wea', such as spats, and stockin's, and gaitas, but I nova did like to speak of such things befoa ladies, and now I stick ex-elusively to shoes. You know that well enough, guls; what's the use?"

He kept a sober face amidst the giggling that his words aroused,—and let his voice sink into a final note of injury.

"Well, if you don't want any shoes, to-day, I guess I must be goin'." He made a feint of jerking his horse's reins, but forebore at the entreaties that went up from the group of girls.

"Yes, we do!" "Let's see them!" "Oh, don't go!" they chorused in an equally histrionic alarm, and the shoeman got down from his perch to show his wares.

"Now, the'a, ladies," he said, pulling out one of the drawers, and dangling a pair of shoes from it by the string that joined their heels, "the'e's a shoe that looks as good as any Sat'd'y-night shoe you eva see. Looks as han'some as if it had a pasteboa'd sole and was split stock all through, like the kind you buy for a dollar at the store, and kick out in the fust walk you take with your fella—'r some other gul's fella, I don't ca'e which. And yet that's an honest shoe, made of the best of material all the way through, and in the best manna. Just look at that shoe, ladies; ex-amine it; sha'n't cost you a cent, and I'll pay for youa lost time myself, if any complaint is made." He began to toss pairs of the shoes into the crowd of girls, who caught them from each other before they fell, with hysterical laughter, and ran away with them in-doors to try them on. "This is a shoe that I'm intaducin'," the shoeman went on, "and every pair is warranted— warranted numba two; don't make any otha size, because we want to cata to a strictly numba two custom. If any lady doos feel 'em a little mite too snug, I'm sorry for her, but I can't do anything to help her in this shoe."

"Too snug!" came a gay voice from in-doors. "Why my foot feels puffectly lost in this one."

"All right," the shoeman shouted back. "Call it a numba one shoe and then see if you can't find that lost foot in it, some'eres. Or try a little flour, and see if it won't feel more at home. I've hea'd of a shoe that give that sensation of looseness by not goin' on at all."

The girls exulted joyfully together at the defeat of their companion, but the shoeman kept a grave face, while he searched out other sorts of shoes and slippers, and offered them, or responded to some definite demand with something as near like as he could hope to make serve. The tumult of talk and laughter grew till the chef put his head out of the kitchen door, and then came sauntering across the grass to the helps' piazza. At the same time the clerk suffered himself to be lured from his post by the excitement. He came and stood beside the chef, who listened to the shoeman's flow of banter with a longing to take his chances with him.

"That's a nice hawss," he said. "What'll you take for him?"

"Why, hello!" said the shoeman, with an eye that dwelt upon the chef's official white cap and apron, "You talk English, don't you? Fust off, I didn't know but it was one of them foreign dukes come ova he'a to marry some oua poor millionai'es daughtas." The girls cried out for joy, and the chef bore their mirth stoically, but not without a personal relish of the shoeman's up-and-comingness. "Want a hawss?" asked the shoeman with an air of business. "What'll you give?"

"I'll give you thutty-seven dollas and a half," said the chef.

"Sorry I can't take it. That hawss is sellin' at present for just one hundred and fifty dollas."

"Well," said the chef, "I'll raise you a dolla and a quahta. Say thutty-eight and seventy-five."

"W-ell now, you're gittin' up among the figgas where you're liable to own a hawss. You just keep right on a raisin' me, while I sell these ladies some shoes, and maybe you'll hit it yit, 'fo'e night."

The girls were trying on shoes on every side now, and they had dispensed with the formality of going in-doors for the purpose. More than one put out her foot to the clerk for his opinion of the fit, and the shoeman was mingling with the crowd, testing with his hand, advising from his professional knowledge, suggesting, urging, and in some cases artfully agreeing with the reluctance shown.

"This man," said the chef, indicating Fane, "says you can tell moa lies to the square inch than any man out o' Boston."

"Doos he?" asked the shoeman, turning with a pair of high-heeled bronze slippers in his hand from the wagon. "Well, now, if I stood as nea' to him as you do, I believe I sh'd hit him."

"Why, man, I can't dispute him!" said the chef, and as if he had now at last scored a point, he threw back his head and laughed. When he brought down his head again, it was to perceive the approach of Clementina. "Hello," he said for her to hear, "he'e comes the Boss. Well, I guess I must be goin'," he added, in mock anxiety. "I'm a goin', Boss, I'm a goin'."

Clementina ignored him. "Mr. Atwell wants to see you a moment, Mr. Fane," she said to the clerk.

"All right, Miss Claxon," Fane answered, with the sorrowful respect which he always showed Clementina, now, "I'll be right there." But he waited a moment, either in expression of his personal independence, or from curiosity to know what the shoeman was going to say of the bronze slippers.

Clementina felt the fascination, too; she thought the slippers were beautiful, and her foot thrilled with a mysterious prescience of its fitness for them.

"Now, the'e, ladies, or as I may say guls, if you'll excuse it in one that's moa like a fatha to you than anything else, in his feelings"—the girls tittered, and some one shouted derisively—"It's true!"—"now there is a shoe, or call it a slippa, that I've rutha hesitated about showin' to you, because I know that you're all rutha serious-minded, I don't ca'e how young ye be, or how good-lookin' ye be; and I don't presume the'e's one among you that's eve' head o' dancin'." In the mirthful hooting and mocking that followed, the shoeman hedged gravely from the extreme position he had taken. "What? Well, maybe you have among some the summa folks, but we all know what summa folks ah', and I don't expect you to patte'n by them. But what I will say is that if any young lady within the sound of my voice,"—he looked round for the applause which did not fail him in his parody of the pulpit style—"should get an invitation to a dance next winta, and should feel it a wo'k of a charity to the young man to go, she'll be sorry—on his account, rememba—that she ha'n't got this pair o' slippas.

"The'a! They're a numba two, and they'll fit any lady here, I don't ca'e how small a foot she's got. Don't all speak at once, sistas! Ample time allowed for meals. That's a custom-made shoe, and if it hadn't b'en too small for the lady they was oddid foh, you couldn't-'a' got 'em for less than seven dollas; but now I'm throwin' on 'em away for three."

A groan of dismay went up from the whole circle, and some who had pressed forward for a sight of the slippers, shrank back again.

"Did I hea' just now," asked the shoeman, with a soft insinuation in his voice, and in the glance he suddenly turned upon Clementina, "a party addressed as Boss?" Clementina flushed, but she did not cower; the chef walked away with a laugh, and the shoeman pursued him with his voice. "Not that I am goin' to folla the wicked example of a man who tries to make spot of young ladies; but if the young lady addressed as Boss—"

"Miss Claxon," said the clerk with ingratiating reverence.

"Miss Claxon—I Stan' corrected," pursued the shoeman. "If Miss Claxon will do me the fava just to try on this slippa, I sh'd be able to tell at the next place I stopped just how it looked on a lady's foot. I see you a'n't any of you disposed to buy 'em this aftanoon, 'and I a'n't complainin'; you done pootty well by me, already, and I don't want to uhge you; but I do want to carry away the picture, in my mind's eye—what you may call a mental photograph—of this slipper on the kind of a foot it was made fob, so't I can praise it truthfully to my next customer. What do you say, ma'am?" he addressed himself with profound respect to Clementina.

"Oh, do let him, Clem!" said one of the girls, and another pleaded, "Just so he needn't tell a story to his next customa," and that made the rest laugh.

Clementina's heart was throbbing, and joyous lights were dancing in her eyes. "I don't care if I do," she said, and she stooped to unlace her shoe, but one of the big girls threw herself on her knees at her feet to prevent her. Clementina remembered too late that there was a hole in her stocking and that her little toe came through it, but she now folded the toe artfully down, and the big girl discovered the hole in time to abet her attempt at concealment. She caught the slipper from the shoeman and harried it on; she tied the ribbons across the instep, and then put on the other. "Now put out youa foot, Clem! Fast dancin' position!" She leaned back upon her own heels, and Clementina daintily lifted the edge of her skirt a little, and peered over at her feet. The slippers might or might not have been of an imperfect taste, in their imitation of the prevalent fashion, but on Clementina's feet they had distinction.

"Them feet was made for them slippas," said the shoeman devoutly.

The clerk was silent; he put his hand helplessly to his mouth, and then dropped it at his side again.

Gregory came round the corner of the building from the dining-room, and the big girl who was crouching before Clementina, and who boasted that she was not afraid of the student, called saucily to him, "Come here, a minute, Mr. Gregory," and as he approached, she tilted aside, to let him see Clementina's slippers.

Clementina beamed up at him with all her happiness in her eyes, but after a faltering instant, his face reddened through its freckles, and he gave her a rebuking frown and passed on.

"Well, I decla'e!" said the big girl. Fane turned uneasily, and said with a sigh, he guessed he must be going, now.

A blight fell upon the gay spirits of the group, and the shoeman asked with an ironical glance after Gregory's retreating figure, "Owna of this propaty?"

"No, just the ea'th," said the big girl, angrily.

The voice of Clementina made itself heard with a cheerfulness which had apparently suffered no chill, but was really a rising rebellion. "How much ah' the slippas?"

"Three dollas," said the shoeman in a surprise which he could not conceal at Clementina's courage.

She laughed, and stooped to untie the slippers. "That's too much for me."

"Let me untie 'em, Clem," said the big girl. "It's a shame for you eva to take 'em off."

"That's right, lady," said the shoeman. "And you don't eva need to," he added, to Clementina, "unless you object to sleepin' in 'em. You pay me what you want to now, and the rest when I come around the latta paht of August."

"Oh keep 'em, Clem!" the big girl urged, passionately, and the rest joined her with their entreaties.

"I guess I betta not," said Clementina, and she completed the work of taking off the slippers in which the big girl could lend her no further aid, such was her affliction of spirit.

"All right, lady," said the shoeman. "Them's youa slippas, and I'll just keep 'em for you till the latta paht of August."

He drove away, and in the woods which he had to pass through on the road to another hotel he overtook the figure of a man pacing rapidly. He easily recognized Gregory, but he bore him no malice. "Like a lift?" he asked, slowing up beside him.

"No, thank you," said Gregory. "I'm out for the walk." He looked round furtively, and then put his hand on the side of the wagon, mechanically, as if to detain it, while he walked on.

"Did you sell the slippers to the young lady?"

"Well, not as you may say sell, exactly," returned the shoeman, cautiously.

"Have you-got them yet?" asked the student.

"Guess so," said the man. "Like to see 'em?"

He pulled up his horse.

Gregory faltered a moment. Then he said, "I'd like to buy them. Quick!"

He looked guiltily about, while the shoeman alertly obeyed, with some delay for a box to put them in. "How much are they?"

"Well, that's a custom made slipper, and the price to the lady that oddid'em was seven dollas. But I'll let you have 'em for three—if you want 'em for a present."—The shoeman was far too discreet to permit himself anything so overt as a smile; he merely let a light of intelligence come into his face.

Gregory paid the money. "Please consider this as confidential," he said, and he made swiftly away. Before the shoeman could lock the drawer that had held the slippers, and clamber to his perch under the buggy-hood, Gregory was running back to him again.

"Stop!" he called, and as he came up panting in an excitement which the shoeman might well have mistaken for indignation attending the discovery of some blemish in his purchase. "Do you regard this as in any manner a deception?" he palpitated.

"Why," the shoeman began cautiously, "it wa'n't what you may call a promise, exactly. More of a joke than anything else, I looked on it. I just said I'd keep 'em for her; but—"

"You don't understand. If I seemed to disapprove—if I led any one to suppose, by my manner, or by—anything—that I thought it unwise or unbecoming to buy the shoes, and then bought them myself, do you think it is in the nature of an acted falsehood?"

"Lo'd no!" said the shoeman, and he caught up the slack of his reins to drive on, as if he thought this amusing maniac might also be dangerous.

Gregory stopped him with another question. "And shall—will you—think it necessary to speak of—of this transaction? I leave you free!"

"Well," said the shoeman. "I don't know what you're after, exactly, but if you think I'm so shot on for subjects that I've got to tell the folks at the next stop that I sold a fellar a pair of slippas for his gul—Go 'long!" he called to his horse, and left Gregory standing in the middle of the road.

VIII.

The people who came to the Middlemount in July were ordinarily the nicest, but that year the August folks were nicer than usual and there were some students among them, and several graduates just going into business, who chose to take their outing there instead of going to the sea-side or the North Woods. This was a chance that might not happen in years again, and it made the house very gay for the young ladies; they ceased to pay court to the clerk, and asked him for letters only at mail-time. Five or six couples were often on the floor together, at the hops, and the young people sat so thick upon the stairs that one could scarcely get up or down.

So many young men made it gay not only for the young ladies, but also for a certain young married lady, when she managed to shirk her rather filial duties to her husband, who was much about the verandas, purblindly feeling his way with a stick, as he walked up and down, or sitting opaque behind the glasses that preserved what was left of his sight, while his wife read to him. She was soon acquainted with a good many more people than he knew, and was in constant request for such occasions as needed a chaperon not averse to mountain climbing, or drives to other hotels for dancing and supper and return by moonlight, or the more boisterous sorts of charades; no sheet and pillow case party was complete without her; for welsh-rarebits her presence was essential. The event of the conflict between these social claims and her duties to her husband was her appeal to Mrs. Atwell on a point which the landlady referred to Clementina.

"She wants somebody to read to her husband, and I don't believe but what you could do it, Clem. You're a good reader, as good as I want to hear, and while you may say that you don't put in a great deal of elocution, I guess you can read full well enough. All he wants is just something to keep him occupied, and all she wants is a chance to occupy herself with otha folks. Well, she is moa their own age. I d'know as the's any hahm in her. And my foot's so much betta, now, that I don't need you the whole while, any moa."

"Did you speak to her about me?" asked the girl.

"Well, I told her I'd tell you. I couldn't say how you'd like."

"Oh, I guess I should like," said Clementina, with her eyes shining. "But—I should have to ask motha."

"I don't believe but what your motha'd be willin'," said Mrs. Atwell. "You just go down and see her about it."

The next day Mrs. Milray was able to take leave of her husband, in setting off to matronize a coaching party, with an exuberance of good conscience that she shared with the spectators. She kissed him with lively affection, and charged him not to let the child read herself to death for him. She captioned Clementina that Mr. Milray never knew when he was tired, and she had better go by the clock in her reading, and not trust to any sign from him.

Clementina promised, and when the public had followed Mrs. Milray away, to watch her ascent to the topmost seat of the towering coach, by means of the ladder held in place by two porters, and by help of the down-stretched hands of all the young men on the coach, Clementina opened the book at the mark she found in it, and began to read to Mr. Milray.

The book was a metaphysical essay, which he professed to find a lighter sort of reading than fiction; he said most novelists were too seriously employed in preventing the marriage of the lovers, up to a certain point, to be amusing; but you could always trust a metaphysician for entertainment if he was very much in earnest, and most metaphysicians were. He let Clementina read on a good while in her tender voice, which had still so many notes of childhood in it, before he manifested any consciousness of being read to. He kept the smile on his delicate face which had come there when his wife said at parting, "I don't believe I should leave her with you if you could see how prettty she was," and he held his head almost motionlessly at the same poise he had given it in listening to her final charges. It was a fine head, still well covered with soft hair, which lay upon it in little sculpturesque masses, like chiseled silver, and the acquiline profile had a purity of line in the arch of the high nose and the jut of the thin lips and delicate chin, which had not been lost in the change from youth to age. One could never have taken it for the profile of a New York lawyer who had early found New York politics more profitable than law, and after a long time passed in city affairs, had emerged with a name shadowed by certain doubtful transactions. But this was Milray's history, which in the rapid progress of American events, was so far forgotten that you had first to remind people of what he had helped do before you could enjoy their surprise in realizing that this gentle person, with the cast of intellectual refinement which distinguished his face, was the notorious Milray, who was once in all the papers. When he made his game and retired from politics, his family would have sacrificed itself a good deal to reclaim him socially, though they were of a severer social than spiritual conscience, in the decay of some ancestral ideals. But he had rendered their willingness hopeless by marrying, rather late in life, a young girl from the farther West who had come East with a general purpose to get on. She got on very well with Milray, and it was perhaps not altogether her own fault that she did not get on so well with his family, when she began to substitute a society aim for the artistic ambition that had brought her to New York. They might have forgiven him for marrying her, but they could not forgive her for marrying him. They were of New England origin and they were perhaps a little more critical with her than if they had been New Yorkers of Dutch strain. They said that she was a little Western hoyden, but that the stage would have been a good place for her if she could have got over her Pike county accent; in the hush of family councils they confided to one another the belief that there were phases of the variety business in which her accent would have been no barrier to her success, since it could not have been heard in the dance, and might have been disguised in the song.

"Will you kindly read that passage over again?" Milray asked as Clementina paused at the end of a certain paragraph. She read it, while he listened attentively. "Could you tell me just what you understand by that?" he pursued, as if he really expected Clementina to instruct him.

She hesitated a moment before she answered, "I don't believe I undastand anything at all."

"Do you know," said Milray, "that's exactly my own case? And I've an idea that the author is in the same box," and Clementina perceived she might laugh, and laughed discreetly.

Milray seemed to feel the note of discreetness in her laugh, and he asked, smiling, "How old did you tell me you were?"

"I'm sixteen," said Clementina.

"It's a great age," said Milray. "I remember being sixteen myself; I have never been so old since. But I was very old for my age, then. Do you think you are?"

"I don't believe I am," said Clementina, laughing again, but still very discreetly.

"Then I should like to tell you that you have a very agreeable voice. Do you sing?"

"No'm—no, sir—no," said Clementina, "I can't sing at all."

"Ah, that's very interesting," said Milray, "but it's not surprising. I wish I could see your face distinctly; I've a great curiosity about matching voices and faces; I must get Mrs. Milray to tell me how you look. Where did you pick up your pretty knack at reading? In school, here?"

"I don't know," answered Clementina. "Do I read-the way you want?"

"Oh, perfectly. You let the meaning come through—when there is any."

"Sometimes," said Clementina ingenuously, "I read too fast; the children ah' so impatient when I'm reading to them at home, and they hurry me. But I can read a great deal slower if you want me to."

"No, I'm impatient, too," said Milray. "Are there many of them,—the children?"

"There ah' six in all."

"And are you the oldest?"

"Yes," said Clementina. She still felt it very blunt not to say sir, too, but she tried to make her tone imply the sir, as Mr. Gregory had bidden her.

"You've got a very pretty name."

Clementina brightened. "Do you like it? Motha gave it to me; she took it out of a book that fatha was reading to her."

"I like it very much," said Milray. "Are you tall for your age?"

"I guess I am pretty tall."

"You're fair, of course. I can tell that by your voice; you've got a light-haired voice. And what are your eyes?"

"Blue!" Clementina laughed at his pursuit.

"Ah, of course! It isn't a gray-eyed blonde voice. Do you think—has anybody ever told you-that you were graceful?"

"I don't know as they have," said Clementina, after thinking.

"And what is your own opinion?" Clementina began to feel her dignity infringed; she did not answer, and now Milray laughed. "I felt the little tilt in your step as you came up. It's all right. Shall we try for our friend's meaning, now?"

Clementina began again, and again Milray stopped her. "You mustn't bear malice. I can hear the grudge in your voice; but I didn't mean to laugh at you. You don't like being made fun of, do you?"

"I don't believe anybody does," said Clementina.

"No, indeed," said Milray. "If I had tried such a thing I should be afraid you would make it uncomfortable for me. But I haven't, have I?"

"I don't know," said Clementina, reluctantly.

Milray laughed gleefully. "Well, you'll forgive me, because I'm an old fellow. If I were young, you wouldn't, would you?"

Clementina thought of the clerk; she had certainly never forgiven him. "Shall I read on?" she asked.

"Yes, yes. Read on," he said, respectfully. Once he interrupted her to say that she pronounced admirable, but he would like now and then to differ with her about a word if she did not mind. She answered, Oh no, indeed; she should like it ever so much, if he would tell her when she was wrong. After that he corrected her, and he amused himself by studying forms of respect so delicate that they should not alarm her pride; Clementina reassured him in terms as fine as his own. She did not accept his instructions implicitly; she meant to bring them to the bar of Gregory's knowledge. If he approved of them, then she would submit.

Milray easily possessed himself of the history of her life and of all its circumstances, and he said he would like to meet her father and make the acquaintance of a man whose mind, as Clementina interpreted it to him, he found so original.

He authorized his wife to arrange with Mrs. Atwell for a monopoly of Clementina's time while he stayed at Middlemount, and neither he nor Mrs. Milray seemed surprised at the good round sum, as the landlady thought it, which she asked in the girl's behalf.

IX

The Milrays stayed through August, and Mrs. Milray was the ruling spirit of the great holiday of the summer, at Middlemount. It was this year that the landlords of the central mountain region had decided to compete in a coaching parade, and to rival by their common glory the splendor of the East Side and the West Side parades. The boarding-houses were to take part, as well as the hotels; the farms where only three or four summer folks were received, were to send their mountain-wagons, and all were to be decorated with bunting. An arch draped with flags and covered with flowers spanned the entrance to the main street at Middlemount Centre, and every shop in the village was adorned for the event.

Mrs. Milray made the landlord tell her all about coaching parades, and the champions of former years on the East Side and the West Side, and then she said that the Middlemount House must take the prize from them all this year, or she should never come near his house again. He answered, with a dignity and spirit he rarely showed with Mrs. Milray's class of custom, "I'm goin' to drive our hossis myself."

She gave her whole time to imagining and organizing the personal display on the coach. She consulted with the other ladies as to the kind of dresses that were to be worn, but she decided everything herself; and when the time came she had all the young men ravaging the lanes and pastures for the goldenrod and asters which formed the keynote of her decoration for the coach.

She made peace and kept it between factions that declared themselves early in the affair, and of all who could have criticized her for taking the lead perhaps none would have willingly relieved her of the trouble. She freely declared that it was killing her, and she sounded her accents of despair all over the place. When their dresses were finished she made the persons of her drama rehearse it on the coach top in the secret of the barn, where no one but the stable men were suffered to see the effects she aimed at. But on the eve of realizing these in public she was overwhelmed by disaster. The crowning glory of her composition was to be a young girl standing on the highest seat of the coach, in the character of the Spirit of Summer, wreathed and garlanded with flowers, and invisibly sustained by the twelve months of the year, equally divided as to sex, but with the more difficult and painful attitudes assigned to the gentlemen who were to figure as the fall and winter months. It had been all worked out and the actors drilled in their parts, when the Spirit of Summer, who had been chosen for the inoffensiveness of her extreme youth, was taken with mumps, and withdrawn by the doctor's orders. Mrs. Milray had now not only to improvise another Spirit of Summer, but had to choose her from a group of young ladies, with the chance of alienating and embittering those who were not chosen. In her calamity she asked her husband what she should do, with but the least hope that he could tell her. But he answered promptly, "Take Clementina; I'll let you have her for the day," and then waited for the storm of her renunciations and denunciations to spend itself.

"To be sure," she said, when this had happened, "it isn't as if she were a servant in the house; and the position can be regarded as a kind of public function, anyhow. I can't say that I've hired her to take the part, but I can give her a present afterwards, and it will be the same thing."

The question of clothes for Clementina Mrs. Milray declared was almost as sweeping in its implication as the question of the child's creation. "She has got to be dressed new from head to foot," she said, "every stitch, and how am I to manage it in twenty-four hours?"

By a succession of miracles with cheese-cloth, and sashes and ribbons, it was managed; and ended in a triumph so great that Mrs. Milray took the girl in her arms and kissed her for looking the Spirit of Summer to a perfection that the victim of the mumps could not have approached. The victory was not lastingly marred by the failure of Clementina's shoes to look the Spirit of Summer as well as the rest of her costume. No shoes at all world have been the very thing, but shoes so shabby and worn down at one side of the heel as Clementina's were very far from the thing. Mrs. Milray decided that another fold of cheese-cloth would add to the statuesque charm of her figure, and give her more height; and she was richly satisfied with the effect when the Middlemount coach drove up to the great veranda the next morning, with all the figures of her picture in position on its roof, and Clementina supreme among them. She herself mounted in simple, undramatized authority to her official seat beside the landlord, who in coachman's dress, with a bouquet of autumnal flowers in his lapel, sat holding his garlanded reins over the backs of his six horses; and then the coach as she intended it to appear in the parade set out as soon as the turnouts of the other houses joined it. They were all to meet at the Middlemount, which was thickly draped and festooned in flags, with knots of evergreen and the first red boughs of the young swamp maples holding them in place over its irregular facade. The coach itself was amass of foliage and flowers, from which it defined itself as a wheeled vehicle in vague and partial outline; the other wagons and coaches, as they drove tremulously up, with an effect of having been mired in blossoms about their spokes and hubs, had the unwieldiness which seems inseparable from spectacularity. They represented motives in color and design sometimes tasteless enough, and sometimes so nearly very good that Mrs. Milray's heart was a great deal in her mouth, as they arrived, each with its hotel-cry roared and shrilled from a score of masculine and feminine throats, and finally spelled for distinctness sake, with an ultimate yell or growl. But she had not finished giving the lady-representative of a Sunday newspaper the points of her own tableau, before she regained the courage and the faith in which she remained serenely steadfast throughout the parade.

It was when all the equipages of the neighborhood had arrived that she climbed to her place; the ladder was taken away; the landlord spoke to his horses, and the Middlemount coach led the parade, amid the renewed slogans, and the cries and fluttered handkerchiefs of the guests crowding the verandas.

The line of march was by one road to Middlemount Centre, where the prize was to be awarded at the judges' stand, and then the coaches were to escort the triumphant vehicle homeward by another route, so as to pass as many houses on the way as possible. It was a curious expression of the carnival spirit in a region immemorially starved of beauty in the lives of its people; and whatever was the origin of the mountain coaching parade, or from whatever impulse of sentimentality or advertising it came, the effect was of undeniable splendor, and of phantasmagoric strangeness.

Gregory watched its progress from a hill-side pasture as it trailed slowly along the rising and falling road. The songs of the young girls, interrupted by the explosion of hotel slogans and college cries from the young men, floated off to him on the thin breeze of the cloudless August morning, like the hymns and shouts of a saturnalian rout going in holiday processional to sacrifice to their gods. Words of fierce Hebrew poetry burned in his thought; the warnings and the accusals and the condemnations of the angry prophets; and he stood rapt from his own time and place in a dream of days when the Most High stooped to commune face to face with His ministers, while the young voices of those forgetful or ignorant of Him, called to his own youth, and the garlanded chariots, with their banners and their streamers passed on the road beneath him and out of sight in the shadow of the woods beyond.

When the prize was given to the Middlemount coach at the Center the landlord took the flag, and gallantly transferred it to Mrs. Milray, and Mrs. Milray passed it up to Clementina, and bade her, "Wave it, wave it!"

The village street was thronged with people that cheered, and swung their hats and handkerchiefs to the coach as it left the judges' stand and drove under the triumphal arch, with the other coaches behind it. Then Atwell turned his horses heads homewards, and at the brisker pace with which people always return from festivals or from funerals, he left the village and struck out upon the country road with his long escort before him. The crowd was quick to catch the courteous intention of the victors, and followed them with applause as far beyond the village borders as wind and limb would allow; but the last noisy boy had dropped off breathless before they reached a half-finished house in the edge of some woods. A line of little children was drawn up by the road-side before it, who watched the retinue with grave eagerness, till the Middlemount coach came in full sight. Then they sprang into the air, and beating their hands together, screamed, "Clem! Clem! Oh it's Clem!" and jumped up and down, and a shabby looking work worn woman came round the corner of the house and stared up at Clementina waving her banner wildly to the children, and shouting unintelligible words to them. The young people on the coach joined in response to the children, some simply, some ironically, and one of the men caught up a great wreath of flowers which lay at Clementina's feet, and flung it down to them; the shabby woman quickly vanished round the corner of the house again. Mrs. Milray leaned over to ask the landlord, "Who in the world are Clementina's friends?"

"Why don't you know?" he retorted in abated voice. "Them's her brothas and sistas."

"And that woman?"

"The lady at the conna? That's her motha."

When the event was over, and all the things had been said and said again, and there was nothing more to keep the spring and summer months from going up to their rooms to lie down, and the fall and winter months from trying to get something to eat, Mrs. Milray found herself alone with Clementina.

The child seemed anxious about something, and Mrs. Milray, who wanted to go and lie down, too, asked a little impatiently, "What is it, Clementina?"

"Oh, nothing. Only I was afraid maybe you didn't like my waving to the children, when you saw how queea they looked." Clementina's lips quivered.

"Did any of the rest say anything?"

"I know what they thought. But I don't care! I should do it right over again!"

Mrs. Milray's happiness in the day's triumph was so great that she could indulge a generous emotion. She caught the girl in her arms. "I want to kiss you; I want to hug you, Clementina!"

X.

The notion of a dance for the following night to celebrate the success of the house in the coaching parade came to Mrs. Milray aver a welsh-rarebit which she gave at the close of the evening. The party was in the charge of Gregory, who silently served them at their orgy with an austerity that might have conspired with the viand itself against their dreams, if they had not been so used to the gloom of his ministrations. He would not allow the waitresses to be disturbed in their evening leisure, or kept from their sleep by such belated pleasures; and when he had provided the materials for the rarebit, he stood aloof, and left their combination to Mrs. Milray and her chafing-dish.

She had excluded Clementina on account of her youth, as she said to one of the fall and winter months, who came in late, and noticed Clementina's absence with a "Hello! Anything the matter with the Spirit of Summer?" Clementina had become both a pet and a joke with these months before the parade was over, and now they clamored together, and said they must have her at the dance anyway. They were more tepidly seconded by the spring and summer months, and Mrs. Milray said, "Well, then, you'll have to all subscribe and get her a pair of dancing slippers." They pressed her for her meaning, and she had to explain the fact of Clementina's destitution, which that additional fold of cheese-cloth had hidden so well in the coaching tableau that it had never been suspected. The young men entreated her to let them each buy a pair of slippers for the Spirit of Summer, which she should wear in turn for the dance that she must give each of them; and this made Mrs. Milray declare that, no, the child should not come to the dance at all, and that she was not going to have her spoiled. But, before the party broke up, she promised that she would see what could be done, and she put it very prettily to the child the next day, and waited for her to say, as she knew she must, that she could not go, and why. They agreed that the cheese-cloth draperies of the Spirit of Summer were surpassingly fit for the dance; but they had to agree that this still left the question of slippers untouched. It remained even more hopeless when Clementina tried on all of Mrs. Milray's festive shoes, and none of her razorpoints and high heels would avail. She went away disappointed, but not yet disheartened; youth does not so easily renounce a pleasure pressed to the lips; and Clementina had it in her head to ask some of the table girls to help her out. She meant to try first with that big girl who had helped her put on the shoeman's bronze slippers; and she hurried through the office, pushing purblindly past Fane without looking his way, when he called to her in the deference which he now always used with her, "Here's a package here for you, Clementina—Miss Claxon," and he gave her an oblong parcel, addressed in a hand strange to her. "Who is it from?" she asked, innocently, and Fane replied with the same ingenuousness: "I'm sure I don't know." Afterwards he thought of having retorted, "I haven't opened it," but still without being certain that he would have had the courage to say it.

Clementina did not think of opening it herself, even when she was alone in her little room above Mrs. Atwell's, until she had carefully felt it over, and ascertained that it was a box of pasteboard, three or four inches deep and wide, and eight or ten inches long. She looked at the address again, "Miss Clementina Claxon," and at the narrow notched ribbon which tied it, and noted that the paper it was wrapped in was very white and clean. Then she sighed, and loosed the knot, and the paper slipped off the box, and at the same time the lid fell off, and the shoe man's bronze slippers fell out upon the floor.

Either it must be a dream or it must be a joke; it could not be both real and earnest; somebody was trying to tease her; such flattery of fortune could not be honestly meant. But it went to her head, and she was so giddy with it as she caught the slippers from the floor, and ran down to Mrs. Atwell, that she knocked against the sides of the narrow staircase.

"What is it? What does it mean? Who did it?" she panted, with the slippers in her hand. "Whe'e did they come from?" She poured out the history of her trying on these shoes, and of her present need of them and of their mysterious coming, to meet her longing after it had almost ceased to be a hope. Mrs. Atwell closed with her in an exultation hardly short of a clapping the hands. Her hair was gray, and the girl's hair still hung in braids down her back, but they were of the same age in their transport, which they referred to Mrs. Milray, and joined with her in glad but fruitless wonder who had sent Clementina the shoes. Mrs. Atwell held that the help who had seen the girl trying them on had clubbed together and got them for her at the time; and had now given them to her for the honor she had done the Middlemount House in the parade. Mrs. Milray argued that the spring and summer months had secretly dispatched some fall and winter month to ransack the stores at Middlemount Centre for them. Clementina believed that they came from the shoe man himself, who had always wanted to send them, in the hope that she would keep them, and had merely happened to send them just then in that moment of extremity when she was helpless against them. Each conjecture involved improbabilities so gross that it left the field free to any opposite theory.

Rumor of the fact could not fail to go through the house, and long before his day's work was done it reached the chef, and amused him as a piece of the Boss's luck. He was smoking his evening pipe at the kitchen door after supper, when Clementina passed him on one of the many errands that took her between Mrs. Milray's room and her own, and he called to her: "Boss, what's this I hear about a pair o' glass slippas droppin' out the sky int' youa lap?"

Clementina was so happy that she thought she might trust him for once, and she said, "Oh, yes, Mr. Mahtin! Who do you suppose sent them?" she entreated him so sweetly that it would have softened any heart but the heart of a tease.

"I believe I could give a pootty good guess if I had the facts."

Clementina innocently gave them to him, and he listened with a well-affected sympathy.

"Say Fane fust told you about 'em?"

"Yes. 'He'e's a package for you,' he said. Just that way; and he couldn't tell me who left it, or anything."

"Anybody asked him about it since?"

"Oh, yes! Mrs. Milray, and Mrs. Atwell, and Mr. Atwell, and everybody."

"Everybody." The chef smiled with a peculiar droop of one eye. "And he didn't know when the slippas got into the landlo'd's box?"

"No. The fust thing he knew, the' they we'e!" Clementina stood expectant, but the chef smoked on as if that were all there was to say, and seemed to have forgotten her. "Who do you think put them thea, Mr. Mahtin?"

The chef looked up as if surprised to find her still there. "Oh! Oh, yes! Who d' I think? Why, I know, Boss. But I don't believe I'd betta tell you."

"Oh, do, Mr. Mahtin! If you knew how I felt about it—"

"No, no! I guess I betta not. 'Twouldn't do you any good. I guess I won't say anything moa. But if I was in youa place, and I really wanted to know whe'e them slippas come from—"

"I do—I do indeed—"

The chef paused before he added, "I should go at Fane. I guess what he don't know ain't wo'th knowin', and I guess nobody else knows anything. Thea! I don't know but I said mo'n I ought, now."

What the chef said was of a piece with what had been more than once in Clementina's mind; but she had driven it out, not because it might not be true, but because she would not have it true. Her head drooped; she turned limp and springless away. Even the heart of the tease was touched; he had not known that it would worry her so much, though he knew that she disliked the clerk.

"Mind," he called after her, too late, "I ain't got no proof 't he done it."

She did not answer him, or look round. She went to her room, and sat down in the growing dusk to think, with a hot lump in her throat.

Mrs. Atwell found her there an hour later, when she climbed to the chamber where she thought she ought to have heard Clementina moving about over her own room.

"Didn't know but I could help you do youa dressin'," she began, and then at sight of the dim figure she broke off: "Why, Clem! What's the matte? Ah' you asleep? Ah' you sick? It's half an hour of the time and—"

"I'm not going," Clementina answered, and she did not move.

"Not goin'! Why the land o'—"

"Oh, I can't go, Mrs. Atwell. Don't ask me! Tell Mrs. Milray, please!"

"I will, when I got something to tell," said Mrs. Atwell. "Now, you just say what's happened, Clementina Claxon!" Clementina suffered the woful truth to be drawn from her. "But you don't know whether it's so or not," the landlady protested.

"Yes, yes, I do! It was the last thing I thought of, and the chef wouldn't have said it if he didn't believe it."

"That's just what he would done," cried Mrs. Atwell. "And I'll give him such a goin' ova, for his teasin', as he ain't had in one while. He just said it to tease. What you goin' to say to Mrs. Milray?"

"Oh, tell her I'm not a bit well, Mrs. Atwell! My head does ache, truly."

"Why, listen," said Mrs. Atwell, recklessly. "If you believe he done it—and he no business to—why don't you just go to the dance, in 'em, and then give 'em back to him after it's ova? It would suv him right."

Clementina listened for a moment of temptation, and then shook her head. "It wouldn't do, Mrs. Atwell; you know it wouldn't," she said, and Mrs. Atwell had too little faith in her suggestion to make it prevail. She went away to carry Clementina's message to Mrs. Milray, and her task was greatly eased by the increasing difficulty Mrs. Milray had begun to find, since the way was perfectly smoothed for her, in imagining the management of Clementina at the dance: neither child nor woman, neither servant nor lady, how was she to be carried successfully through it, without sorrow to herself or offence to others? In proportion to the relief she felt, Mrs. Milray protested her irreconcilable grief; but when the simpler Mrs. Atwell proposed her going and reasoning with Clementina, she said, No, no; better let her alone, if she felt as she did; and perhaps after all she was right.

XI.

Clementina listened to the music of the dance, till the last note was played; and she heard the gay shouts and laughter of the dancers as they issued from the ball room and began to disperse about the halls and verandas, and presently to call good night to one another. Then she lighted her lamp, and put the slippers back into the box and wrapped it up in the nice paper it had come in, and tied it with the notched ribbon. She thought how she had meant to put the slippers away so, after the dance, when she had danced her fill in them, and how differently she was doing it all now. She wrote the clerk's name on the parcel, and then she took the box, and descended to the office with it. There seemed to be nobody there, but at the noise of her step Fane came round the case of letter-boxes, and advanced to meet her at the long desk.

"What's wanted, Miss Claxon?" he asked, with his hopeless respectfulness. "Anything I can do for you?"

She did not answer, but looked him solemnly in the eyes and laid the parcel down on the open register, and then went out.

He looked at the address on the parcel, and when he untied it, the box fell open and the shoes fell out of it, as they had with Clementina. He ran with them behind the letter-box frame, and held them up before Gregory, who was seated there on the stool he usually occupied, gloomily nursing his knee.

"What do you suppose this means, Frank?"

Gregory looked at the shoes frowningly. "They're the slippers she got to-day.

She thinks you sent them to her."

"And she wouldn't have them because she thought I sent them! As sure as I'm standing here, I never did it," said the clerk, solemnly.

"I know it," said Gregory. "I sent them."

"You!"

"What's so wonderful?" Gregory retorted. "I saw that she wanted them that day when the shoe peddler was here. I could see it, and you could."

"Yes."

"I went across into the woods, and the man overtook me with his wagon. I was tempted, and I bought the slippers of him. I wanted to give them to her then, but I resisted, and I thought I should never give them. To-day, when I heard that she was going to that dance, I sent them to her anonymously. That's all there is about it."

The clerk had a moment of bitterness. "If she'd known it was you, she wouldn't have given them back."

"That's to be seen. I shall tell her, now. I never meant her to know, but she must, because she's doing you wrong in her ignorance."

Gregory was silent, and Fane was trying to measure the extent of his own suffering, and to get the whole bearing of the incident in his mind. In the end his attempt was a failure. He asked Gregory, "And do you think you've done just right by me?"

"I've done right by nobody," said Gregory, "not even by myself; and I can see that it was my own pleasure I had in mind. I must tell her the truth, and then I must leave this place."

"I suppose you want I should keep it quiet," said Fane.

"I don't ask anything of you."

"And she wouldn't," said Fane, after reflection. "But I know she'd be glad of it, and I sha'n't say anything. Of course, she never can care for me; and—there's my hand with my word, if you want it." Gregory silently took the hand stretched toward him and Fane added: "All I'll ask is that you'll tell her I wouldn't have presumed to send her the shoes. She wouldn't be mad at you for it."

Gregory took the box, and after some efforts to speak, he went away. It was an old trouble, an old error, an old folly; he had yielded to impulse at every step, and at every step he had sinned against another or against himself. What pain he had now given the simple soul of Fane; what pain he had given that poor child who had so mistaken and punished the simple soul! With Fane it was over now, but with Clementina the worst was perhaps to come yet. He could not hope to see the girl before morning, and then, what should he say to her? At sight of a lamp burning in Mrs. Atwell's room, which was on a level with the veranda where he was walking, it came to him that first of all he ought to go to her, and confess the whole affair; if her husband were with her, he ought to confess before him; they were there in the place of the child's father and mother, and it was due to them. As he pressed rapidly toward the light he framed in his thought the things he should say, and he did not notice, as he turned to enter the private hallway leading to Mrs. Atwell's apartment, a figure at the door. It shrank back from his contact, and he recognized Clementina. His purpose instantly changed, and he said, "Is that you, Miss Claxon? I want to speak with you. Will you come a moment where I can?"

"I—I don't know as I'd betta," she faltered. But she saw the box under his arm, and she thought that he wished to speak to her about that, and she wanted to hear what he would say. She had been waiting at the door there, because she could not bear to go to her room without having something more happen.

"You needn't be afraid. I shall not keep you. Come with me a moment. There is something I must tell you at once. You have made a mistake. And it is my fault. Come!"

Clementina stepped out into the moonlight with him, and they walked across the grass that sloped between the hotel and the river. There were still people about, late smokers singly, and in groups along the piazzas, and young couples, like themselves, strolling in the dry air, under the pure sky.

Gregory made several failures in trying to begin, before he said: "I have to tell you that you are mistaken about Mr. Fane. I was there behind the letter boxes when you came in, and I know that you left these shoes because you thought he sent them to you. He didn't send them." Clementina did not say anything, and Gregory was forced to ask: "Do you wish to know who sent them? I won't tell you unless you do wish it."

"I think I ought to know," she said, and she asked, "Don't you?"

"Yes; for you must blame some one else now, for what you thought Fane did. I sent them to you."

Clementina's heart gave a leap in her breast, and she could not say anything. He went on.

"I saw that you wanted them that day, and when the peddler happened to overtake me in the woods where I was walking, after I left you, I acted on a sudden impulse, and I bought them for you. I meant to send them to you anonymously, then. I had committed one error in acting upon impulse-my rashness is my besetting sin—and I wished to add a species of deceit to that. But I was kept from it until-to-day. I hoped you would like to wear them to the dance to-night, and I put them in the post-office for you myself. Mr. Fane didn't know anything about it. That is all. I am to blame, and no one else."

He waited for her to speak, but Clementina could only say, "I don't know what to say."

"You can't say anything that would be punishment enough for me. I have acted foolishly, cruelly."

Clementina did not think so. She was not indignant, as she was when she thought Fane had taken this liberty with her, but if Mr. Gregory thought it was so very bad, it must be something much more serious than she had imagined. She said, "I don't see why you wanted to do it," hoping that he would be able to tell her something that would make his behavior seem less dreadful than he appeared to think it was.

"There is only one thing that could justify it, and that is something that I cannot justify." It was very mysterious, but youth loves mystery, and Clementina was very young. "I did it," said Gregory solemnly, and he felt that now he was acting from no impulse, but from a wisely considered decision which he might not fail in without culpability, "because I love you."

"Oh!" said Clementina, and she started away from him.

"I knew that it would make me detestable!" he cried, bitterly. "I had to tell you, to explain what I did. I couldn't help doing it. But now if you can forget it, and never think of me again, I can go away, and try to atone for it somehow. I shall be guided."

Clementina did not know why she ought to feel affronted or injured by what he had said to her; but if Mr. Gregory thought it was wrong for him to have spoken so, it must be wrong. She did not wish him to feel badly, even if he had done wrong, but she had to take his view of what he had done. "Why, suttainly, Mr. Gregory," she answered. "You mustn't mind it."

"But I do mind it. I have been very, very selfish, very thoughtless. We are both too young. I can't ask you to wait for me till I could marry—"

The word really frightened Clementina. She said, "I don't believe I betta promise."

"Oh, I know it!" said Gregory. "I am going away from here. I am going to-morrow as soon as I can arrange—as soon as I can get away. Good-night—I"—Clementina in her agitation put her hands up to her face. "Oh, don't cry—I can't bear to have you cry."

She took down her hands. "I'm not crying! But I wish I had neva seen those slippas."

They had come to the bank of the river, whose current quivered at that point in a scaly ripple in the moonlight. At her words Gregory suddenly pulled the box from under his arm, and flung it into the stream as far as he could. It caught upon a shallow of the ripple, hung there a moment, then loosed itself, and swam swiftly down the stream.

"Oh!" Clementina moaned.

"Do you want them back?" he demanded. "I will go in for them!"

"No, no! No. But it seemed such a—waste!"

"Yes, that is a sin, too." They climbed silently to the hotel. At Mrs. Atwell's door, he spoke. "Try to forget what I said, and forgive me, if you can."

"Yes—yes, I will, Mr. Gregory. You mustn't think of it any moa."

XII

Clementina did not sleep till well toward morning, and she was still sleeping when Mrs. Atwell knocked and called in to her that her brother Jim wanted to see her. She hurried down, and in the confusion of mind left over from the night before she cooed sweetly at Jim as if he had been Mr. Gregory, "What is it, Jim? What do you want me for?"

The boy answered with the disgust a sister's company manners always rouse in a brother. "Motha wants you. Says she's wo'ked down, and she wants you to come and help." Then he went his way.

Mrs. Atwell was used to having help snatched from her by their families at a moment's notice. "I presume you've got to go, Clem," she said.

"Oh, yes, I've got to go," Clementina assented, with a note of relief which mystified Mrs. Atwell.

"You tied readin' to Mr. Milray?"

"Oh, no'm-no, I mean. But I guess I betta go home. I guess I've been away long enough."

"Well, you're a good gul, Clem. I presume your motha's got a right to have you home if she wants you." Clementina said nothing to this, but turned briskly, and started upstairs toward her room again. The landlady called after her, "Shall you speak to Mis' Milray, or do you want I should?"

Clementina looked back at her over her shoulder to warble, "Why, if you would, Mrs. Atwell," and kept on to her room.

Mrs. Milray was not wholly sorry to have her go; she was going herself very soon, and Clementina's earlier departure simplified the question of getting rid of her; but she overwhelmed her with reproaches which Clementina received with such sweet sincerity that another than Mrs. Milray might have blamed herself for having abused her ingenuousness.

The Atwells could very well have let the girl walk home, but they sent her in a buckboard, with one of the stablemen to drive her. The landlord put her neat bundle under the seat of the buckboard with his own hand. There was something in the child's bearing, her dignity and her amiability, which made people offer her, half in fun, and half in earnest, the deference paid to age and state.

She did not know whether Gregory would try to see her before she went. She thought he must have known she was going, but since he neither came to take leave of her, nor sent her any message, she decided that she had not expected him to do so. About the third week of September she heard that he had left Middlemount and gone back to college.

She kept at her work in the house and helped her mother, and looked after the little ones; she followed her father in the woods, in his quest of stuff for walking sticks, and advised with both concerning the taste of summer folks in dress and in canes. The winter came, and she read many books in its long leisure, mostly novels, out of the rector's library. He had a whole set of Miss Edgeworth, and nearly all of Miss Austen and Miss Gurney, and he gave of them to Clementina, as the best thing for her mind as well as her morals; he believed nothing could be better for any one than these old English novels, which he had nearly forgotten in their details. She colored the faded English life of the stories afresh from her Yankee circumstance; and it seemed the consensus of their testimony that she had really been made love to, and not so very much too soon, at her age of sixteen, for most of their heroines were not much older. The terms of Gregory's declaration and of its withdrawal were mystifying, but not more mystifying than many such things, and from what happened in the novels she read, the affair might be trusted to come out all right of itself in time. She was rather thoughtfuller for it, and once her mother asked her what was the matter with her. "Oh, I guess I'm getting old, motha," she said, and turned the question off. She would not have minded telling her mother about Gregory, but it would not have been the custom; and her mother would have worried, and would have blamed him. Clementina could have more easily trusted her father with the case, but so far as she knew fathers never were trusted with anything of the kind. She would have been willing that accident should bring it to the knowledge of Mrs. Richling; but the moment never came when she could voluntarily confide in her, though she was a great deal with her that winter. She was Mrs. Richling's lieutenant in the social affairs of the parish, which the rector's wife took under her care. She helped her get up entertainments of the kind that could be given in the church parlor, and they managed together some dances which had to be exiled to the town hall. They contrived to make the young people of the village feel that they were having a gay time, and Clementina did not herself feel that it was a dull one. She taught them some of the new steps and figures which the help used to pick up from the summer folks at the Middlemount, and practise together; she liked doing that; her mother said the child would rather dance than eat, any time. She was never sad, but so much dignity got into her sweetness that the rector now and then complained of feeling put down by her.

She did not know whether she expected Gregory to write to her or not; but when no letters came she decided that she had not expected them. She wondered if he would come back to the Middlemount the next summer; but when the summer came, she heard that they had another student in his place. She heard that they had a new clerk, and that the boarders were not so pleasant. Another year passed, and towards the end of the season Mrs. Atwell wished her to come and help her again, and Clementina went over to the hotel to soften her refusal. She explained that her mother had so much sewing now that she could not spare her; and Mrs. Atwell said: Well, that was right, and that she must be the greatest kind of dependence for her mother. "You ah' going on seventeen this year, ain't you?"

"I was nineteen the last day of August," said Clementina, and Mrs. Atwell sighed, and said, How the time did fly.

It was the second week of September, but Mrs. Atwell said they were going to keep the house open till the middle of October, if they could, for the autumnal foliage, which there was getting to be quite a class of custom for.

"I presume you knew Mr. Landa was dead," she added, and at Clementina's look of astonishment, she said with a natural satisfaction, "Mm! died the thutteenth day of August. I presumed somehow you'd know it, though you didn't see a great deal of 'em, come to think of it. I guess he was a good man; too good for her, I guess," she concluded, in the New England necessity of blaming some one. "She sent us the papah."

There was an early frost; and people said there was going to be a hard winter, but it was not this that made Clementina's father set to work finishing his house. His turning business was well started, now, and he had got together money enough to pay for the work. He had lately enlarged the scope of his industry by turning gate-posts and urns for the tops of them, which had become very popular, for the front yards of the farm and village houses in a wide stretch of country. They sold more steadily than the smaller wares, the cups, and tops, and little vases and platters which had once been the output of his lathe; after the first season the interest of the summer folks in these fell off; but the gate posts and the urns appealed to a lasting taste in the natives.

Claxon wished to put the finishing touches on the house himself, and he was willing to suspend more profitable labors to do so. After some attempts at plastering he was forced to leave that to the plasterers, but he managed the clap-boarding, with Clementina to hand him boards and nails, and to keep him supplied with the hammer he was apt to drop at critical moments. They talked pretty constantly at their labors, and in their leisure, which they spent on the brown needles under the pines at the side of the house. Sometimes the hammering or the talking would be interrupted by a voice calling, from a passing vehicle in the hidden roadway, something about urns. Claxon would answer, without troubling himself to verify the inquirer; or moving from his place, that he would get round to them, and then would hammer on, or talk on with Clementina.

One day in October a carriage drove up to the door, after the work on the house had been carried as far as Claxon's mood and money allowed, and he and Clementina were picking up the litter of his carpentering. He had replaced the block of wood which once served at the front door by some steps under an arbor of rustic work; but this was still so novel that the younger children had not outgrown their pride in it and were playing at house-keeping there. Clementina ran around to the back door and out through the front entry in time to save the visitor and the children from the misunderstanding they began to fall into, and met her with a smile of hospitable brilliancy, and a recognition full of compassionate welcome.

Mrs. Lander gave way to her tears as she broke out, "Oh, it ain't the way it was the last time I was he'a! You hea'd that he—that Mr. Landa—"

"Mrs. Atwell told me," said Clementina. "Won't you come in, and sit down?"

"Why, yes." Mrs. Lander pushed in through the narrow door of what was to be the parlor. Her crapes swept about her and exhaled a strong scent of their dyes. Her veil softened her heavy face; but she had not grown thinner in her bereavement.

"I just got to the Middlemount last night," she said, "and I wanted to see you and your payrents, both, Miss Claxon. It doos bring him back so! You won't neva know how much he thought of you, and you'll all think I'm crazy. I wouldn't come as long as he was with me, and now I have to come without him; I held out ag'inst him as long as I had him to hold out ag'inst. Not that he was eva one to push, and I don't know as he so much as spoke of it, afta we left the hotel two yea's ago; but I presume it wa'n't out of his mind a single minute. Time and time again I'd say to him, 'Now, Albe't, do you feel about it just the way you done?' and he'd say, 'I ha'r't had any call to charge my mind about it,' and then I'd begin tryin' to ahgue him out of it, and keep a hectorin', till he'd say, 'Well, I'm not askin' you to do it,' and that's all I could get out of him. But I see all the while 't he wanted me to do it, whateva he asked, and now I've got to do it when it can't give him any pleasure." Mrs. Lander put up her black-bordered handkerchief and sobbed into it, and Clementina waited till her grief had spent itself; then she gave her a fan, and Mrs. Lander gratefully cooled her hot wet face. The children had found the noises of her affliction and the turbid tones of her monologue annoying, and had gone off to play in the woods; Claxon kept incuriously about the work that Clementina had left him to; his wife maintained the confidence which she always felt in Clementina's ability to treat with the world when it presented itself, and though she was curious enough, she did not offer to interrupt the girl's interview with Mrs. Lander; Clementina would know how to behave.

Mrs. Lander, when she had refreshed herself with the fan, seemed to get a fresh grip of her theme, and she told Clementina all abort Mr. Lander's last sickness. It had been so short that it gave her no time to try the climate of Colorado upon him, which she now felt sure would have brought him right up; and she had remembered, when too late, to give him a liver-medicine of her own, though it did not appear that it was his liver which was affected; that was the strange part of it. But, brief as his sickness was, he had felt that it was to be his last, and had solemnly talked over her future with her, which he seemed to think would be lonely. He had not named Clementina, but Mrs. Lander had known well enough what he meant; and now she wished to ask her, and her father and mother, how they would all like Clementina to come and spend the winter with her at Boston first, and then further South, and wherever she should happen to go. She apologized for not having come sooner upon this errand; she had resolved upon it as soon as Mr. Lander was gone, but she had been sick herself, and had only just now got out of bed.

Clementina was too young to feel the pathos of the case fully, or perhaps even to follow the tortuous course of Mrs. Lander's motives, but she was moved by her grief; and she could not help a thrill of pleasure in the vague splendor of the future outlined by Mrs. Lander's proposal. For a time she had thought that Mrs. Milray was going to ask her to visit her in New York; Mrs. Milray had thrown out a hint of something of the kind at parting, but that was the last of it; and now she at once made up her mind that she would like to go with Mrs. Lander, while discreetly saying that she would ask her father and mother to come and talk with her.

XIII

Her parents objected to leaving their work; each suggested that the other had better go; but they both came at Clementina's urgence. Her father laughed and her mother frowned when she told them what Mrs. Lander wanted, from the same misgiving of her sanity. They partly abandoned this theory for a conviction of Mrs. Lander's mere folly when she began to talk, and this slowly yielded to the perception that she had some streaks of sense. It was sense in the first place to want to have Clementina with her, and though it might not be sense to suppose that they would be anxious to let her go, they did not find so much want of it as Mrs. Lander talked on. It was one of her necessities to talk away her emotions before arriving at her ideas, which were often found in a tangle, but were not without a certain propriety. She was now, after her interview with Clementina, in the immediate presence of these, and it was her ideas that she began to produce for the girl's father and mother. She said, frankly, that she had more money than she knew what to do with, and they must not think she supposed she was doing a favor, for she was really asking one.

She was alone in the world, without near connections of her own, or relatives of her husband's, and it would be a mercy if they could let their daughter come and visit her; she would not call it more than a visit; that would be the best thing on both sides; she told of her great fancy for Clementina the first time she saw her, and of her husband's wish that she would come and visit with them then for the winter. As for that money she had tried to make the child take, she presumed that they knew about it, and she wished to say that she did it because she was afraid Mr. Lander had said so much about the sewing, that they would be disappointed. She gave way to her tears at the recollection, and confessed that she wanted the child to have the money anyway. She ended by asking Mrs. Claxon if she would please to let her have a drink of water; and she looked about the room, and said that they had got it finished up a great deal, now, had not they? She made other remarks upon it, so apt that Mrs. Claxon gave her a sort of permissive invitation to look about the whole lower floor, ending with the kitchen.

Mrs. Lander sat down there while Mrs. Claxon drew from the pipes a glass of water, which she proudly explained was pumped all over the house by the wind mill that supplied the power for her husband's turning lathes.

"Well, I wish mah husband could have tasted that wata," said Mrs. Lander, as if reminded of husbands by the word, and by the action of putting down the glass. "He was always such a great hand for good, cold wata. My! He'd 'a liked youa kitchen, Mrs. Claxon. He always was such a home-body, and he did get so ti'ed of hotels. For all he had such an appearance, when you see him, of bein'—well!—stiff and proud, he was fah moa common in his tastes—I don't mean common, exactly, eitha—than what I was; and many a time when we'd be drivin' through the country, and we'd pass some o' them long-strung-out houses, don't you know, with the kitchen next to the wood shed, and then an ahchway befoa you get to the stable, Mr. Landa he'd get out, and make an urrand, just so's to look in at the kitchen dooa; he said it made him think of his own motha's kitchen. We was both brought up in the country, that's a fact, and I guess if the truth was known we both expected to settle down and die thea, some time; but now he's gone, and I don't know what'll become o' me, and sometimes I don't much care. I guess if Mr. Landa'd 'a seen youa kitchen, it wouldn't 'a' been so easy to git him out of it; and I do believe if he's livin' anywhe' now he takes as much comfo't in my settin' here as what I do. I presume I shall settle down somewhe's before a great while, and if you could make up youa mind to let your daughta come to me for a little visit till spring, you couldn't do a thing that 'd please Mr. Landa moa."

Mrs. Claxon said that she would talk it over with the child's father; and then Mrs. Lander pressed her to let her take Clementina back to the Middlemount with her for supper, if they wouldn't let her stay the night. After Clementina had driven away, Mrs. Claxon accused herself to her husband of being the greatest fool in the State, but he said that the carriage was one of the Middlemount rigs, and he guessed it was all right. He could see that Clem was wild to go, and he didn't see why she shouldn't.

"Well, I do, then," his wife retorted. "We don't know anything about the woman, or who she is."

"I guess no harm'll come to Clem for one night," said Claxon, and Mrs. Claxon was forced back upon the larger question for the maintenance of her anxiety. She asked what he was going to do about letting Clem go the whole winter with a perfect stranger; and he answered that he had not got round to that yet, and that there were a good many things to be thought of first. He got round to see the rector before dark, and in the light of his larger horizon, was better able to orient Mrs. Lander and her motives than he had been before.

When she came back with the girl the next morning, she had thought of something in the nature of credentials. It was the letter from her church in Boston, which she took whenever she left home, so that if she wished she might unite with the church in any place where she happened to be stopping. It did not make a great impression upon the Klaxons, who were of no religion, though they allowed their children to go to the Episcopal church and Sunday-school, and always meant to go themselves. They said they would like to talk the matter over with the rector, if Mrs. Lander did not object; she offered to send her carriage for him, and the rector was brought at once.

He was one of those men who have, in the breaking down of the old Puritanical faith, and the dying out of the later Unitarian rationalism, advanced and established the Anglican church so notably in the New England hill-country, by a wise conformity to the necessities and exactions of the native temperament. On the ecclesiastical side he was conscientiously uncompromising, but personally he was as simple-mannered as he was simple-hearted. He was a tall lean man in rusty black, with a clerical waistcoat that buttoned high, and scholarly glasses, but with a belated straw hat that had counted more than one summer, and a farmer's tan on his face and hands. He pronounced the church-letter, though quite outside of his own church, a document of the highest respectability, and he listened with patient deference to the autobiography which Mrs. Lander poured out upon him, and her identifications, through reference to this or that person in Boston whom he knew either at first or second hand. He had not to pronounce upon her syntax, or her social quality; it was enough for him, in behalf of the Claxons, to find her what she professed to be.

"You must think," he said, laughing, "that we are over-particular; but the fact is that we value Clementina rather highly, and we wish to be sure that your hospitable offer will be for her real good."

"Of cou'se," said Mrs. Lander. "I should be just so myself abort her."

"I don't know," he continued, "that I've ever said how much we think of her, Mrs. Richling and I, but this seems a good opportunity, as she is not present.

"She is not perfect, but she comes as near being a thoroughly good girl as she can without knowing it. She has a great deal of common-sense, and we all want her to have the best chance."

"Well, that's just the way I feel about her, and that's just what I mean to give her," said Mrs. Lander.

"I am not sure that I make myself quite clear," said the rector. "I mean, a chance to prove how useful and helpful she can be. Do you think you can make life hard for her occasionally? Can you be peevish and exacting, and unreasonable? Can you do something to make her value superfluity and luxury at their true worth?"

Mrs. Lander looked a little alarmed and a little offended. "I don't know as I undastand what you mean, exactly," she said, frowning rather with perplexity than resentment. "But the child sha'n't have a care, and her own motha couldn't be betta to her than me. There a'n't anything money can buy that she sha'n't have, if she wants it, and all I'll ask of her is 't she'll enjoy herself as much as she knows how. I want her with me because I should love to have her round; and we did from the very fust minute she spoke, Mr. Lander and me, both. She shall have her own money, and spend it for anything she pleases, and she needn't do a stitch o' work from mohnin' till night. But if you're afraid I shall put upon her."

"No, no," said the rector, and he threw back his head with a laugh.

When it was all arranged, a few days later, after the verification of certain of Mrs. Lander's references by letters to Boston, he said to Clementina's father and mother, "There's only one danger, now, and that is that she will spoil Clementina; but there's a reasonable hope that she won't know how." He found the Claxons struggling with a fresh misgiving, which Claxon expressed. "The way I look at it is like this. I don't want that woman should eva think Clem was after her money. On the face of it there a'n't very much to her that would make anybody think but what we was after it; and I should want it pootty well undastood that we wa'n't that kind. But I don't seem to see any way of tellin' her."

"No," said the rector, with a sympathetic twinkle, "that would be difficult."

"It's plain to be seen," Mrs. Claxon interposed, "that she thinks a good deal of her money; and I d' know but what she'd think she was doin' Clem most too much of a favor anyway. If it can't be a puffectly even thing, all round, I d' know as I should want it to be at all."

"You're quite right, Mrs. Claxon, quite right. But I believe Mrs. Lander may be safely left to look out for her own interests. After all, she has merely asked Clementina to pass the winter with her. It will be a good opportunity for her to see something of the world; and perhaps it may bring her the chance of placing herself in life. We have got to consider these things with reference to a young girl."

Mrs. Claxon said, "Of cou'se," but Claxon did not assent so readily.

"I don't feel as if I should want Clem to look at it in that light. If the chance don't come to her, I don't want she should go huntin' round for it."

"I thoroughly agree with you," said the rector. "But I was thinking that there was not only no chance worthy of her in Middlemount, but there is no chance at all."

"I guess that's so," Claxon owned with a laugh. "Well, I guess we can leave it to Clem to do what's right and proper everyway. As you say, she's got lots of sense."

From that moment he emptied his mind of care concerning the matter; but husband and wife are never both quite free of care on the same point of common interest, and Mrs. Claxon assumed more and more of the anxieties which he had abandoned. She fretted under the load, and expressed an exasperated tenderness for Clementina when the girl seemed forgetful of any of the little steps to be taken before the great one in getting her clothes ready for leaving home. She said finally that she presumed they were doing a wild thing, and that it looked crazier and crazier the more she thought of it; but all was, if Clem didn't like, she could come home. By this time her husband was in something of that insensate eagerness to have the affair over that people feel in a house where there is a funeral.

At the station, when Clementina started for Boston with Mrs. Lander, her father and mother, with the rector and his wife, came to see her off. Other friends mistakenly made themselves of the party, and kept her talking vacuities when her heart was full, till the train drew up. Her father went with her into the parlor car, where the porter of the Middlemount House set down Mrs. Lander's hand baggage and took the final fee she thrust upon him. When Claxon came out he was not so satisfactory about the car as he might have been to his wife, who had never been inside a parlor car, and who had remained proudly in the background, where she could not see into it from the outside. He said that he had felt so bad about Clem that he did not notice what the car was like. But he was able to report that she looked as well as any of the folks in it, and that, if there were any better dressed, he did not see them. He owned that she cried some, when he said good-bye to her.

"I guess," said his wife, grimly, "we're a passel o' fools to let her go. Even if she don't like, the'a, with that crazy-head, she won't be the same Clem when she comes back."

They were too heavy-hearted to dispute much, and were mostly silent as they drove home behind Claxon's self-broken colt: a creature that had taken voluntarily to harness almost from its birth, and was an example to its kind in sobriety and industry.

The children ran out from the house to meet them, with a story of having seen Clem at a point in the woods where the train always slowed up before a crossing, and where they had all gone to wait for her. She had seen them through the car-window, and had come out on the car platform, and waved her handkerchief, as she passed, and called something to them, but they could not hear what it was, they were all cheering so.

At this their mother broke down, and went crying into the house. Not to have had the last words of the child whom she should never see the same again if she ever saw her at all, was more, she said, than heart could bear.

The rector's wife arrived home with her husband in a mood of mounting hopefulness, which soared to tops commanding a view of perhaps more of this world's kingdoms than a clergyman's wife ought ever to see, even for another. She decided that Clementina's chances of making a splendid match, somewhere, were about of the nature of certainties, and she contended that she would adorn any station, with experience, and with her native tact, especially if it were a very high station in Europe, where Mrs. Lander would now be sure to take her. If she did not take her to Europe, however, she would be sure to leave her all her money, and this would serve the same end, though more indirectly.

Mr. Richling scoffed at this ideal of Clementina's future with a contempt which was as little becoming to his cloth. He made his wife reflect that, with all her inherent grace and charm, Clementina was an ignorant little country girl, who had neither the hardness of heart nor the greediness of soul, which gets people on in the world, and repair for them the disadvantages of birth and education. He represented that even if favorable chances for success in society showed themselves to the girl, the intense and inexpugnable vulgarity of Mrs. Lander would spoil them; and he was glad of this, he said, for he believed that the best thing which could happen to the child would be to come home as sweet and good as she had gone away; he added this was what they ought both to pray for.

His wife admitted this, but she retorted by asking if he thought such a thing was possible, and he was obliged to own that it was not possible. He marred the effect of his concession by subjoining that it was no more possible than her making a brilliant and triumphant social figure in society, either at home or in Europe.

XIV

So far from embarking at once for Europe, Mrs. Lander went to that hotel in a suburb of Boston, where she had the habit of passing the late autumn months, in order to fortify herself for the climate of the early winter months in the city. She was a little puzzled how to provide for Clementina, with respect to herself, but she decided that the best thing would be to have her sleep in a room opening out of her own, with a folding bed in it, so that it could be used as a sort of parlor for both of them during the day, and be within easy reach, for conversation, at all times.

On her part, Clementina began by looking after Mrs. Lander's comforts, large and little, like a daughter, to her own conception and to that of Mrs. Lander, but to other eyes, like a servant. Mrs. Lander shyly shrank from acquaintance among the other ladies, and in the absence of this, she could not introduce Clementina, who went down to an early breakfast alone, and sat apart with her at lunch and dinner, ministering to her in public as she did in private. She ran back to their rooms to fetch her shawl, or her handkerchief, or whichever drops or powders she happened to be taking with her meals, and adjusted with closer care the hassock which the head waiter had officially placed at her feet. They seldom sat in the parlor where the ladies met, after dinner; they talked only to each other; and there, as elsewhere, the girl kept her filial care of the old woman. The question of her relation to Mrs. Lander became so pressing among several of the guests that, after Clementina had watched over the banisters, with throbbing heart and feet, a little dance one night which the other girls had got up among themselves, and had fled back to her room at the approach of one of the kindlier and bolder of them, the landlord felt forced to learn from Mrs. Lander how Miss Claxon was to be regarded. He managed delicately, by saying he would give the Sunday paper she had ordered to her nurse, "Or, I beg your pardon," he added, as if he had made a mistake. "Why, she a'n't my nuhse," Mrs. Lander explained, simply, neither annoyed nor amused; "she's just a young lady that's visiting me, as you may say," and this put an end to the misgiving among the ladies. But it suggested something to Mrs. Lander, and a few days afterwards, when they came out from Boston where they had been shopping, and she had been lavishing a bewildering waste of gloves, hats, shoes, capes and gowns upon Clementina, she said, "I'll tell you what. We've got to have a maid."

"A maid?" cried the girl.

"It isn't me, or my things I want her for," said Mrs. Lander. "It's you and these dresses of youas. I presume you could look afta them, come to give youa mind to it; but I don't want to have you tied up to a lot of clothes; and I presume we should find her a comfo't in moa ways than one, both of us. I don't know what we shall want her to do, exactly; but I guess she will, if she undastands her business, and I want you should go in with me, to-morror, and find one. I'll speak to some of the ladies, and find out whe's the best place to go, and we'll get the best there is."

A lady whom Mrs. Lander spoke to entered into the affair with zeal born of a lurking sense of the wrong she had helped do Clementina in the common doubt whether she was not herself Mrs. Lander's maid. She offered to go into Boston with them to an intelligence office, where you could get nice girls of all kinds; but she ended by giving Mrs. Lander the address, and instructions as to what she was to require in a maid. She was chiefly to get an English maid, if at all possible, for the qualifications would more or less naturally follow from her nationality. There proved to be no English maid, but there was a Swedish one who had received a rigid training in an English family living on the Continent, and had come immediately from that service to seek her first place in America. The manager of the office pronounced her character, as set down in writing, faultless, and Mrs. Lander engaged her. "You want to look afta this young lady," she said, indicating Clementina. "I can look afta myself," but Ellida took charge of them both on the train out from Boston with prompt intelligence.

"We got to get used to it, I guess," Mrs. Lander confided at the first chance of whispering to Clementina.

Within a month after washing the faces and combing the hair of all her brothers and sisters who would suffer it at her hands, Clementina's own head was under the brush of a lady's maid, who was of as great a discreetness in her own way as Clementina herself. She supplied the defects of Mrs. Lander's elementary habits by simply asking if she should get this thing and that thing for the toilet, without criticising its absence,—and then asking whether she should get the same things for her young lady. She appeared to let Mrs. Lander decide between having her brushes in ivory or silver, but there was really no choice for her, and they came in silver. She knew not only her own place, but the places of her two ladies, and she presently had them in such training that they were as proficient in what they might and might not do for themselves and for each other, as if making these distinctions were the custom of their lives.

Their hearts would both have gone out to Ellida, but Ellida kept them at a distance with the smooth respectfulness of the iron hand in the glove of velvet; and Clementina first learned from her to imagine the impassable gulf between mistress and maid.

At the end of her month she gave them, out of a clear sky, a week's warning. She professed no grievance, and was not moved by Mrs. Lander's appeal to say what wages she wanted. She would only say that she was going to take a place an Commonwealth Avenue, where a friend of hers was living, and when the week was up, she went, and left her late mistresses feeling rather blank. "I presume we shall have to get anotha," said Mrs. Lander.

"Oh, not right away!" Clementina pleaded.

"Well, not right away," Mrs. Lander assented; and provisionally they each took the other into her keeping, and were much freer and happier together.

Soon after Clementina was startled one morning, as she was going in to breakfast, by seeing Mr. Fane at the clerk's desk. He did not see her; he was looking down at the hotel register, to compute the bill of a departing guest; but when she passed out she found him watching for her, with some letters.

"I didn't know you were with us," he said, with his pensive smile, "till I found your letters here, addressed to Mrs. Lander's care; and then I put two and two together. It only shows how small the world is, don't you think so? I've just got back from my vacation; I prefer to take it in the fall of the year, because it's so much pleasanter to travel, then. I suppose you didn't know I was here?"

"No, I didn't," said Clementina. "I never dreamed of such a thing."

"To be sure; why should you?" Fane reflected. "I've been here ever since last spring. But I'll say this, Miss Claxon, that if it's the least unpleasant to you, or the least disagreeable, or awakens any kind of associations—"

"Oh, no!" Clementina protested, and Fane was spared the pain of saying what he would do if it were.

He bowed, and she said sweetly, "It's pleasant to meet any one I've seen before. I suppose you don't know how much it's changed at Middlemount since you we' e thea." Fane answered blankly, while he felt in his breast pocket, Oh, he presumed so; and she added: "Ha'dly any of the same guests came back this summer, and they had more in July than they had in August,

Mrs. Atwell said. Mr. Mahtin, the chef, is gone, and newly all the help is different."

Fane kept feeling in one pocket and then slapped himself over the other pockets. "No," he said, "I haven't got it with me. I must have left it in my room. I just received a letter from Frank—Mr. Gregory, you know, I always call him Frank—and I thought I had it with me. He was asking about Middlemount; and I wanted to read you what he said. But I'll find it upstairs. He's out of college, now, and he's begun his studies in the divinity school. He's at Andover. I don't know what to make of Frank, oftentimes," the clerk continued, confidentially. "I tell him he's a kind of a survival, in religion; he's so aesthetic." It seemed to Fane that he had not meant aesthetic, exactly, but he could not ask Clementina what the word was. He went on to say, "He's a grand good fellow, Frank is, but he don't make enough allowance for human nature. He's more like one of those old fashioned orthodox. I go in for having a good time, so long as you don't do anybody else any hurt."

He left her, and went to receive the commands of a lady who was leaning over the desk, and saying severely, "My mail, if you please," and Clementina could not wait for him to come back; she had to go to Mrs. Lander, and get her ready for breakfast; Ellida had taught Mrs. Lander a luxury of helplessness in which she persisted after the maid's help was withdrawn.

Clementina went about the whole day with the wonder what Gregory had said about Middlemount filling her mind. It must have had something to do with her; he could not have forgotten the words he had asked her to forget. She remembered them now with a curiosity, which had no rancor in it, to know why he really took them back. She had never blamed him, and she had outlived the hurt she had felt at not hearing from him. But she had never lost the hope of hearing from him, or rather the expectation, and now she found that she was eager for his message; she decided that it must be something like a message, although it could not be anything direct. No one else had come to his place in her fancy, and she was willing to try what they would think of each other now, to measure her own obligation to the past by a knowledge of his. There was scarcely more than this in her heart when she allowed herself to drift near Fane's place that night, that he might speak to her, and tell her what Gregory had said. But he had apparently forgotten about his letter, and only wished to talk about himself. He wished to analyze himself, to tell her what sort of person he was. He dealt impartially with the subject; he did not spare some faults of his; and after a week, he proposed a correspondence with her, in a letter of carefully studied spelling, as a means of mutual improvement as well as further acquaintance.

It cost Clementina a good deal of trouble to answer him as she wished and not hurt his feelings. She declined in terms she thought so cold that they must offend him beyond the point of speaking to her again; but he sought her out, as soon after as he could, and thanked her for her kindness, and begged her pardon. He said he knew that she was a very busy person, with all the lessons she was taking, and that she had no time for carrying on a correspondence. He regretted that he could not write French, because then the correspondence would have been good practice for her. Clementina had begun taking French lessons, of a teacher who came out from Boston. She lunched three times a week with her and Mrs. Lander, and spoke the language with Clementina, whose accent she praised for its purity; purity of accent was characteristic of all this lady's pupils; but what was really extraordinary in Mademoiselle Claxon was her sense of grammatical structure; she wrote the language even more perfectly than she spoke it; but beautifully, but wonderfully; her exercises were something marvellous.

Mrs. Lander would have liked Clementina to take all the lessons that she heard any of the other young ladies in the hotel were taking. One of them went in town every day, and studied drawing at an art-school, and she wanted Clementina to do that, too. But Clementina would not do that; she had tried often enough at home, when her brother Jim was drawing, and her father was designing the patterns of his woodwork; she knew that she never could do it, and the time would be wasted. She decided against piano lessons and singing lessons, too; she did not care for either, and she pleaded that it would be a waste to study them; but she suggested dancing lessons, and her gift for dancing won greater praise, and perhaps sincerer, than her accent won from Mademoiselle Blanc, though Mrs. Lander said that she would not have believed any one could be more complimentary. She learned the new steps and figures in all the fashionable dances; she mastered some fancy dances, which society was then beginning to borrow from the stage; and she gave these before Mrs. Lander with a success which she felt herself.

"I believe I could teach dancing," she said.

"Well, you won't eve' haf to, child," returned Mrs. Lander, with an eye on the side of the case that seldom escaped her.

In spite of his wish to respect these preoccupations, Fane could not keep from offering Clementina attentions, which took the form of persecution when they changed from flowers for Mrs. Lander's table to letters for herself. He apologized for his letters whenever he met her; but at last one of them came to her before breakfast with a special delivery stamp from Boston. He had withdrawn to the city to write it, and he said that if she could not make him a favorable answer, he should not come back to Woodlake.

She had to show this letter to Mrs. Lander, who asked: "You want he should come back?"

"No, indeed! I don't want eva to see him again."

"Well, then, I guess you'll know how to tell him so."

The girl went into her own room to write, and when she brought her answer to show it to Mrs. Lander she found her in frowning thought. "I don't know but you'll have to go back and write it all over again, Clementina," she said, "if you've told him not to come. I've been thinkin', if you don't want to have anything to do with him, we betta go ouaselves."

"Yes," answered Clementina, "that's what I've said."

"You have? Well, the witch is in it! How came you to—"

"I just wanted to talk with you about it. But I thought maybe you'd like to go. Or at least I should. I should like to go home, Mrs. Landa."

"Home!" retorted Mrs. Lander. "The'e's plenty of places where you can be safe from the fella besides home, though I'll take you back the'a this minute if you say so. But you needn't to feel wo'ked up about it."

"Oh, I'm not," said Clementina, but with a gulp which betrayed her nervousness.

"I did think," Mrs. Lander went on, "that I should go into the Vonndome, for December and January, but just as likely as not he'd come pesterin' the'a, too, and I wouldn't go, now, if you was to give me the whole city of Boston. Why shouldn't we go to Florid?"

When Mrs. Lander had once imagined the move, the nomadic impulse mounted irresistably in her. She spoke of hotels in the South, where they could renew the summer, and she mapped out a campaign which she put into instant action so far as to advance upon New York.

XV

Mrs. Lander went to a hotel in New York where she had been in the habit of staying with her husband, on their way South or North. The clerk knew her, and shook hands with her across the register, and said she could have her old rooms if she wanted them; the bell-boy who took up their hand-baggage recalled himself to her; the elevator-boy welcomed her with a smile of remembrance.

Since she was already up, from coming off the sleeping-car, she had no excuse for not going to breakfast like other people; and she went with Clementina to the dining-room, where the head-waiter, who found them places, spoke with an outlandish accent, and the waiter who served them had a parlance that seemed superficially English, but was inwardly something else; there was even a touch in the cooking of the familiar dishes, that needed translation for the girl's inexperienced palate. She was finding a refuge in the strangeness of everything, when she was startled by the sound of a familiar voice calling, "Clementina Claxon! Well, I was sure all along it was you, and I determined I wouldn't stand it another minute. Why, child, how you have changed! Why, I declare you are quite a woman! When did you come? How pretty you are!" Mrs. Milray took Clementina in her arms and kissed her in proof of her admiration before the whole breakfast room. She was very nice to Mrs. Lander, too, who, when Clementina introduced them, made haste to say that Clementina was there on a visit with her. Mrs. Milray answered that she envied her such a visitor as Miss Claxon, and protested that she should steal her away for a visit to herself, if Mr. Milray was not so much in love with her that it made her jealous. "Mr. Milray has to have his breakfast in his room," she explained to Clementina. "He's not been so well, since he lost his mother. Yes," she said, with decorous solemnity, "I'm still in mourning for her," and Clementina saw that she was in a tempered black. "She died last year, and now I'm taking Mr. Milray abroad to see if it won't cheer him up a little. Are you going South for the winter?" she inquired, politely, of Mrs. Lander. "I wish I was going," she said, when Mrs. Lander guessed they should go, later on. "Well, you must come in and see me all you can, Clementina; and I shall have the pleasure of calling upon you," she added to Mrs. Lander with state that was lost in the soubrette-like volatility of her flight from them the next moment. "Goodness, I forgot all about Mr. Milray's breakfast!" She ran back to the table she had left on the other side of the room.

"Who is that, Clementina?" asked Mrs. Lander, on their way to their rooms. Clementina explained as well as she could, and Mrs. Lander summed up her feeling in the verdict, "Well, she's a lady, if ever I saw a lady; and you don't see many of 'em, nowadays."

The girl remembered how Mrs. Milray had once before seemed very fond of her, and had afterwards forgotten the pretty promises and professions she had made her. But she went with Mrs. Lander to see her, and she saw Mr. Milray, too, for a little while. He seemed glad of their meeting, but still depressed by the bereavement which Mrs. Milray supported almost with gayety. When he left them she explained that he was a good deal away from her, with his family, as she approved of his being, though she had apparently no wish to join him in all the steps of the reconciliation which the mother's death had brought about among them. Sometimes his sisters came to the hotel to see her, but she amused herself perfectly without them, and she gave much more of her leisure to Clementina and Mrs. Lander.

She soon knew the whole history of the relation between them, and the first time that Clementina found her alone with Mrs. Lander she could have divined that Mrs. Lander had been telling her of the Fane affair, even if Mrs. Milray had not at once called out to her, "I know all about it; and I'll tell you what, Clementina, I'm going to take you over with me and marry you to an English Duke. Mrs. Lander and I have been planning it all out, and I'm going to send down to the steamer office, and engage your passage. It's all settled!"

When she was gone, Mrs. Lander asked, "What do you s'pose your folks would say to your goin' to Europe, anyway, Clementina?" as if the matter had been already debated between them.

Clementina hesitated. "I should want to be su'a, Mrs. Milray really wanted me to go ova with her."

"Why, didn't you hear her say so?" demanded Mrs. Lander.

"Yes," sighed Clementina. "Mrs. Lander, I think Mrs. Milray means what she says, at the time, but she is one that seems to forget."

"She thinks the wo'ld of you," Mrs. Lander urged.

"She was very nice to me that summer at Middlemount. I guess maybe she would like to have us go with her," the girl relented.

"I guess we'll wait and see," said Mrs. Lander. "I shouldn't want she should change her mind when it was too late, as you say." They were both silent for a time, and then Mrs. Lander resumed, "But I presume she ha'n't got the only steams that's crossin'. What should you say about goin' over on some otha steams? I been South a good many wintas, and I should feel kind of lonesome goin' round to the places where I been with Mr. Landa. I felt it since I been here in this hotel, some, and I can't seem to want to go ova the same ground again, well, not right away."

Clementina said, "Why, of cou'se, Mrs. Landa."

"Should you be willin'," asked Mrs. Lander, after another little pause, "if your folks was willin', to go ova the'a, to some of them European countries, to spend the winta?"

"Oh yes, indeed!" said Clementina.

They discussed the matter in one of the full talks they both liked. At the end Mrs. Lander said, "Well, I guess you betta write home, and ask your motha whetha you can go, so't if we take the notion we can go any time. Tell her to telegraph, if she'll let you, and do write all the ifs and ands, so't she'll know just how to answa, without havin' to have you write again."

That evening Mrs. Milray came to their table from where she had been dining alone, and asked in banter: "Well, have you made up your minds to go over with me?"

Mrs. Lander said bluntly, "We can't ha'dly believe you really want us to, Mrs. Milray."

"I don't want you? Who put such an idea into your head! Oh, I know!" She threatened Clementina with the door-key, which she was carrying in her hand. "It was you, was it? What an artful, suspicious thing! What's got into you, child? Do you hate me?" She did not give Clementina time to protest. "Well, now, I can just tell you I do want you, and I'll be quite heart-broken if you don't come."

"Well, she wrote to her friends this mohning," Mrs. Lander said, "but I guess she won't git an answa in time for youa steamer, even if they do let her go."

"Oh, yes she will," Mrs. Milray protested. "It's all right, now; you've got to go, and there's no use trying to get out of it."

She came to them whenever she could find them in the dining-room, and she knocked daily at their door till she knew that Clementina had heard from home. The girl's mother wrote, without a punctuation mark in her letter, but with a great deal of sense, that such a thing as her going to Europe could not be settled by telegraph. She did not think it worth while to report all the facts of a consultation with the rector which they had held upon getting Clementina's request, and which had renewed all the original question of her relations with Mrs. Lander in an intensified form. He had disposed of this upon much the same terms as before; and they had yielded more readily because the experiment had so far succeeded. Clementina had apparently no complaint to make of Mrs. Lander; she was eager to go, and the rector and his wife, who had been invited to be of the council, were both of the opinion that a course of European travel would be of the greatest advantage to the girl, if she wished to fit herself for teaching. It was an opportunity that they must not think of throwing away. If Mrs. Lander went to Florence, as it seemed from

Clementina's letter she thought of doing, the girl would pass a delightful winter in study of one of the most interesting cities in the world, and she would learn things which would enable her to do better for herself when she came home than she could ever hope to do otherwise. She might never marry, Mr. Richling suggested, and it was only right and fair that she should be equipped with as much culture as possible for the struggle of life; Mrs. Richling agreed with this rather vague theory, but she was sure that Clementina would get married to greater advantage in Florence than anywhere else. They neither of them really knew anything at first hand about Florence; the rector's opinion was grounded on the thought of the joy that a sojourn in Italy would have been to him; his wife derived her hope of a Florentine marriage for Clementina from several romances in which love and travel had gone hand in hand, to the lasting credit of triumphant American girlhood.

The Claxons were not able to enter into their view of the case, but if Mrs. Lander wanted to go to Florence instead of Florida they did not see why Clementina should not go with her to one place as well as the other. They were not without a sense of flattery from the fact that their daughter was going to Europe; but they put that as far from them as they could, the mother severely and the father ironically, as something too silly, and they tried not to let it weigh with them in making up their mind, but to consider only Clementina's best good, and not even to regard her pleasure. Her mother put before her the most crucial questions she could think of, in her letter, and then gave her full leave from her father as well as herself to go if she wished.

Clementina had rather it had been too late to go with the Milrays, but she felt bound to own her decision when she reached it; and Mrs. Milray, whatever her real wish was, made it a point of honor to help get Mrs. Lander berths on her steamer. It did not require much effort; there are plenty of berths for the latest-comers on a winter passage, and Clementina found herself the fellow passenger of Mrs. Milray.

XVI

As soon as Mrs. Lander could make her way to her state-room, she got into her berth, and began to take the different remedies for sea-sickness which she had brought with her. Mrs. Milray said that was nice, and that now she and Clementina could have a good time. But before it came to that she had taken pity on a number of lonely young men whom she found on board. She cheered them up by walking round the ship with them; but if any of them continued dull in spite of this, she dropped him, and took another; and before she had been two days out she had gone through with nearly all the lonely young men on the list of cabin passengers. She introduced some of them to Clementina, but at such times as she had them in charge; and for the most part she left her to Milray. Once, as the girl sat beside him in her steamer-chair, Mrs. Milray shed a wrap on his knees in whirring by on the arm of one of her young men, with some laughed and shouted charge about it.

"What did she say?" he asked Clementina, slanting the down-pulled brim of his soft hat purblindly toward her.

She said she had not understood, and then Milray asked, "What sort of person is that Boston youth of Mrs. Milray's? Is he a donkey or a lamb?"

Clementina said ingenuously, "Oh, she's walking with that English gentleman now—that lo'd."

"Ah, yes," said Milray. "He's not very much to look at, I hear."

"Well, not very much," Clementina admitted; she did not like to talk against people.

"Lords are sometimes disappointing, Clementina," Milray said, "but then, so are other great men. I've seen politicians on our side who were disappointing, and there are clergymen and gamblers who don't look it." He laughed sadly. "That's the way people talk who are a little disappointing themselves. I hope you don't expect too much of yourself, Clementina?"

"I don't know what you mean," she said, stiffening with a suspicion that he might be going to make fun of her.

He laughed more gayly. "Well, I mean we must hold the other fellows up to their duty, or we can't do our own. We need their example. Charity may begin at home, but duty certainly begins abroad." He went on, as if it were a branch of the same inquiry, "Did you ever meet my sisters? They came to the hotel in New York to see Mrs. Milray."

"Yes, I was in the room once when they came in."

"Did you like them?"

"Yes—I sca'cely spoke to them—I only stayed a moment."

"Would you like to see any more of the family?"

"Why, of cou'se!" Clementina was amused at his asking, but he seemed in earnest.

"One of my sisters lives in Florence, and Mrs. Milray says you think of going there, too."

"Mrs. Landa thought it would be a good place to spend the winter. Is it a pleasant place?"

"Oh, delightful! Do you know much about Italy?"

"Not very much, I don't believe."

"Well, my sister has lived a good while in Florence. I should like to give you a letter to her."

"Oh, thank you!" said Clementina.

Milray smiled at her spare acknowledgment, but inquired gravely: "What do you expect to do in Florence?"

"Why, I presume, whateva Mrs. Landa wants to do."

"Do you think Mrs. Lander will want to go into society?"

This question had not occurred to Clementina. "I don't believe she will," she said, thoughtfully.

"Shall you?"

Clementina laughed, "Why, do you think," she ventured, "that society would want me to?"

"Yes, I think it would, if you're as charming as you've tried to make me believe. Oh, I don't mean, to your own knowledge; but some people have ways of being charming without knowing it. If Mrs. Lander isn't going into society, and there should be a way found for you to go, don't refuse, will you?"

"I shall wait and see if I'm asked, fust."

"Yes, that will be best," said Milray. "But I shall give you a letter to my sister. She and I used to be famous cronies, and we went to a great many parties together when we were young people. We thought the world was a fine thing, then. But it changes."

He fell into a muse, and they were both sitting quite silent when Mrs. Milray came round the corner of the music room in the course of her twentieth or thirtieth compass of the deck, and introduced her lord to her husband and to Clementina. He promptly ignored Milray, and devoted himself to the girl, leaning over her with his hand against the bulkhead behind her and talking down upon her.

Lord Lioncourt must have been about thirty, but he had the heated and broken complexion of a man who has taken more than is good for him in twice that number of years. This was one of the wrongs nature had done him in apparent resentment of the social advantages he was born to, for he was rather abstemious, as Englishmen go. He looked a very shy person till he spoke, and then you found that he was not in the least shy. He looked so English that you would have expected a strong English accent of him, but his speech was more that of an American, without the nasality. This was not apparently because he had been much in America; he was returning from his first visit to the States, which had been spent chiefly in the Territories; after a brief interval of Newport he had preferred the West; he liked rather to hunt than to be hunted, though even in the West his main business had been to kill time, which he found more plentiful there than other game. The natives, everywhere, were much the same thing to him; if he distinguished it was in favor of those who did not suppose themselves cultivated. If again he had a choice it was for the females; they seemed to him more amusing than the males, who struck him as having an exaggerated reputation for humor. He did not care much for Clementina's past, as he knew it from Mrs. Milray, and if it did not touch his fancy, it certainly did not offend his taste. A real aristocracy is above social prejudice, when it will; he had known some of his order choose the mothers of their heirs from the music halls, and when it came to a question of distinctions among Americans, he could not feel them. They might be richer or poorer; but they could not be more patrician or more plebeian.

The passengers, he told Clementina, were getting up, at this point of the ship's run, an entertainment for the benefit of the seaman's hospital in Liverpool, that well-known convention of ocean-travel, which is sure at some time or other, to enlist all the talent on board every English steamer in some sort of public appeal. He was not very clear how he came to be on the committee for drumming up talent for the occasion; his distinction seemed to have been conferred by a popular vote in the smoking room, as nearly as he could make out; but here he was, and he was counting upon Miss Claxon to help him out. He said Mrs. Milray had told him about that charming affair they had got up in the mountains, and he was sure they could have something of the kind again. "Perhaps not a coaching party; that mightn't be so easy to manage at sea. But isn't there something else—some tableaux or something? If we couldn't have the months of the year we might have the points of the compass, and you could take your choice."

He tried to get something out of the notion, but nothing came of it that Mrs. Milray thought possible. She said, across her husband, on whose further side she had sunk into a chair, that they must have something very informal; everybody must do what they could, separately. "I know you can do anything you like, Clementina. Can't you play something, or sing?" At Clementina's look of utter denial, she added, desperately, "Or dance something?" A light came into the girl's face at which she caught. "I know you can dance something! Why, of course! Now, what is it?"

Clementina smiled at her vehemence. "Why, it's nothing. And I don't know whether I should like to."

"Oh, yes," urged Lord Lioncourt. "Such a good cause, you know."

"What is it?" Mrs. Milray insisted. "Is it something you could do alone?"

"It's just a dance that I learned at Woodlake. The teacha said that all the young ladies we'e leaning it. It's a skut-dance—"

"The very thing!" Mrs. Milray shouted. "It'll be the hit of the evening."

"But I've never done it before any one," Clementina faltered.

"They'll all be doing their turns," the Englishman said. "Speaking, and singing, and playing."

Clementina felt herself giving way, and she pleaded in final reluctance, "But I haven't got a pleated skut in my steama trunk."

"No matter! We can manage that." Mrs. Milray jumped to her feet and took Lord Lioncourt's arm. "Now we must go and drum up somebody else." He did not seem eager to go, but he started. "Then that's all settled," she shouted over her shoulder to Clementina.

"No, no, Mrs. Milray!" Clementina called after her. "The ship tilts so—"

"Nonsense! It's the smoothest run she ever made in December. And I'll engage to have the sea as steady as a rock for you. Remember, now, you've promised."

Mrs. Milray whirled her Englishman away, and left Clementina sitting beside her husband.

"Did you want to dance for them, Clementina?" he asked.

"I don't know," she said, with the vague smile of one to whom a pleasant hope has occurred.

"I thought perhaps you were letting Mrs. Milray bully you into it. She's a frightful tyrant."

"Oh, I guess I should like to do it, if you think it would be—nice."

"I dare say it will be the nicest thing at their ridiculous show." Milray laughed as if her willingness to do the dance had defeated a sentimental sympathy in him.

"I don't believe it will be that," said Clementina, beaming joyously. "But I guess I shall try it, if I can find the right kind of a dress."

"Is a pleated skirt absolutely necessary," asked Milray, gravely.

"I don't see how I could get on without it," said Clementina.

She was so serious still when she went down to her state-room that Mrs. Lander was distracted from her potential ailments to ask: "What is it, Clementina?"

"Oh, nothing. Mrs. Milray has got me to say that I would do something at a concert they ah' going to have on the ship." She explained, "It's that skut dance I learnt at Woodlake of Miss Wilson."

"Well, I guess if you're worryin' about that you needn't to."

"Oh, I'm not worrying about the dance. I was just thinking what I should wear. If I could only get at the trunks!"

"It won't make any matte what you wear," said Mrs. Lander. "It'll be the greatest thing; and if 't wa'n't for this sea-sickness that I have to keep fightin' off he'a, night and day, I should come up and see you myself. You ah' just lovely in that dance, Clementina."

"Do you think so, Mrs. Landa?" asked the girl, gratefully. "Well, Mr. Milray didn't seem to think that I need to have a pleated skut. Any rate, I'm going to look over my things, and see if I can't make something else do."

XVII

The entertainment was to be the second night after that, and Mrs. Milray at first took the whole affair into her own hands. She was willing to let the others consult with her, but she made all the decisions, and she became so prepotent that she drove Lord Lioncourt to rebellion in the case of some theatrical people whom he wanted in the programme. He wished her to let them feel that they were favoring rather than favored, and she insisted that it should be quite the other way. She professed a scruple against having theatrical people in the programme at all, which she might not have felt if her own past had been different, and she spoke with an abhorrence of the stage which he could by no means tolerate in the case. She submitted with dignity when she could not help it. Perhaps she submitted with too much dignity. Her concession verged upon hauteur; and in her arrogant meekness she went back to another of her young men, whom she began to post again as the companion of her promenades.

He had rather an anxious air in the enjoyment of the honor, but the Englishman seemed unconscious of its loss, or else he chose to ignore it. He frankly gave his leisure to Clementina, and she thought he was very pleasant. There was something different in his way from that of any of the other men she had met; something very natural and simple, a way of being easy in what he was, and not caring whether he was like others or not; he was not ashamed of being ignorant of anything he did not know, and she was able to instruct him on some points. He took her quite seriously when she told him about Middlemount, and how her family came to settle there, and then how she came to be going to Europe with Mrs. Lander. He said Mrs. Milray had spoken about it; but he had not understood quite how it was before; and he hoped Mrs. Lander was coming to the entertainment.

He did not seem aware that Mrs. Milray was leaving the affair more and more to him. He went forward with it and was as amiable with her as she would allow. He was so amiable with everybody that he reconciled many true Americans to his leadership, who felt that as nearly all the passengers were Americans, the chief patron of the entertainment ought to have been some distinguished American. The want of an American who was very distinguished did something to pacify them; but the behavior of an English lord who put on no airs was the main agency. When the night came they filled the large music room of the 'Asia Minor', and stood about in front of the sofas and chairs so many deep that it was hard to see or hear through them.

They each paid a shilling admittance; they were prepared to give munificently besides when the hat came round; and after the first burst of blundering from Lord Lioncourt, they led the magnanimous applause. He said he never minded making a bad speech in a good cause, and he made as bad a one as very well could be. He closed it by telling Mark Twain's whistling story so that those who knew it by heart missed the paint; but that might have been because he hurried it, to get himself out of the way of the others following. When he had done, one of the most ardent of the Americans proposed three cheers for him.

The actress whom he had secured in spite of Mrs. Milray appeared in woman's dress contrary to her inveterate professional habit, and followed him with great acceptance in her favorite variety-stage song; and then her husband gave imitations of Sir Henry Irving, and of Miss Maggie Kline in "T'row him down, McCloskey," with a cockney accent. A frightened little girl, whose mother had volunteered her talent, gasped a ballad to her mother's accompaniment, and two young girls played a duet on the mandolin and guitar. A gentleman of cosmopolitan military tradition, who sold the pools in the smoking-room, and was the friend of all the men present, and the acquaintance of several, gave selections of his autobiography prefatory to bellowing in a deep bass voice, "They're hanging Danny Deaver," and then a lady interpolated herself into the programme with a kindness which Lord Lioncourt acknowledged, in saying "The more the merrier," and sang Bonnie Dundee, thumping the piano out of all proportion to her size and apparent strength.

Some advances which Clementina had made for Mrs. Milray's help about the dress she should wear in her dance met with bewildering indifference, and she had fallen back upon her own devices. She did not think of taking back her promise, and she had come to look forward to her part with a happiness which the good weather and the even sway of the ship encouraged. But her pulses fluttered, as she glided into the music room, and sank into a chair next Mrs. Milray. She had on an accordion skirt which she had been able to get out of her trunk in the hold, and she felt that the glance of Mrs. Milray did not refuse it approval.

"That will do nicely, Clementina," she said. She added, in careless acknowledgement of her own failure to direct her choice, "I see you didn't need my help after all," and the thorny point which Clementina felt in her praise was rankling, when Lord Lioncourt began to introduce her.

He made rather a mess of it, but as soon as he came to an end of his well-meant blunders, she stood up and began her poses and paces. It was all very innocent, with something courageous as well as appealing. She had a kind of tender dignity in her dance, and the delicate beauty of her face translated itself into the grace of her movements. It was not impersonal; there was her own quality of sylvan, of elegant in it; but it was unconscious, and so far it was typical, it was classic; Mrs. Milray's Bostonian achieved a snub from her by saying it was like a Botticelli; and in fact it was merely the skirt-dance which society had borrowed from the stage at that period, leaving behind the footlights its more acrobatic phases, but keeping its pretty turns and bows and bends. Clementina did it not only with tender dignity, but when she was fairly launched in it, with a passion to which her sense of Mrs. Milray's strange unkindness lent defiance. The dance was still so new a thing then, that it had a surprise to which the girl's gentleness lent a curious charm, and it had some adventitious fascinations from the necessity she was in of weaving it in and out among the stationary armchairs and sofas which still further cramped the narrow space where she gave it. Her own delight in it shone from her smiling face, which was appealingly happy. Just before it should have ended, one of those wandering waves that roam the smoothest sea struck the ship, and Clementina caught herself skilfully from falling, and reeled to her seat, while the room rang with the applause and sympathetic laughter for the mischance she had baffled. There was a storm of encores, but Clementina called out, "The ship tilts so!" and her naivete won her another burst of favor, which was at its height when Lord Lioncourt had an inspiration.

He jumped up and said, "Miss Claxon is going to oblige us with a little bit of dramatics, now, and I'm sure you'll all enjoy that quite as much as her beautiful dancing. She's going to take the principal part in the laughable after-piece of Passing round the Hat, and I hope the audience will—a—a—a—do the rest. She's consented on this occasion to use a hat—or cap, rather—of her own, the charming Tam O'Shanter in which we've all seen her, and—a—admired her about the ship for the week past."

He caught up the flat woolen steamer-cap which Clementina had left in her seat beside Mrs. Milray when she rose to dance, and held it aloft. Some one called out, "Chorus! For he's a jolly good fellow," and led off in his praise. Lord Lioncourt shouted through the uproar the announcement that while Miss Claxon was taking up the collection, Mr. Ewins, of Boston, would sing one of the student songs of Cambridge—no! Harvard—University; the music being his own.

Everyone wanted to make some joke or some compliment to Clementina about the cap which grew momently heavier under the sovereigns and half sovereigns, half crowns and half dollars, shillings, quarters, greenbacks and every fraction of English and American silver; and the actor who had given the imitations, made bold, as he said, to ask his lordship if the audience might not hope, before they dispersed, for something more from Miss Claxon. He was sure she could do something more; he for one would be glad of anything; and Clementina turned from putting her cap into Mrs. Milray's lap, to find Lord Lioncourt bowing at her elbow, and offering her his arm to lead her to the spot where she had stood in dancing.

The joy of her triumph went to her head; she wished to retrieve herself from any shadow of defeat.

She stood panting a moment, and then, if she had had the professional instinct, she would have given her admirers the surprise of something altogether different from what had pleased them before. That was what the actor would have done, but Clementina thought of how her dance had been brought to an untimely close by the rolling of the ship; she burned to do it all as she knew it, no matter how the sea behaved, and in another moment she struck into it again. This time the sea behaved perfectly, and the dance ended with just the swoop and swirl she had meant it to have at first. The spectators went generously wild over her; they cheered and clapped her, and crowded upon her to tell how lovely it was; but she escaped from them, and ran back to the place where she had left Mrs. Milray. She was not there, and Clementina's cap full of alms lay abandoned on the chair. Lord Lioncourt said he would take charge of the money, if she would lend him her cap to carry it in to the purser, and she made her way into the saloon. In a distant corner she saw Mrs. Milray with Mr. Ewins.

She advanced in a vague dismay toward them, and as she came near Mrs. Milray said to Mr. Ewins, "I don't like this place. Let's go over yonder." She rose and rushed him to the other end of the saloon.

Lord Lioncourt came in looking about. "Ah, have you found her?" he asked, gayly. "There were twenty pounds in your cap, and two hundred dollars."

"Yes," said Clementina, "she's over the'a." She pointed, and then shrank and slipped away.

XVIII

At breakfast Mrs. Milray would not meet Clementina's eye; she talked to the people across the table in a loud, lively voice, and then suddenly rose, and swept past her out of the saloon.

The girl did not see her again till Mrs. Milray came up on the promenade at the hour when people who have eaten too much breakfast begin to spoil their appetite for luncheon with the tea and bouillon of the deck-stewards. She looked fiercely about, and saw Clementina seated in her usual place, but with Lord Lioncourt in her own chair next her husband, and Ewins on foot before her. They were both talking to Clementina, whom Lord Lioncourt was accusing of being in low spirits unworthy of her last night's triumphs. He jumped up, and offered his place, "I've got your chair, Mrs. Milray."

"Oh, no," she said, coldly, "I was just coming to look after Mr. Milray. But I see he's in good hands."

She turned away, as if to make the round of the deck, and Ewins hurried after her. He came back directly, and said that Mrs. Milray had gone into the library to write letters. He stayed, uneasily, trying to talk, but with the air of a man who has been snubbed, and has not got back his composure.

Lord Lioncourt talked on until he had used up the incidents of the night before, and the probabilities of their getting into Queenstown before morning; then he and Mr. Ewins went to the smoking-room together, and Clementina was left alone with Milray.

"Clementina," he said, gently, "I don't see everything; but isn't there some trouble between you and Mrs. Milray?"

"Why, I don't know what it can be," answered the girl, with trembling lips. "I've been trying to find out, and I can't undastand it."

"Ah, those things are often very obscure," said Milray, with a patient smile.

Clementina wanted to ask him if Mrs. Milray had said anything to him about her, but she could not, and he did not speak again till he heard her stir in rising from her chair. Then he said, "I haven't forgotten that letter to my sister, Clementina. I will give it to you before we leave the steamer. Are you going to stay in Liverpool, over night, or shall you go up to London at once?"

"I don't know. It will depend upon how Mrs. Landa feels."

"Well, we shall see each other again. Don't be worried." He looked up at her with a smile, and he could not see how forlornly she returned it.

As the day passed, Mrs. Milray's angry eyes seemed to search her out for scorn whenever Clementina found herself the centre of her last night's celebrity. Many people came up and spoke to her, at first with a certain expectation of knowingness in her, which her simplicity baffled. Then they either dropped her, and went away, or stayed and tried to make friends with her because of this; an elderly English clergyman and his wife were at first compassionately anxious about her, and then affectionately attentive to her in her obvious isolation. Clementina's simple-hearted response to their advances appeared to win while it puzzled them; and they seemed trying to divine her in the strange double character she wore to their more single civilization. The theatrical people thought none the worse of her for her simple-hearted ness, apparently; they were both very sweet to her, and wanted her to promise to come and see them in their little box in St. John's Wood. Once, indeed, Clementina thought she saw relenting in Mrs. Milray's glance, but it hardened again as Lord Lioncourt and Mr. Ewins came up to her, and began to talk with her. She could not go to her chair beside Milray, for his wife was now keeping guard of him on the other side with unexampled devotion. Lord Lioncourt asked her to walk with him and she consented. She thought that Mr. Ewins would go and sit by Mrs. Milray, of course, but when she came round in her tour of the ship, Mrs. Milray was sitting alone beside her husband.

After dinner she went to the library and got a book, but she could not read there; every chair was taken by people writing letters to send back from Queenstown in the morning; and she strayed into the ladies' sitting room, where no ladies seemed ever to sit, and lost herself in a miserable muse over her open page.

Some one looked in at the door, and then advanced within and came straight to Clementina; she knew without looking up that it was Mrs. Milray. "I have been hunting for you, Miss Claxon," she said, in a voice frostily fierce, and with a bearing furiously formal. "I have a letter to Miss Milray that my husband wished me to write for you, and give you with his compliments."

"Thank you," said Clementina. She rose mechanically to her feet, and at the same time Mrs. Milray sat down.

"You will find Miss Milray," she continued, with the same glacial hauteur, "a very agreeable and cultivated lady."

Clementina said nothing; and Mrs. Milray added,

"And I hope she may have the happiness of being more useful to you than I have."

"What do you mean, Mrs. Milray?" Clementina asked with unexpected spirit and courage.

"I mean simply this, that I have not succeeded in putting you on your guard against your love of admiration—especially the admiration of gentlemen. A young girl can't be too careful how she accepts the attentions of gentlemen, and if she seems to invite them—"

"Mrs. Milray!" cried Clementina. "How can you say such a thing to me?"

"How? I shall have to be plain with you, I see. Perhaps I have not considered that, after all, you know nothing about life and are not to blame for things that a person born and bred in the world would understand from childhood. If you don't know already, I can tell you that the way you have behaved with Lord Lioncourt during the last two or three days, and the way you showed your pleasure the other night in his ridiculous flatteries of you, was enough to make you the talk of the whole steamer. I advise you for your own sake to take my warning in time. You are very young, and inexperienced and ignorant, but that will not save you in the eyes of the world if you keep on." Mrs. Milray rose. "And now I will leave you to think of what I have said. Here is the letter for Miss Milray—"

Clementina shook her head. "I don't want it."

"You don't want it? But I have written it at Mr. Milray's request, and I shall certainly leave it with you!"

"If you do," said Clementina, "I shall not take it!"

"And what shall I say to Mr. Milray?"

"What you have just said to me."

"What have I said to you?"

"That I'm a bold girl, and that I've tried to make men admi'a me."

Mrs. Milray stopped as if suddenly daunted by a fact that had not occurred to her before. "Did I say that?"

"The same as that."

"I didn't mean that—I—merely meant to put you on your guard. It may be because you are so innocent yourself, that you can't imagine what others think, and—I did it out of my regard for you."

Clementina did not answer.

Mrs. Milray went on, "That was why I was so provoked with you. I think that for a young girl to stand up and dance alone before a whole steamer full of strangers"—Clementina looked at her without speaking, and Mrs. Milray hastened to say, "To be sure I advised you to do it, but I certainly was surprised that you should give an encore. But no matter, now. This letter—"

"I can't take it, Mrs. Milray," said Clementina, with a swelling heart.

"Now, listen!" urged Mrs. Milray. "You think I'm just saying it because, if you don't take it I shall have to tell Mr. Milray I was so hateful to you, you couldn't. Well, I should hate to tell him that; but that isn't the reason. There!" She tore the letter in pieces, and threw it on the floor. Clementina did not make any sign of seeing this, and Mrs. Milray dropped upon her chair again. "Oh, how hard you are! Can't you say something to me?"

Clementina did not lift her eyes. "I don't feel like saying anything just now."

Mrs. Milray was silent a moment. Then she sighed. "Well, you may hate me, but I shall always be your friend. What hotel are you going to in Liverpool?

"I don't know," said Clementina.

"You had better come to the one where we go. I'm afraid Mrs. Lander won't know how to manage very well, and we've been in Liverpool so often. May I speak to her about it?"

"If you want to," Clementina coldly assented.

"I see!" said Mrs. Milray. "You don't want to be under the same roof with me. Well, you needn't! But I'll tell you a good hotel: the one that the trains start out of; and I'll send you that letter for Miss Milray." Clemeutina was silent. "Well, I'll send it, anyway."

Mrs. Milray went away in sudden tears, but the girl remained dry-eyed.

XIX

Mrs. Lander realized when the ship came to anchor in the stream at Liverpool that she had not been seasick a moment during the voyage. In the brisk cold of the winter morning, as they came ashore in the tug, she fancied a property of health in the European atmosphere, which she was sure would bring her right up, if she stayed long enough; and a regret that she had never tried it with Mr. Lander mingled with her new hopes for herself.

But Clementina looked with home-sick eyes at the strangeness of the alien scene: the pale, low heaven which seemed not to be clouded and yet was so dim; the flat shores with the little railroad trains running in and out over them; the grimy bulks of the city, and the shipping in the river, sparse and sombre after the gay forest of sails and stacks at New York.

She did not see the Milrays after she left the tug, in the rapid dispersal of the steamer's passengers. They both took leave of her at the dock, and Mrs. Milray whispered with penitence in her voice and eyes, "I will write," but the girl did not answer.

Before Mrs. Lander's trunks and her own were passed, she saw Lord Lioncourt going away with his heavily laden man at his heels. Mr. Ewins came up to see if he could help her through the customs, but she believed that he had come at Mrs. Milray's bidding, and she thanked him so prohibitively that he could not insist. The English clergyman who had spoken to her the morning after the charity entertainment left his wife with Mrs. Lander, and came to her help, and then Mr. Ewins went his way.

The clergyman, who appeared to feel the friendlessness of the young girl and the old woman a charge laid upon him, bestowed a sort of fatherly protection upon them both. He advised them to stop at a hotel for a few hours and take the later train for London that he and his wife were going up by; they drove to the hotel together, where Mrs. Lander could not be kept from paying the omnibus, and made them have luncheon with her. She allowed the clergyman to get her tickets, and she could not believe that he had taken second class tickets for himself and his wife. She said that she had never heard of anyone travelling second class before, and she assured him that they never did it in America. She begged him to let her pay the difference, and bring his wife into her compartment, which the guard had reserved for her. She urged that the money was nothing to her, compared with the comfort of being with some one you knew; and the clergyman had to promise that as they should be neighbors, he would look in upon her, whenever the train stopped long enough.

Before it began to move, Clementina thought she saw Lord Lioncourt hurrying past their carriage-window. At Rugby the clergyman appeared, but almost before he could speak, Lord Lioncourt's little red face showed at his elbow. He asked Clementina to present him to Mrs. Lander, who pressed him to get into her compartment; the clergyman vanished, and Lord Lioncourt yielded.

Mrs. Lander found him able to tell her the best way to get to Florence, whose situation he seemed to know perfectly; he confessed that he had been there rather often. He made out a little itinerary for going straight through by sleeping-car as soon as you crossed the Channel; she had said that she always liked a through train when she could get it, and the less stops the better. She bade Clementina take charge of the plan and not lose it; without it she did not see what they could do. She conceived of him as a friend of Clementina's, and she lost in the strange environment the shyness she had with most people. She told him how Mr. Lander had made his money, and from what beginnings he rose to be ignorant of what he really was worth when he died. She dwelt upon the diseases they had suffered, and at the thought of his death, so unnecessary in view of the good that the air was already doing her in Europe, she shed tears.

Lord Lioncourt was very polite, but there was no resumption of the ship's comradery in his manner. Clementina could not know how quickly this always drops from people who have been fellow-passengers; and she wondered if he were guarding himself from her because she had danced at the charity entertainment. The poison which Mrs. Milray had instilled worked in her thoughts while she could not help seeing how patient he was with all Mrs.

Lander's questions; he answered them with a simplicity of his own, or laughed and put them by, when they were quite impossible. Many of them related to the comparative merits of English and American railroads, and what he thought himself of these. Mrs. Lander noted the difference of the English stations; but she did not see much in the landscape to examine him upon. She required him to tell her why the rooks they saw were not crows, and she was not satisfied that he should say the country seat she pointed out was a castle when it was plainly deficient in battlements. She based upon his immovable confidence in respect to it an inquiry into the structure of English society, and she made him tell her what a lord was, and a commoner, and how the royal family differed from both. She asked him how he came to be a lord, and when he said that it was a peerage of George the Third's creation, she remembered that George III. was the one we took up arms against. She found that Lord Lioncourt knew of our revolution generally, but was ignorant of such particulars as the Battle of Bunker Hill, and the Surrender of Cornwallis, as well as the throwing of the Tea into Boston Harbor; he was much struck by this incident, and said, And quite right, he was sure.

He told Clementina that her friends the Milrays had taken the steamer for London in the morning. He believed they were going to Egypt for the winter. Cairo, he said, was great fun, and he advised Mrs. Lander, if she found Florence a bit dull, to push on there. She asked if it was an easy place to get to, and he assured her that it was very easy from Italy.

Mrs. Lander was again at home in her world of railroads and hotels; but she confessed, after he left them at the next station, that she should have felt more at home if he had been going on to London with them. She philosophized him to the disadvantage of her own countrymen as much less offish than a great many New York and Boston peuple. He had given her a good opinion of the whole English nation; and the clergyman, who had been so nice to them at Liverpool, confirmed her friendly impressions of England by getting her a small omnibus at the station in London before he got a cab for himself and his wife, and drove away to complete his own journey on another road. She celebrated the omnibus as if it were an effect of his goodness in her behalf. She admired its capacity for receiving all their trunks, and saving the trouble and delay of the express, which always vexed her so much in New York, and which had nearly failed in getting her baggage to the steamer in time.

The omnibus remained her chief association with London, for she decided to take the first through train for Italy in the morning. She wished to be settled, by which she meant placed in a Florentine hotel for the winter. That lord, as she now began and always continued to call Lioncourt, had first given her the name of the best little hotel in Florence, but as it had neither elevator nor furnace heat in it, he agreed in the end that it would not do for her, and mentioned the most modern and expensive house on the Lungarno. He told her he did not think she need telegraph for rooms; but she took this precaution before leaving London, and was able to secure them at a price which seemed to her quite as much as she would have had to pay for the same rooms at a first class hotel on the Back Bay.

The manager had reserved for her one of the best suites, which had just been vacated by a Russian princess. "I guess you better cable to your folks where you ah', Clementina," she said. "Because if you're satisfied, I am, and I presume we sha'n't want to change as long as we stay in Florence. My, but it's sightly!" She joined Clementina a moment at the windows looking upon the Arno, and the hills beyond it. "I guess you'll spend most of your time settin' at this winder, and I sha'n't blame you."

They had arrived late in the dull, soft winter afternoon. The landlord led the way himself to their apartment, and asked if they would have fire; a facchino came in and kindled roaring blazes on the hearths; at the same time a servant lighted all the candles on the tables and mantels. They both gracefully accepted the fees that Mrs. Lander made Clementina give them; the facchino kissed the girl's hand. "My!" said Mrs. Lander, "I guess you never had your hand kissed before."

The hotel developed advantages which, if not those she was used to, were still advantages. The halls were warmed by a furnace, and she came to like the little logs burning in her rooms. In the care of her own fire, she went back to the simple time of her life in the country, and chose to kindle it herself when it died out, with the fagots of broom that blazed up so briskly.

In the first days of her stay she made inquiry for the best American doctor in Florence; and she found him so intelligent that she at once put her liver in his charge, with a history of her diseases and symptoms of every kind. She told him that she was sure that he could have cured Mr. Lander, if he had only had him in time; she exacted a new prescription from him for herself, and made him order some quinine pills for Clementina against the event of her feeling debilitated by the air of Florence.

XX

In these first days a letter came to Clementina from Mrs. Lander's banker, enclosing the introduction which Mrs. Milray had promised to her sister-in-law. It was from Mr. Milray, as before, and it was in Mrs. Milray's handwriting; but no message from her came with it. To Clementina it explained itself, but she had to explain it to Mrs. Lander. She had to tell her of Mrs. Milray's behavior after the entertainment on the steamer, and Mrs. Lander said that Clementina had done just exactly right; and they both decided, against some impulses of curiosity in Clementina's heart, that she should not make use of the introduction.

The 'Hotel des Financieres' was mainly frequented by rich Americans full of ready money, and by rich Russians of large credit. Better Americans and worse, went, like the English, to smaller and cheaper hotels; and Clementina's acquaintance was confined to mothers as shy and ungrammatical as Mrs. Lander herself, and daughters blankly indifferent to her. Mrs. Lander drove out every day when it did not rain, and she took Clementina with her, because the doctor said it would do them both good; but otherwise the girl remained pent in their apartment. The doctor found her a teacher, and she kept on with her French, and began to take lessons in Italian; she spoke with no one but her teacher, except when the doctor came. At the table d'hote she heard talk of the things that people seemed to come to Florence for: pictures, statues, palaces, famous places; and it made her ashamed of not knowing about them. But she could not go to see these things alone, and Mrs. Lander, in the content she felt with all her circumstances, seemed not to suppose that Clementina could care for anything but the comfort of the hotel and the doctor's visits. When the girl began to get letters from home in answer to the first she had written back, boasting how beautiful Florence was, they assumed that she was very gay, and demanded full accounts of her pleasures. Her brother Jim gave something of the village news, but he said he supposed that she would not care for that, and she would probably be too proud to speak to them when she came home. The Richlings had called in to share the family satisfaction in Clementina's first experiences, and Mrs. Richling wrote her very sweetly of their happiness in them. She charged her from the rector not to forget any chance of self-improvement in the allurements of society, but to make the most of her rare opportunities. She said that they had got a guide-book to Florence, with a plan of the city, and were following her in the expeditions they decided she must be making every day; they were reading up the Florentine history in Sismondi's Italian Republics, and she bade Clementina be sure and see all the scenes of Savonarola's martyrdom, so that they could talk them over together when she returned.

Clementina wondered what Mrs. Richling would think if she told her that all she knew of Florence was what she overheard in the talk of the girls in the hotel, who spoke before her of their dances and afternoon teas, and evenings at the opera, and drives in the Cascine, and parties to Fiesole, as if she were not by.

The days and weeks passed, until Carnival was half gone, and Mrs. Lander noticed one day that Clementina appeared dull. "You don't seem to get much acquainted?" she suggested.

"Oh, the'e's plenty of time," said Clementina.

"I wish the'e was somebody you could go round with, and see the place. Shouldn't you like to see the place?" Mrs. Lander pursued.

"There's no hurry about it, Mrs. Lander. It will stay as long as we do."

Mrs. Lander was thoughtfully silent. Then she said, "I declare, I've got half a mind to make you send that letta to Miss Milray, after all. What difference if Mrs. Milray did act so ugly to you? He never did, and she's his sista."

"Oh, I don't want to send it, Mrs. Landa; you mustn't ask me to. I shall get along," said Clementina. The recognition of her forlornness deepened it, but she was cheerfuller, for no reason, the next morning; and that afternoon, the doctor unexpectedly came upon a call which he made haste to say was not professional.

"I've just come from another patient of mine, and I promised to ask if you had not crossed on the same ship with a brother of hers,—Mr. Milray."

Celementina and Mrs. Lander looked guiltily at each other. "I guess we did," Mrs. Lander owned at last, with a reluctant sigh.

"Then, she says you have a letter for her."

The doctor spoke to both, but his looks confessed that he was not ignorant of the fact when Mrs. Lander admitted, "Well Clementina, he'e, has."

"She wants to know why you haven't delivered it," the doctor blurted out.

Mrs. Lander looked at Clementina. "I guess she ha'n't quite got round to it yet, have you, Clementina?"

The doctor put in: "Well, Miss Milray is rather a dangerous person to keep waiting. If you don't deliver it pretty soon, I shouldn't be surprised if she came to get it." Dr. Welwright was a young man in the early thirties, with a laugh that a great many ladies said had done more than any one thing for them, and he now prescribed it for Clementina. But it did not seem to help her in the trouble her face betrayed.

Mrs. Lander took the word, "Well, I wouldn't say it to everybody. But you're our doctor, and I guess you won't mind it. We don't like the way Mrs. Milray acted to Clementina, in the ship, and we don't want to be beholden to any of her folks. I don't know as Clementina wants me to tell you just what it was, and I won't; but that's the long and sho't of it."

"I'm sorry," the doctor said. "I've never met Mrs. Milray, but Miss Milray has such a pleasant house, and likes to get young people about her. There are a good many young people in your hotel, though, and I suppose you all have a very good time here together." He ended by speaking to Clementina, and now he said he had done his errand, and must be going.

When he was gone, Mrs. Lander faltered, "I don't know but what we made a mistake, Clementina."

"It's too late to worry about it now," said the girl.

"We ha'n't bound to stay in Florence," said Mrs. Lander, thoughtfully. "I only took the rooms by the week, and we can go, any time, Clementina, if you are uncomf'table bein' here on Miss Milray's account. We could go to Rome; they say Rome's a nice place; or to Egypt."

"Mrs. Milray's in Egypt," Clementina suggested.

"That's true," Mrs. Lander admitted, with a sigh. After a while she went on, "I don't know as we've got any right to keep the letter. It belongs to her, don't it?"

"I guess it belongs to me, as much as it does to her," said Clementina. "If it's to her, it's for me. I am not going to send it, Mrs. Landa."

They were still in this conclusion when early in the following afternoon Miss Milray's cards were brought up for Mrs. Lander and Miss Claxon.

"Well, I decla'e!" cried Mrs. Lander. "That docta: must have gone straight and told her what we said."

"He had no right to," said Clementina, but neither of them was displeased, and after it was over, Mrs. Lander said that any one would have thought the call was for her, instead of Clementina, from the way Miss Milray kept talking to her. She formed a high opinion of her; and Miss Milray put Clementina in mind of Mr. Milray; she had the same hair of chiseled silver, and the same smile; she moved like him, and talked like him; but with a greater liveliness. She asked fondly after him, and made Clementina tell her if he seemed quite well, and in good spirits; she was civilly interested in Mrs. Milray's health. At the embarrassment which showed itself in the girl, she laughed and said, "Don't imagine I don't know all about it, Miss Claxon! My sister-in-law has owned up very handsomely; she isn't half bad, as the English say, and I think she likes owning up if she can do it safely."

"And you don't think," asked Mrs. Lander, "that Clementina done wrong to dance that way?"

Clementina blushed, and Miss Milray laughed again. "If you'll let Miss Claxon come to a little party I'm giving she may do her dance at my house; but she sha'n't be obliged to do it, or anything she doesn't like. Don't say she hasn't a gown ready, or something of that kind! You don't know the resources of Florence, and how the dress makers here doat upon doing impossible things in no time at all, and being ready before they promise. If you'll put Miss Claxon in my hands, I'll see that she's dressed for my dance. I live out on one of the hills over there, that you see from your windows"—she nodded toward them —"in a beautiful villa, too cold for winter, and too hot for summer, but I think Miss Claxon can endure its discomfort for a day, if you can spare her, and she will consent to leave you to the tender mercies of your maid, and—" Miss Milray paused at the kind of unresponsive blank to which she found herself talking, and put up her lorgnette, to glance from Mrs. Lander to Clementina. The girl said, with embarrassment, "I don't think I ought to leave Mrs. Landa, just now. She isn't very well, and I shouldn't like to leave her alone."

"But we're just as much obliged to you as if she could come," Mrs. Lander interrupted; "and later on, maybe she can. You see, we han't got any maid, yit. Well, we did have one at Woodlake, but she made us do so many things for her, that we thought we should like to do a few things for ouaselves, awhile."

If Miss Milray perhaps did not conceive the situation, exactly, she said, Oh, they were quite right in that; but she might count upon Miss Claxon for her dance, might not she; and might not she do anything in her power for them? She rose to go, but Mrs. Lander took her at her word, so far as to say, Why, yes, if she could tell Clementina the best place to get a dress she guessed the child would be glad enough to come to the dance.

"Tell her!" Miss Milray cried. "I'll take her! Put on your hat, my dear," she said to Clementina, "and come with me now. My carriage is at your door."

Clementina looked at Mrs. Lander, who said, "Go, of cou'se, child. I wish I could go, too."

"Do come, too," Miss Milray entreated.

"No, no," said Mrs. Lander, flattered. "I a'n't feeling very well, to-day. I guess I'm better off at home. But don't you hurry back on my account, Clementina." While the girl was gone to put on her hat she talked on about her. "She's the best gul in the wo'ld, and she won't be one of the poorest; and I shall feel that I'm doin' just what Mr. Landa would have wanted I should. He picked her out himself, moa than three yea's ago, when we was drivin' past her house at Middlemount, and it was to humor him afta he was gone, moa than anything else, that I took her. Well, she wa'n't so very easy to git, either, I can tell you." She cut short her history of the affair to say when Clementina came back, "I want you should do the odderin' yourself, Miss Milray, and not let her scrimp with the money. She wants to git some visitin' cahds; and if you miss anything about her that she'd ought to have, or that any otha yong lady's got, won't you just git it for her?"

As soon as she imagined the case, Miss Milray set herself to overcome Mrs. Lander's reluctance from a maid. She prevailed with her to try the Italian woman whom she sent her, and in a day the genial Maddalena had effaced the whole tradition of the bleak Ellida. It was not essential to the understanding which instantly established itself between them that they should have any language in common. They babbled at each other, Mrs. Lander in her Bostonized Yankee, and Maddalena in her gutteral Florentine, and Mrs. Lander was flattered to find how well she knew Italian.

Miss Milray had begun being nice to Clementina in fealty to her brother, who so seldom made any proof of her devotion to him, and to whom she bad remained passionately true through his shady past. She was eager to humor his whim for the little country girl who had taken his fancy, because it was his whim, and not because she had any hopes that Clementina would justify it. She had made Dr. Welwright tell her all he knew about her, and his report of her grace and beauty had piqued her curiosity; his account of the forlorn dullness of her life with Mrs. Lander in their hotel had touched her heart. But she was still skeptical when she went to get her letter of introduction; when she brought Clementina home from the dressmaker's she asked if she might kiss her, and said she was already in love with her.

Her love might have made her wish to do everything for her that she now began to do, but it simplified the situation to account for her to the world as the ward of Mrs. Lander, who was as rich as she was vulgar, and it was with Clementina in this character that Miss Milray began to make the round of afternoon teas, and inspired invitations for her at pleasant houses, by giving a young ladies' lunch for her at her own. Before the night of her little dance, she had lost any misgiving she had felt at first, in the delight of seeing Clementina take the world as if she had thought it would always behave as amiably as that, and as if she had forgotten her unkind experiences to the contrary. She knew from Mrs. Lander how the girls at their hotel had left her out, but Miss Milray could not see that Clementina met them with rancor, when her authority brought them together. If the child was humiliated by her past in the gross lonely luxury of Mrs. Lander's life or the unconscious poverty of her own home, she did not show it in the presence of the world that now opened its arms to her. She remained so tranquil in the midst of all the novel differences, that it made her friend feel rather vulgar in her anxieties for her, and it was not always enough to find that she had not gone wrong simply because she had hold still, and had the gift of waiting for things to happen. Sometimes when Miss Milray had almost decided that her passivity was the calm of a savage, she betrayed so sweet and grateful a sense of all that was done for her, that her benefactress decided that, she was not rustic, but was sylvan in a way of her own, and not so much ignorant as innocent. She discovered that she was not ignorant even of books, but with no literary effect from them she had transmitted her reading into the substance of her native gentleness, and had both ideas and convictions. When Clementina most affected her as an untried wilderness in the conventional things she most felt her equality to any social fortune that might befall her, and then she would have liked to see her married to a title, and taking the glory of this world with an unconsciousness that experience would never wholly penetrate. But then again she felt that this would be somehow a profanation, and she wanted to pack her up and get her back to Middlemount before anything of the kind should happen. She gave Milray these impressions of Clementina in the letter she wrote to thank him for her, and to scold him for sending the girl to her. She accused him of wishing to get off on her a riddle which he could not read himself; but she owned that the charm of Clementina's mystery was worth a thousand times the fatigue of trying to guess her out and that she was more and more infatuated with her every day.

In the meantime, Miss Milray's little dance grew upon her till it became a very large one that filled her villa to overflowing when the time came for it. She lived on one of the fine avenues of the Oltrarno region, laid out in the brief period of prosperity which Florence enjoyed as the capital of Italy. The villa was built at that time, and it was much newer than the house on Seventeenth street in New York, where she spent the girlhood that had since prolonged itself beyond middle life with her. She had first lived abroad in the Paris of the Second Empire, and she had been one winter in Rome, but she had settled definitely in Florence before London became an American colony, so that her friends were chiefly Americans, though she had a wide international acquaintance. Perhaps her habit of taking her brother's part, when he was a black sheep, inclined her to mercy with people who had not been so blameless in their morals as they were in their minds and manners. She exacted that they should be interesting and agreeable, and not too threadbare; but if they had something that decently buttoned over the frayed places, she did not frown upon their poverty. Bohemians of all kinds liked her; Philistines liked her too;

and in such a place as Florence, where the Philistines themselves are a little Bohemian, she might be said to be very popular. You met persons whom you did not quite wish to meet at her house, but if these did not meet you there, it was your loss.

XI

On the night of the dance the line of private carriages, remises and cabs, lined the Viale Ariosto for a mile up and down before her gates, where young artists of both sexes arrived on foot. By this time her passion for Clementina was at its height. She had Maddalena bring her out early in the evening, and made her dress under her own eye and her French maid's, while Maddalena went back to comfort Mrs. Lander.

"I hated to leave her," said Clementina. "I don't believe she's very well."

"Isn't she always ill?" demanded Miss Milray. She embraced the girl again, as if once were not enough. "Clementina, if Mrs. Lander won't give you to me, I'm going to steal you. Do you know what I want you to do tonight? I want you to stand up with me, and receive, till the dancing begins, as if it were your coming-out. I mean to introduce everybody to you. You'll be easily the prettiest girl, there, and you'll have the nicest gown, and I don't mean that any of your charms shall be thrown away. You won't be frightened?"

"No, I don't believe I shall," said Clementina. "You can tell me what to do."

The dress she wore was of pale green, like the light seen in thin woods; out of it shone her white shoulders, and her young face, as if rising through the verdurous light. The artists, to a man and woman, wished to paint her, and severally told her so, during the evening which lasted till morning. She was not surprised when Lord Lioncourt appeared, toward midnight, and astonished Miss Milray by claiming acquaintance with Clementina. He asked about Mrs. Lander, and whether she had got to Florence without losing the way; he laughed but he seemed really to care. He took Clementina out to supper, when the time came; and she would have topped him by half a head as she leaned on his arm, if she had not considerately drooped and trailed a little after him.

She could not know what a triumph he was making for her; and it was merely part of the magic of the time that Mr. Ewins should come in presently with one of the ladies. He had arrived in Florence that day, and had to be brought unasked. He put on the effect of an old friend with her; but Clementina's curiosity was chiefly taken with a tall American, whom she thought very handsome. His light yellow hair was brushed smooth across his forehead like a well-behaving boy's; he was dressed like the other men, but he seemed not quite happy in his evening coat, and his gloves which he smote together uneasily from time to time. He appeared to think that somehow the radiant Clementina would know how he felt; he did not dance, and he professed to have found himself at the party by a species of accident. He told her that he was out in Europe looking after a patent right that he had just taken hold of, and was having only a middling good time. He pretended surprise to hear her say that she was having a first-rate time, and he tried to reason her out of it. He confessed that from the moment he came into the room he had made up his mind to take her to supper, and had never been so disgusted in his life as when he saw that little lord toddling off with her, and trying to look as large as life. He asked her what a lord was like, anyway, and he made her laugh all the time.

He told her his name, G. W. Hinkle, and asked whether she would be likely to remember it if they ever met again.

Another man who interested her very much was a young Russian, with curling hair and neat, small features who spoke better English than she did, and said he was going to be a writer, but had not yet decided whether to write in Russian or French; she supposed he had wanted her advice, but he did not wait for it, or seem to expect it. He was very much in earnest, while he fanned her, and his earnestness amused her as much as the American's irony. He asked which city of America she came from, and when she said none, he asked which part of America. She answered New England, and he said, "Oh, yes, that is where they have the conscience." She did not know what he meant, and he put before her the ideal of New England girlhood which he had evolved from reading American novels. "Are you like that?" he demanded.

She laughed, and said, "Not a bit," and asked him if he had ever met such an American girl, and he said, frankly, No; the American girls were all mercenary, and cared for nothing but money, or marrying titles. He added that he had a title, but he would not wear it.

Clementina said she did not believe she cared for titles, and then he said, "But you care for money." She denied it, but as if she had confessed it, he went on: "The only American that I have seen with that conscience was a man. I will tell you of him, if you wish."

He did not wait for her answer. "It was in Naples—at Pompeii. I saw at the first glance that he was different from other Americans, and I resolved to know him. He was there in company with a stupid boy, whose tutor he was;

and he told me that he was studying to be a minister of the Protestant church. Next year he will go home to be consecrated. He promised to pass through Florence in the spring, and he will keep his word. Every act, every word, every thought of his is regulated by conscience. It is terrible, but it is beautiful." All the time, the Russian was fanning Clementina, with every outward appearance of flirtation. "Will you dance again? No? I should like to draw such a character as his in a romance."

XXII.

It was six o'clock in the morning before Miss Milray sent Clementina home in her carriage. She would have kept her to breakfast, but Clementina said she ought to go on Mrs. Lander's account, and she wished to go on her own.

She thought she would steal to bed without waking her, but she was stopped by the sound of groans when she entered their apartment; the light gushed from Mrs. Lander's door. Maddalena came out, and blessed the name of her Latin deity (so much more familiar and approachable than the Anglo-Saxon divinity) that Clementina had come at last, and poured upon her the story of a night of suffering for Mrs. Lander. Through her story came the sound of Mrs. Lander's voice plaintively reproachful, summoning Clementina to her bedside. "Oh, how could you go away and leave me? I've been in such misery the whole night long, and the docta didn't do a thing for me. I'm puffectly wohn out, and I couldn't make my wants known with that Italian crazy-head. If it hadn't been for the portyary comin' in and interpretin', when the docta left, I don't know what I should have done. I want you should give him a twenty-leary note just as quick as you see him; and oh, isn't the docta comin'?"

Clementina set about helping Maddalena put the room, which was in an impassioned disorder, to rights; and she made Mrs. Lander a cup of her own tea, which she had brought from S. S. Pierces in passing through Boston; it was the first thing, the sufferer said, that had saved her life. Clementina comforted her, and promised her that the doctor should be there very soon; and before Mrs. Lander fell away to sleep, she was so far out of danger as to be able to ask how Clementina had enjoyed herself, and to be glad that she had such a good time.

The doctor would not wake her when he came; he said that she had been through a pretty sharp gastric attack, which would not recur, if she ate less of the most unwholesome things she could get, and went more into the air, and walked a little. He did not seem alarmed, and he made Clementina tell him about the dance, which he had been called from to Mrs. Lander's bed of pain. He joked her for not having missed him; in the midst of their fun, she caught herself in the act of yawning, and the doctor laughed, and went away.

Maddalena had to call her, just before dinner, when Mrs. Lander had been awake long enough to have sent for the doctor to explain the sort of gone feeling which she was now the victim of. It proved, when he came, to be hunger, and he prescribed tea and toast and a small bit of steak. Before he came she had wished to arrange for going home at once, and dying in her own country. But his opinion so far prevailed with her that she consented not to telegraph for berths. "I presume," she said, "it'll do, any time before the icebugs begin to run. But I d' know, afta this, Clementina, as I can let you leave me quite as you be'n doin'. There was a lot of flowas come for you, this aftanoon, but I made Maddalena put 'em on the balcony, for I don't want you should get poisoned with 'em in your sleep; I always head they was dangerous in a person's 'bed room. I d' know as they are, eitha."

Maddalena seemed to know that Mrs. Lander was speaking of the flowers. She got them and gave them to Clementina, who found they were from some of the men she had danced with. Mr. Hinkle had sent a vast bunch of violets, which presently began to give out their sweetness in the warmth of the room, and the odor brought him before her with his yellow hair, scrupulously parted at the side, and smoothly brushed, showing his forehead very high up. Most of the gentlemen wore their hair parted in the middle, or falling in a fringe over their brows; the Russian's was too curly to part, and Lord Lioncourt had none except at the sides.

She laughed, and Mrs. Lander said, "Tell about it, Clementina," and she began with Mr. Hinkle, and kept coming back to him from the others. Mrs. Lander wished most to know how that lord had got down to Florence; and Clementina said he was coming to see her.

"Well, I hope to goodness he won't come to-day, I a'n't fit to see anybody."

"Oh, I guess he won't come till to-morrow," said Clementina; she repeated some of the compliments she had got, and she told of all Miss Milray's kindness to her, but Mrs. Lander said, "Well, the next time, I'll thank her not to keep you so late." She was astonished to hear that Mr. Ewins was there, and "Any of the nasty things out of the hotel the'e?" she asked.

"Yes," Clementina said, "the'e we'e, and some of them we'e very nice. They wanted to know if I wouldn't join them, and have an aftanoon of our own here in the hotel, so that people could come to us all at once."

She went back to the party, and described the rest of it. When she came to the part about the Russian, she told what he had said of American girls being fond of money, and wanting to marry foreign noblemen.

Mrs. Lander said, "Well, I hope you a'n't a going to get married in a hurry, anyway, and when you do I hope you'll pick out a nice American."

"Oh, yes," said Clementina.

Mrs. Lander had their dinner brought to their apartment. She cheered up, and she was in some danger of eating too much, but with Clementina's help she denied herself. Their short evening was one of the gayest; Clementina declared she was not the least sleepy, but she went to bed at nine, and slept till nine the next day.

Mrs. Lander, the doctor confessed, the second morning, was more shaken up by, her little attack than he had expected; but she decided to see the gentleman who had asked to call on Clementina. Lord Lioncourt did not come quite so soon as she was afraid he might, and when he came he talked mostly to Clementina. He did not get to Mrs. Lander until just before he was going. She hospitably asked him what his hurry was, and then he said that he was off for Rome, that evening at seven. He was nice about hoping she was comfortable in the hotel, and he sympathized with her in her wish that there was a set-bowl in her room; she told him that she always tried to have one, and he agreed that it must be very convenient where any one was, as she said, sick so much.

Mr. Hinkle came a day later; and then it appeared that he had a mother whose complaints almost exactly matched Mrs. Lander's. He had her photograph with him, and showed it; he said if you had no wife to carry round a photograph of, you had better carry your mother's; and Mrs. Lander praised him for being a good son. A good son, she added, always made a good husband; and he said that was just what he told the young ladies himself, but it did not seem to make much impression on them. He kept Clementina laughing; and he pretended that he was going to bring a diagram of his patent right for her to see, because she would be interested in a gleaner like that; and he said he wished her father could see it, for it would be sure to interest the kind of man Mrs. Lander described him to be. "I'll be along up there just about the time you get home, Miss Clementina. Then did you say it would be?"

"I don't know; pretty ea'ly in the spring, I guess."

She looked at Mrs. Lander, who said, "Well, it depends upon how I git up my health. I couldn't bea' the voyage now."

Mr. Hinkle said, "No, best look out for your health, if it takes all summer. I shouldn't want you to hurry on my account. Your time is my time. All I want is for Miss Clementina, here, to personally conduct me to her father. If I could get him to take hold of my gleaner in New England, we could make the blueberry crop worth twice what it is."

Mrs. Lander perceived that he was joking; and she asked what he wanted to run away for when the young Russian's card came up. He said, "Oh, give every man a chance," and he promised that he would look in every few days, and see how she was getting along. He opened the door after he had gone out, and put his head in to say in confidence to Mrs. Lander, but so loud that Clementina could hear, "I suppose she's told you who the belle of the ball was, the other night? Went out to supper with a lord!" He seemed to think a lord was such a good joke that if you mentioned one you had to laugh.

The Russian's card bore the name Baron Belsky, with the baron crossed out in pencil, and he began to attack in Mrs. Lander the demerits of the American character, as he had divined them. He instructed her that her countrymen existed chiefly to make money; that they were more shopkeepers than the English and worse snobs; that their women were trivial and their men sordid; that their ambition was to unite their families with the European aristocracies; and their doctrine of liberty and equality was a shameless hypocrisy. This followed hard upon her asking, as she did very promptly, why he had scratched out the title on his card. He told her that he wished to be known solely as an artist, and he had to explain to her that he was not a painter, but was going to be a novelist. She taxed him with never having been in America, but he contended that as all America came to Europe he had the materials for a study of the national character at hand, without the trouble of crossing the ocean. In return she told him that she had not been the least sea-sick during the voyage, and that it was no trouble at all; then he abruptly left her and went over to beg a cup of tea from Clementina, who sat behind the kettle by the window.

"I have heard this morning from that American I met in Pompeii" he began. "He is coming northward, and I am going down to meet him in Rome."

Mrs. Lander caught the word, and called across the room, "Why, a'n't that whe'e that lo'd's gone?"

Clementina said yes, and while the kettle boiled, she asked if Baron Belsky were going soon.

"Oh, in a week or ten days, perhaps. I shall know when he arrives. Then I shall go. We write to each other every day." He drew a letter from his breast pocket. "This will give you the idea of his character," and he read, "If we believe that the hand of God directs all our actions, how can we set up our theories of conduct against what we feel to be his inspiration?"

"What do you think of that?" he demanded.

"I don't believe that God directs our wrong actions," said Clementina.

"How! Is there anything outside of God?

"I don't know whether there is or not. But there is something that tempts me to do wrong, sometimes, and I don't believe that is God."

The Russian seemed struck. "I will write that to him!"

"No," said Clementina, "I don't want you to say anything about me to him."

"No, no!" said Baron Belsky, waving his band reassuringly. "I would not mention your name!"

Mr. Ewins came in, and the Russian said he must go. Mrs. Lander tried to detain him, too, as she had tried to keep Mr. Hinkle, but he was inexorable. Mr. Ewins looked at the door when it had closed upon him. Mrs. Lander said, "That is one of the gentlemen that Clementina met the otha night at the dance. He is a baron, but he scratches it out. You'd ought to head him go on about Americans."

"Yes," said Mr. Ewins coldly. "He's at our hotel, and he airs his peculiar opinions at the table d'hote pretty freely. He's a revolutionist of some kind, I fancy." He pronounced the epithet with an abhorrence befitting the citizen of a state born of revolution and a city that had cradled the revolt. "He's a Nihilist, I believe."

Mrs. Lander wished to know what that was, and he explained that it was a Russian who wanted to overthrow the Czar, and set up a government of the people, when they were not prepared for liberty.

"Then, maybe he isn't a baron at all," said Mrs. Lander.

"Oh, I believe he has a right to his title," Ewins answered. "It's a German one."

He said he thought that sort of man was all the more mischievous on account of his sincerity. He instanced a Russian whom a friend of his knew in Berlin, a man of rank like this fellow: he got to brooding upon the condition of working people and that kind of thing, till he renounced his title and fortune and went to work in an iron foundry.

Mr. Ewins also spoke critically of Mrs. Milray. He had met her in Egypt; but you soon exhausted the interest of that kind of woman. He professed a great concern that Clementina should see Florence in just the right way, and he offered his services in showing her the place.

The Russian came the next day, and almost daily after that, in the interest with which Clementina's novel difference from other American girls seemed to inspire him. His imagination had transmuted her simple Yankee facts into something appreciable to a Slav of his temperament. He conceived of her as the daughter of a peasant, whose beauty had charmed the widow of a rich citizen, and who was to inherit the wealth of her adoptive mother. He imagined that the adoption had taken place at a much earlier period than the time when Clementina's visit to Mrs. Lander actually began, and that all which could be done had been done to efface her real character by indulgence and luxury.

His curiosity concerning her childhood, her home, her father and mother, her brothers and sisters, and his misunderstanding of everything she told him, amused her. But she liked him, and she tried to give him some notion of the things he wished so much to know. It always ended in a dissatisfaction, more or less vehement, with the outcome of American conditions as he conceived them.

"But you," he urged one day, "you who are a daughter of the fields and woods, why should you forsake that pure life, and come to waste yourself here?"

"Why, don't you think it's very nice in Florence?" she asked, with eyes of innocent interest.

"Nice! Nice! Do we live for what is nice? Is it enough that you have what you Americans call a nice time?"

Clementina reflected. "I wasn't doing much of anything at home, and I thought I might as well come with Mrs. Lander, if she wanted me so much." She thought in a certain way, that he was meddling with what was not his affair, but she believed that he was sincere in his zeal for the ideal life he wished her to lead, and there were some things she had heard about him that made her pity and respect him; his self-exile and his renunciation of home and country for his principles, whatever they were; she did not understand exactly. She would not have liked never being able to go back to Middlemount, or to be cut off from all her friends as this poor young Nihilist was, and she said, now, "I didn't expect that it was going to be anything but a visit, and I always supposed we should go back in the spring; but now Mrs. Lander is beginning to think she won't be well enough till fall."

"And why need you stay with her?"

"Because she's not very well," answered Clementina, and she smiled, a little triumphantly as well as tolerantly.

"She could hire nurses and doctors, all she wants with her money."

"I don't believe it would be the same thing, exactly, and what should I do if I went back?"

"Do? Teach! Uplift the lives about you."

"But you say it is better for people to live simply, and not read and think so much."

"Then labor in the fields with them."

Clementina laughed outright. "I guess if anyone saw me wo'king in the fields they would think I was a disgrace to the neighbahood."

Belsky gave her a stupified glare through his spectacles. "I cannot understand you Americans."

"Well, you must come ova to America, then, Mr. Belsky"—he had asked her not to call him by his title—"and then you would."

"No, I could not endure the disappointment. You have the great opportunity of the earth. You could be equal and just, and simple and kind. There is nothing to hinder you. But all you try to do is to get more and more money."

"Now, that isn't faia, Mr. Belsky, and you know it."

Well, then, you joke, joke—always joke. Like that Mr. Hinkle. He wants to make money with his patent of a gleaner, that will take the last grain of wheat from the poor, and he wants to joke—joke!'

Clementina said, "I won't let you say that about Mr. Hinkle. You don't know him, or you wouldn't. If he jokes, why shouldn't he?"

Belsky made a gesture of rejection. "Oh, you are an American, too."

She had not grown less American, certainly, since she had left home; even the little conformities to Europe that she practiced were traits of Americanism. Clementina was not becoming sophisticated, but perhaps she was becoming more conventionalized. The knowledge of good and evil in things that had all seemed indifferently good to her once, had crept upon her, and she distinguished in her actions. She sinned as little as any young lady in Florence against the superstitions of society; but though she would not now have done a skirt-dance before a shipful of people, she did not afflict herself about her past errors. She put on the world, but she wore it simply and in most matters unconsciously. Some things were imparted to her without her asking or wishing, and merely in virtue of her youth and impressionability. She took them from her environment without knowing it, and in this way she was coming by an English manner and an English tone; she was only the less American for being rather English without trying, when other Americans tried so hard. In the region of harsh nasals, Clementina had never spoken through her nose, and she was now as unaffected in these alien inflections as in the tender cooings which used to rouse the misgivings of her brother Jim. When she was with English people she employed them involuntarily, and when she was with Americans she measurably lost them, so that after half an hour with Mr. Hinkle, she had scarcely a trace of them, and with Mrs. Lander she always spoke with her native accent.

XXIII

One Sunday night, toward the end of Lent, Mrs. Lander had another of her attacks; she now began to call them so as if she had established an ownership in them. It came on from her cumulative over-eating, again, but the doctor was not so smiling as he had been with regard to the first. Clementina had got ready to drive out to Miss Milray's for one of her Sunday teas, but she put off her things, and prepared to spend the night at Mrs. Lander's bedside. "Well, I should think you would want to," said the sufferer. "I'm goin' to do everything for you, and you'd ought to be willing to give up one of youa junketin's for me. I'm sure I don't know what you see in 'em, anyway."

"Oh, I am willing, Mrs. Lander; I'm glad I hadn't stahted before it began." Clementina busied herself with the pillows under Mrs. Lander's dishevelled head, and the bedclothes disordered by her throes, while Mrs. Lander went on.

"I don't see what's the use of so much gaddin', anyway. I don't see as anything comes of it, but just to get a passal of wo'thless fellas afta you that think you'a going to have money. There's such a thing as two sides to everything, and if the favas is goin' to be all on one side I guess there'd betta be a clear undastandin' about it. I think I got a right to a little attention, as well as them that ha'n't done anything; and if I'm goin' to be left alone he'e to die among strangers every time one of my attacks comes on—"

The doctor interposed, "I don't think you're going to have a very bad attack, this time, Mrs. Lander."

"Oh, thank you, thank you, docta! But you can undastand, can't you, how I shall want to have somebody around that can undastand a little English?"

The doctor said, "Oh yes. And Miss Claxon and I can understand a good deal, between us, and we're going to stay, and see how a little morphine behaves with you."

Mrs. Lander protested, "Oh, I can't bea' mo'phine, docta."

"Did you ever try it?" he asked, preparing his little instrument to imbibe the solution.

"No; but Mr. Landa did, and it 'most killed him; it made him sick."

"Well, you're about as sick as you can be, now, Mrs. Lander, and if you don't die of this pin-prick"—he pushed the needle-point under the skin of her massive fore-arm—"I guess you'll live through it."

She shrieked, but as the pain began to abate, she gathered courage, and broke forth joyfully. "Why, it's beautiful, a'n't it? I declare it wo'ks like a cha'm. Well, I shall always keep mo'phine around after this, and when, I feel one of these attacks comin' on—"

"Send for a physician, Mrs. Lander," said Dr. Welwright, "and he'll know what to do."

"I an't so sure of that," returned Mrs. Lander fondly. "He would if you was the one. I declare I believe I could get up and walk right off, I feel so well."

"That's good. If you'll take a walk day after tomorrow it will help you a great deal more."

"Well, I shall always say that you've saved my life, this time, doctor; and Clementina she's stood by, nobly; I'll say that for her." She twisted her big head round on the pillow to get sight of the girl. "I'm all right, now; and don't you mind what I said. It's just my misery talkin'; I don't know what I did say; I felt so bad. But I'm fustrate, now, and I believe I could drop off to sleep, this minute. Why don't you go to your tea? You can, just as well as not!"

"Oh, I don't want to go, now, Mrs. Lander; I'd ratha stay."

"But there a'n't any more danger now, is the'e, docta?" Mrs. Lander appealed.

"No. There wasn't any danger before. But when you're quite yourself, I want to have a little talk with you, Mrs. Lander, about your diet. We must look after that."

"Why, docta, that's what I do do, now. I eat all the healthy things I lay my hands on, don't I, Clementina? And ha'n't you always at me about it?"

Clementina did not answer, and the doctor laughed. "Well, I should like to know what more I could do!"

"Perhaps you could do less. We'll see about that. Better go to sleep, now, if you feel like it."

"Well, I will, if you'll make this silly child go to her tea. I s'pose she won't because I scolded her. She's an awful hand to lay anything up against you. You know you ah', Clementina! But I can say this, doctor: a betta child don't breathe, and I just couldn't live without her. Come he'e, Clementina, I want to kiss you once, before I go to sleep, so's to make su'a you don't bea' malice." She pulled Clementina down to kiss her, and babbled on affectionately and optimistically, till her talk became the voice of her dreams, and then ceased altogether.

"You could go, perfectly well, Miss Claxon," said the doctor.

"No, I don't ca'e to go," answered Clementina. "I'd ratha stay. If she should wake—"

"She won't wake, until long after you've got back; I'll answer for that. I'm going to stay here awhile. Go! I'll take the responsibility."

Clementina's face brightened. She wanted very much to go. She should meet some pleasant people; she always did, at Miss Milray's. Then the light died out of her gay eyes, and she set her lips. "No, I told her I shouldn't go."

"I didn't hear you," said Dr. Welwright. "A doctor has no eyes and ears except for the symptoms of his patients."

"Oh, I know," said Clementina. She had liked Dr. Welwright from the first, and she thought it was very nice of him to stay on, after he left Mrs. Lander's bedside, and help to make her lonesome evening pass pleasantly in the parlor. He jumped up finally, and looked at his watch. "Bless my soul!" he said, and he went in for another look at Mrs. Lander. When he came back, he said, "She's all right. But you've made me break an engagement, Miss Claxon. I was going to tea at Miss Milray's. She promised me I should meet you there."

It seemed a great joke; and Clementina offered to carry his excuses to Miss Milray, when she went to make her own.

She, went the next morning. Mrs. Lander insisted that she should go; she said that she was not going to have Miss Milray thinking that she wanted to keep her all to herself.

Miss Milray kissed the girl in full forgiveness, but she asked, "Did Dr. Welwright think it a very bad attack?"

"Has he been he'a?" returned Clementina.

Miss Milray laughed. "Doctors don't betray their patients—good doctors. No, he hasn't been here, if that will help you. I wish it would help me, but it won't, quite. I don't like to think of that old woman using you up, Clementina."

"Oh, she doesn't, Miss Milray. You mustn't think so. You don't know how good she is to me."

"Does she ever remind you of it?"

Clementina's eyes fell. "She isn't like herself when she doesn't feel well."

"I knew it!" Miss Milray triumphed. "I always knew that she was a dreadful old tabby. I wish you were safely out of her clutches. Come and live with me, my dear, when Mrs. Lander gets tired of you. But she'll never get tired of you. You're just the kind of helpless mouse that such an old tabby would make her natural prey. But she sha'n't, even if another sort of cat has to get you! I'm sorry you couldn't come last night. Your little Russian was here, and went away early and very bitterly because you didn't come. He seemed to think there was nobody, and said so, in everything but words."

"Oh!" said Clementina. "Don't you think he's very nice, Miss Milray?"

"He's very mystical, or else so very simple that he seems so. I hope you can make him out."

Don't you think he's very much in ea'nest?

"Oh, as the grave, or the asylum. I shouldn't like him to be in earnest about me, if I were you."

"But that's just what he is!" Clementina told how the Russian had lectured her, and wished her to go back to the country and work in the fields.

"Oh, if that's all!" cried Miss Milray. "I was afraid it was another kind of earnestness: the kind I shouldn't like if I were you."

"There's no danger of that, I guess." Clementina laughed, and Miss Milray went on:

"Another of your admirers was here; but he was not so inconsolable, or else be found consolation in staying on and talking about you, or joking."

"Oh, yes; Mr. Hinkle," cried Clementina with the smile that the thought of him always brought. "He's lovely."

"Lovely? Well, I don't know why it isn't the word. It suits him a great deal better than some insipid girls that people give it to. Yes, I could really fall in love with Mr. Hinkle. He's the only man I ever saw who would know how to break the fall!"

It was lunch-time before their talk had begun to run low, and it swelled again over the meal. Miss Milray returned to Mrs. Lander, and she made Clementina confess that she was a little trying sometimes. But she insisted that she was always good, and in remorse she went away as soon as Miss Milray rose from table.

She found Mrs. Lander very much better, and willing to have had her stay the whole afternoon with Miss Milray. "I don't want she should have anything to say against me, to you, Clementina; she'd be glad enough to. But I guess it's just as well you'a back. That scratched-out baron has been he'e twice, and he's waitin' for you in the pahla', now. I presume he'll keep comin' till you do see him. I guess you betta have it ova; whatever it is."

"I guess you're right, Mrs. Lander."

Clementina found the Russian walking up and down the room, and as soon as their greeting was over, he asked leave to continue his promenade, but he stopped abruptly before her when she had sunk upon a sofa.

"I have come to tell you a strange story," he said.

"It is the story of that American friend of mine. I tell it to you because I think you can understand, and will know what to advise, what to do."

He turned upon his heel, and walked the length of the room and back before he spoke again.

"Since several years," he said, growing a little less idiomatic in his English as his excitement mounted, "he met a young girl, a child, when he was still not a man's full age. It was in the country, in the mountains of America, and—he loved her. Both were very poor; he, a student, earning the means to complete his education in the university. He had dedicated himself to his church, and with the temperament of the Puritans, he forbade himself all thoughts of love. But he was of a passionate and impulsive nature, and in a moment of abandon he confessed his love. The child was bewildered, frightened; she shrank from his avowal, and he, filled with remorse for his self-betrayal, bade her let it be as if it had not been; he bade her think of him no more."

Clementina sat as if powerless to move, staring at Belsky. He paused in his walk, and allowed an impressive silence to ensue upon his words.

"Time passed: days, months, years; and he did not see her again. He pursued his studies in the university; at their completion, he entered upon the course of divinity, and he is soon to be a minister of his church. In all that time the image of the young girl has remained in his heart, and has held him true to the only love he has ever known. He will know no other while he lives."

Again he stopped in front of Clementina; she looked helplessly up at him, and he resumed his walk.

"He, with his dreams of renunciation, of abnegation, had thought some day to return to her and ask her to be his. He believed her capable of equal sacrifice with himself, and he hoped to win her not for himself alone, but for the religion which he put before himself. He would have invited her to join her fate with his that they might go together on some mission to the pagan—in the South Seas, in the heart of Africa, in the jungle of India. He had always thought of her as gay but good, unworldly in soul, and exalted in spirit. She has remained with him a vision of angelic loveliness, as he had seen her last in the moonlight, on the banks of a mountain torrent. But he believes that he has disgraced himself before her; that the very scruple for her youth, her ignorance, which made him entreat her to forget him, must have made her doubt and despise him. He has never had the courage to write to her one word since all those years, but he maintains himself bound to her forever." He stopped short before Clementina and seized her hands. "If you knew such a girl, what would you have her do? Should she bid him hope again? Would you have her say to him that she, too, had been faithful to their dream, and that she too—"

"Let me go, Mr. Belsky, let me go, I say!" Clementina wrenched her hands from him, and ran out of the room. Belsky hesitated, then he found his hat, and after a glance at his face in the mirror, left the house.

XXIV

The tide of travel began to set northward in April. Many English, many Americans appeared in Florence from Naples and Rome; many who had wintered in Florence went on to Venice and the towns of northern Italy, on their way to Switzerland and France and Germany.

The spring was cold and rainy, and the irresolute Italian railroads were interrupted by the floods. A tawny deluge rolled down from the mountains through the bed of the Arno, and kept the Florentine fire-department on the alert night and day. "It is a curious thing about this country," said Mr. Hinkle, encountering Baron Belsky on the Ponte Trinita, "that the only thing they ever have here for a fire company to put out is a freshet. If they had a real conflagration once, I reckon they would want to bring their life-preservers."

The Russian was looking down over the parapet at the boiling river. He lifted his head as if he had not heard the American, and stared at him a moment before he spoke. "It is said that the railway to Rome is broken at Grossetto."

"Well, I'm not going to Rome," said Hinkle, easily. "Are you?"

"I was to meet a friend there; but he wrote to me that he was starting to Florence, and now—"

"He's resting on the way? Well, he'll get here about as quick as he would in the ordinary course of travel. One good thing about Italy is, you don't want to hurry; if you did, you'd get left."

Belsky stared at him in the stupefaction to which the American humor commonly reduced him. "If he gets left on the Grossetto line, he can go back and come up by Orvieto, no?"

"He can, if he isn't in a hurry," Hinkle assented.

"It's a good way, if you've got time to burn."

Belsky did not attempt to explore the American's meaning. "Do you know," he asked, "whether Mrs. Lander and her young friend are still in Florence?

"I guess they are."

"It was said they were going to Venice for the summer."

"That's what the doctor advised for the old lady. But they don't start for a week or two yet."

"Oh!"

"Are you going to Miss Milray's, Sunday night? Last of the season, I believe."

Belsky seemed to recall himself from a distance.

"No—no," he said, and he moved away, forgetful of the ceremonious salutation which he commonly used at meeting and parting. Hinkle looked after him with the impression people have of a difference in the appearance and behavior of some one whose appearance and behavior do not particularly concern them.

The day that followed, Belsky haunted the hotel where Gregory was to arrive with his pupil, and where the pupil's family were waiting for them. That night, long after their belated train was due, they came; the pupil was with his father and mother, and Gregory was alone, when Belsky asked for him, the fourth or fifth time.

"You are not well," he said, as they shook hands. "You are fevered!"

"I'm tired," said Gregory. "We've bad a bad time getting through."

"I come inconveniently! You have not dined, perhaps?"

"Yes, Yes. I've had dinner. Sit down. How have you been yourself?"

"Oh, always well." Belsky sat down, and the friends stared at each other. "I have strange news for you."

"For me?"

"You. She is here."

"She?"

"Yes. The young girl of whom you told me. If I had not forbidden myself by my loyalty to you—if I had not said to myself every moment in her presence, 'No, it is for your friend alone that she is beautiful and good!'—But you will have nothing to reproach me in that regard."

"What do you mean?" demanded Gregory.

"I mean that Miss Claxon is in Florence, with her protectress, the rich Mrs. Lander. The most admired young lady in society, going everywhere, and everywhere courted and welcomed; the favorite of the fashionable Miss Milray. But why should this surprise you?"

"You said nothing about it in your letters. You—"

"I was not sure it was she; you never told me her name. When I had divined the fact, I was so soon to see you, that I thought best to keep it till we met."

Gregory tried to speak, but he let Belsky go on.

"If you think that the world has spoiled her, that she will be different from what she was in her home among your mountains, let me reassure you. In her you will find the miracle of a woman whom no flattery can turn the head. I have watched her in your interest; I have tested her. She is what you saw her last."

"Surely," asked Gregory, in an anguish for what he now dreaded, "you haven't spoken to her of me?"

"Not by name, no. I could not have that indiscretion—"

"The name is nothing. Have you said that you knew me—Of course not! But have you hinted at any knowledge—Because—"

"You will hear!" said Belsky; and he poured out upon Gregory the story of what he had done. "She did not deny anything. She was greatly moved, but she did not refuse to let me bid you hope—"

"Oh!" Gregory took his head between his hands. "You have spoiled my life!"

"Spoiled" Belsky stopped aghast.

"I told you my story in a moment of despicable weakness—of impulsive folly. But how could I dream that you would ever meet her? How could I imagine that you would speak to her as you have done?" He groaned, and began to creep giddily about the room in his misery. "Oh, oh, oh! What shall I do?"

"But I do not understand!" Belsky began. "If I have committed an error—"

"Oh, an error that never could be put right in all eternity!"

"Then let me go to her—let me tell her—"

"Keep away from her!" shouted Gregory. "Do you hear? Never go near her again!"

"Gregory!"

"Ah, I beg your pardon! I don't know what I'm doing-saying. What will she think—what will she think of me!" He had ceased to speak to Belsky; he collapsed into a chair, and hid his face in his arms stretched out on the table before him.

Belsky watched him in the stupefaction which the artistic nature feels when life proves sentient under its hand, and not the mere material of situations and effects. He could not conceive the full measure of the disaster he had wrought, the outrage of his own behavior had been lost to him in his preoccupation with the romantic end to be accomplished. He had meant to be the friend, the prophet, to these American lovers, whom he was reconciling and interpreting to each other; but in some point he must have misunderstood. Yet the error was not inexpiable; and in his expiation he could put the seal to his devotion. He left the room, where Gregory made no effort to keep him.

He walked down the street from the hotel to the Arno, and in a few moments he stood on the bridge, where he had talked with that joker in the morning, as they looked down together on the boiling river. He had a strange wish that the joker might have been with him again, to learn that there were some things which could not be joked away.

The night was blustering, and the wind that blew the ragged clouds across the face of the moon, swooped in sudden gusts upon the bridge, and the deluge rolling under it and hoarsely washing against its piers. Belsky leaned over the parapet and looked down into the eddies and currents as the fitful light revealed them. He had a fantastic pleasure in studying them, and choosing the moment when he should leap the parapet and be lost in them. The incident could not be used in any novel of his, and no one else could do such perfect justice to the situation, but perhaps afterwards, when the facts leading to his death should be known through the remorse of the lovers whom he had sought to serve, some other artist-nature could distil their subtlest meaning in a memoir delicate as the aroma of a faded flower.

He was willing to make this sacrifice, too, and he stepped back a pace from the parapet when the fitful blast caught his hat from his head, and whirled it along the bridge. The whole current of his purpose changed, and as if it had been impossible to drown himself in his bare head, he set out in chase of his hat, which rolled and gamboled away, and escaped from his clutch whenever he stooped for it, till a final whiff of wind flung it up and tossed it over the bridge into the river, where he helplessly watched it floating down the flood, till it was carried out of sight.

XXV

Gregory did not sleep, and he did not find peace in the prayers he put up for guidance. He tried to think of some one with whom he might take counsel; but he knew no one in Florence except the parents of his pupil, and they were impossible. He felt himself abandoned to the impulse which he dreaded, in going to Clementina, and he went without hope, willing to suffer whatever penalty she should visit upon him, after he had disavowed Belsky's action, and claimed the responsibility for it.

He was prepared for her refusal to see him; he had imagined her wounded and pathetic; he had fancied her insulted and indignant; but she met him eagerly and with a mystifying appeal in her welcome. He began at once, without attempting to bridge the time since they had met with any formalities.

"I have come to speak to you about—that—Russian, about Baron Belsky—"

"Yes, yes!" she returned, anxiously. "Then you have hea'd"

"He came to me last night, and—I want to say that I feel myself to blame for what he has done."

"You?"

"Yes; I. I never spoke of you by name to him; I didn't dream of his ever seeing you, or that he would dare to speak to you of what I told him. But I believe he meant no wrong; and it was I who did the harm, whether I authorized it or not."

"Yes, yes!" she returned, with the effect of putting his words aside as something of no moment. "Have they head anything more?"

"How, anything more?" he returned, in a daze.

"Then, don't you know? About his falling into the river? I know he didn't drown himself."

Gregory shook his head. "When—what makes them think"—He stopped and stared at her.

"Why, they know that he went down to the Ponte Trinity last night; somebody saw him going: And then that peasant found his hat with his name in it in the drift-wood below the Cascine—"

"Yes," said Gregory, lifelessly. He let his arms drop forward, and his helpless hands hang over his knees; his gaze fell from her face to the floor.

Neither spoke for a time that seemed long, and then it was Clementina who spoke. "But it isn't true!"

"Oh, yes, it is," said Gregory, as before.

"Mr. Hinkle doesn't believe it is," she urged.

"Mr. Hinkle?"

"He's an American who's staying in Florence. He came this mo'ning to tell me about it. Even if he's drowned Mr. Hinkle believes he didn't mean to; he must have just fallen in."

"What does it matter?" demanded Gregory, lifting his heavy eyes. "Whether he meant it or not, I caused it. I drove him to it."

"You drove him?"

"Yes. He told me what he had said to you, and I—said that he had spoiled my life—I don't know!"

"Well, he had no right to do it; but I didn't blame you," Clementina began, compassionately.

"It's too late. It can't be helped now." Gregory turned from the mercy that could no longer save him. He rose dizzily, and tried to get himself away.

"You mustn't go!" she interposed. "I don't believe you made him do it. Mr. Hinkle will be back soon, and he will—"

"If he should bring word that it was true?" Gregory asked.

"Well," said Clementina, "then we should have to bear it."

A sense of something finer than the surface meaning of her words pierced his morbid egotism. "I'm ashamed," he said. "Will you let me stay?"

"Why, yes, you must," she said, and if there was any censure of him at the bottom of her heart, she kept it there, and tried to talk him away from his remorse, which was in his temperament, perhaps, rather than his conscience; she made the time pass till there came a knock at the door, and she opened it to Hinkle.

"I didn't send up my name; I thought I wouldn't stand upon ceremony just now," he said.

"Oh, no!" she returned. "Mr. Hinkle, this is Mr. Gregory. Mr. Gregory knew Mr. Belsky, and he thinks—"

She turned to Gregory for prompting, and he managed to say, "I don't believe he was quite the sort of person to—And yet he might—he was in trouble—"

"Money trouble?" asked Hinkle. "They say these Russians have a perfect genius for debt. I had a little inspiration, since I saw you, but there doesn't seems to be anything in it, so far." He addressed himself to Clementina, but he included Gregory in what he said. "It struck me that he might have been running his board, and had used this drowning episode as a blind. But I've been around to his hotel, and he's settled up, all fair and square enough. The landlord tried to think of something he hadn't paid, but he couldn't; and I never saw a man try harder, either." Clementina smiled; she put her hand to her mouth to keep from laughing; but Gregory frowned his distress in the untimely droning.

"I don't give up my theory that it's a fake of some kind, though. He could leave behind a good many creditors besides his landlord. The authorities have sealed up his effects, and they've done everything but call out the fire department; that's on duty looking after the freshet, and it couldn't be spared. I'll go out now and slop round a little more in the cause," Hinkle looked down at his shoes and his drabbled trousers, and wiped the perspiration from his face, "but I thought I'd drop in, and tell you not to worry about it, Miss Clementina. I would stake anything you pleased on Mr. Belsky's safety. Mr. Gregory, here, looks like he would be willing to take odds," he suggested.

Gregory commanded himself from his misery to say, "I wish I could believe— I mean—"

"Of course, we don't want to think that the man's a fraud, any more than that he's dead. Perhaps we might hit upon some middle course. At any rate, it's worth trying."

"May I—do you object to my joining you?" Gregory asked.

"Why, come!" Hinkle hospitably assented. "Glad to have you. I'll be back again, Miss Clementina!"

Gregory was going away without any form of leavetaking; but he turned back to ask, "Will you let me come back, too?"

"Why, suttainly, Mr. Gregory," said Clementina, and she went to find Mrs. Lander, whom she found in bed.

"I thought I'd lay down," she explained. "I don't believe I'm goin' to be sick, but it's one of my pooa days, and I might just as well be in bed as not." Clementina agreed with her, and Mrs. Lander asked: "You hea'd anything moa?"

"No. Mr. Hinkle has just been he'a, but he hadn't any news."

Mrs. Lander turned her face toward the wall. "Next thing, he'll be drownin' himself. I neva wanted you should have anything to do with the fellas that go to that woman's. There ain't any of 'em to be depended on."

It was the first time that her growing jealousy of Miss Milray had openly declared itself; but Clementina had felt it before, without knowing how to meet it. As an escape from it now she was almost willing to say, "Mrs. Lander, I want to tell you that Mr. Gregory has just been he'a, too."

"Mr. Gregory?"

"Yes. Don't you remember? At the Middlemount? The first summa? He was the headwaita—that student."

Mrs. Lander jerked her head round on the pillow. "Well, of all the—What does he want, over he'a?"

"Nothing. That is—he's travelling with a pupil that he's preparing for college, and—he came to see us—"

"D'you tell him I couldn't see him?"

"Yes"

"I guess he'd think I was a pretty changed pusson! Now, I want you should stay with me, Clementina, and if anybody else comes—"

Maddalena entered the room with a card which she gave to the girl.

"Who is it?" Mrs. Lander demanded.

"Miss Milray."

"Of cou'se! Well, you may just send wo'd that you can't—Or, no; you must! She'd have it all ova the place, by night, that I wouldn't let you see her. But don't you make any excuse for me! If she asks after me, don't you say I'm sick! You say I'm not at home."

"I've come about that little wretch," Miss Milray began, after kissing Clementina. "I didn't know but you had heard something I hadn't, or I had heard something you hadn't. You know I belong to the Hinkle persuasion: I think Belsky's run his board—as Mr. Hinkle calls it."

Clementina explained how this part of the Hinkle theory had failed, and then Miss Milray devolved upon the belief that he had run his tailor's bill or his shoemaker's. "They are delightful, those Russians, but they're born insolvent. I don't believe he's drowned himself. How," she broke off to ask, in a burlesque whisper, "is-the-old-tabby?" She laughed, for answer to her own question, and then with another sudden diversion she demanded of a look in Clementina's face which would not be laughed away, "Well, my dear, what is it?"

"Miss Milray," said the girl, "should you think me very silly, if I told you something—silly?"

"Not in the least!" cried Miss Milray, joyously. "It's the final proof of your wisdom that I've been waiting for?"

"It's because Mr. Belsky is all mixed up in it," said Clementina, as if some excuse were necessary, and then she told the story of her love affair with Gregory. Miss Milray punctuated the several facts with vivid nods, but at the end she did not ask her anything, and the girl somehow felt the freer to add: "I believe I will tell you his name. It is Mr. Gregory—Frank Gregory—"

"And he's been in Egypt?"

"Yes, the whole winta."

"Then he's the one that my sister-in-law has been writing me about!"

"Oh, did he meet her the'a?"

"I should think so! And he'll meet her there, very soon. She's coming, with my poor brother. I meant to tell you, but this ridiculous Belsky business drove it out of my head."

"And do you think," Clementina entreated, "that he was to blame?"

"Why, I don't believe he's done it, you know."

"Oh, I didn't mean Mr. Belsky. I meant—Mr. Gregory. For telling Mr. Belsky?"

"Certainly not. Men always tell those things to some one, I suppose. Nobody was to blame but Belsky, for his meddling."

Miss Milray rose and shook out her plumes for flight, as if she were rather eager for flight, but at the little sigh with which Clementina said, "Yes, that is what I thought," she faltered.

"I was going to run away, for I shouldn't like to mix myself up in your affair—it's certainly a very strange one—unless I was sure I could help you. But if you think I can—"

Clementina shook her head. "I don't believe you can," she said, with a candor so wistful that Miss Milray stopped quite short. "How does Mr. Gregory take this Belsky business?" she asked.

"I guess he feels it moa than I do," said the girl.

"He shows his feeling more?"

"Yes—no—He believes he drove him to it."

Miss Milray took her hand, for parting, but did not kiss her. "I won't advise you, my dear. In fact, you haven't asked me to. You'll know what to do, if you haven't done it already; girls usually have, when they want advice. Was there something you were going to say?"

"Oh, no. Nothing. Do you think," she hesitated, appealingly, "do you think we are-engaged?"

"If he's anything of a man at all, he must think he is."

"Yes," said Clementina, wistfully, "I guess he does."

Miss Milray looked sharply at her. "And does he think you are?"

"I don't know—he didn't say."

"Well," said Miss Milray, rather dryly, "then it's something for you to think over pretty carefully."

XXVI

Hinkle came back in the afternoon to make a hopeful report of his failure to learn anything more of Belsky, but Gregory did not come with him. He came the next morning long before Clementina expected visitors, and he was walking nervously up and down the room when she appeared. As if he could not speak, he held toward her without speaking a telegram in English, dated that day in Rome:

"Deny report of my death. Have written.

"Belsky."

She looked up at Gregory from the paper, when she had read it, with joyful eyes. "Oh, I am so glad for you! I am so glad he is alive."

He took the dispatch from her hand. "I brought it to you as soon as it came."

"Yes, yes! Of cou'se!"

"I must go now and do what he says—I don't know how yet." He stopped, and then went on from a different impulse. "Clementina, it isn't a question now of that wretch's life and death, and I wish I need never speak of him again. But what he told you was true." He looked steadfastly at her, and she realized how handsome he was, and how well dressed. His thick red hair seemed to have grown darker above his forehead; his moustache was heavier, and it curved in at the corners of his mouth; he bore himself with a sort of self-disdain that enhanced his splendor. "I have never changed toward you; I don't say it to make favor with you; I don't expect to do that now; but it is true. That night, there at Middlemount, I tried to take back what I said, because I believed that I ought."

"Oh, yes, I knew that," said Clementina, in the pause he made.

"We were both too young; I had no prospect in life; I saw, the instant after I had spoken, that I had no right to let you promise anything. I tried to forget you; I couldn't. I tried to make you forget me." He faltered, and she did not speak, but her head drooped a little. "I won't ask how far I succeeded. I always hoped that the time would come when I could speak to you again. When I heard from Fane that you were at Woodlake, I wished to come out and see you, but I hadn't the courage, I hadn't the right. I've had to come to you without either, now. Did he speak to you about me?"

"I thought he was beginning to, once; but he neva did."

"It didn't matter; it could only have made bad worse. It can't help me to say that somehow I was wishing and trying to do what was right; but I was."

"Oh, I know that, Mr. Gregory," said Clementina, generously.

"Then you didn't doubt me, in spite of all?"

"I thought you would know what to do. No, I didn't doubt you, exactly."

"I didn't deserve your trust!" he cried. "How came that man to mention me?" he demanded, abruptly, after a moment's silence.

"Mr. Belsky? It was the first night I saw him, and we were talking about Americans, and he began to tell me about an American friend of his, who was very conscientious. I thought it must be you the fust moment," said Clementina, smiling with an impersonal pleasure in the fact.

"From the conscientiousness?" he asked, in bitter self-irony.

"Why, yes," she returned, simply. "That was what made me think of you. And the last time when he began to talk about you, I couldn't stop him, although I knew he had no right to."

"He had no right. But I gave him the power to do it! He meant no harm, but I enabled him to do all the harm."

"Oh, if he's only alive, now, there is no harm!"

He looked into her eyes with a misgiving from which he burst impetuously. "Then you do care for me still, after all that I have done to make you detest me?" He started toward her, but she shrank back.

"I didn't mean that," she hesitated.

"You know that I love you,—that I have always loved you?"

"Yes," she assented. "But you might be sorry again that you had said it." It sounded like coquetry, but he knew it was not coquetry.

"Never! I've wished to say it again, ever since that night at Middlemount; I have always felt bound by what I said then, though I took back my words for your sake. But the promise was always there, and my life was in it. You believe that?"

"Why, I always believed what you said, Mr. Gregory."

"Well?"

Clementina paused, with her head seriously on one side. "I should want to think about it before I said anything."

"You are right," he submitted, dropping his outstretched arms to his side. "I have been thinking only of myself, as usual."

"No," she protested, compassionately. "But doesn't it seem as if we ought to be su'a, this time? I did ca'e for you then, but I was very young, and I don't know yet—I thought I had always felt just; as you did, but now—Don't you think we had both betta wait a little while till we ah' moa suttain?"

They stood looking at each other, and he said, with a kind of passionate self-denial, "Yes, think it over for me, too. I will come back, if you will let me."

"Oh, thank you!" she cried after him, gratefully, as if his forbearance were the greatest favor.

When he was gone she tried to release herself from the kind of abeyance in which she seemed to have gone back and been as subject to him as in the first days when he had awed her and charmed her with his superiority at Middlemount, and he again older and freer as she had grown since.

He came back late in the afternoon, looking jaded and distraught. Hinkle, who looked neither, was with him. "Well," he began, "this is the greatest thing in my experience. Belsky's not only alive and well, but Mr. Gregory and I are both at large. I did think, one time, that the police would take us into custody on account of our morbid interest in the thing, and I don't believe we should have got off, if the Consul hadn't gone bail for us, so to speak. I thought we had better take the Consul in, on our way, and it was lucky we did."

Clementina did not understand all the implications, but she was willing to take Mr. Hinkle's fun on trust. "I don't believe you'll convince Mrs. Landa that Mr. Belsky's alive and well, till you bring him back to say so."

"Is that so!" said Hinkle. "Well, we must have him brought back by the authorities, then. Perhaps they'll bring him, anyway. They can't try him for suicide, but as I understand the police, here, a man can't lose his hat over a bridge in Florence with impunity, especially in a time of high water. Anyway, they're identifying Belsky by due process of law in Rome, now, and I guess Mr. Gregory"—he nodded toward Gregory, who sat silent and absent "will be kept under surveillance till the whole mystery is cleared up."

Clementina responded gayly still, but with less and less sincerity, and she let Hinkle go at last with the feeling that he knew she wished him to go. He made a brave show of not seeing this, and when he was gone, she remembered that she had not thanked him for the trouble he had taken on her account, and her heart ached after him with a sense of his sweetness and goodness, which she had felt from the first through his quaint drolling. It was as if the door which closed upon him shut her out of the life she had been living of late, and into the life of the past where she was subject again to the spell of Gregory's mood; it was hardly his will.

He began at once: "I wished to make you say something this morning that I have no right to hear you say, yet; and I have been trying ever since to think how I could ask you whether you could share my life with me, and yet not ask you to do it. But I can't do anything without knowing—You may not care for what my life is to be, at all!"

Clementina's head drooped a little, but she answered distinctly, "I do ca'e, Mr. Gregory."

"Thank you for that much; I don't count upon more than you have said. Clementina, I am going to be a missionary. I think I shall ask to be sent to China; I've not decided yet. My life will be hard; it will be full of danger and privation; it will be exile. You will have to think of sharing such a life if you think—"

He stopped; the time had come for her to speak, and she said, "I knew you wanted to be a missionary—"

"And—and—you would go with me? You would"—He started toward her, and she did not shrink from him, now; but he checked himself. "But you mustn't, you know, for my sake."

"I don't believe I quite undastand," she faltered.

"You must not do it for me, but for what makes me do it. Without that our life, our work, could have no consecration."

She gazed at him in patient, faintly smiling bewilderment, as if it were something he would unriddle for her when he chose.

"We mustn't err in this; it would be worse than error; it would be sin." He took a turn about the room, and then stopped before her. "Will you—will you join me in a prayer for guidance, Clementina?"

"I—I don't know," she hesitated. "I will, but—do you think I had betta?"

He began, "Why, surely"—After a moment he asked gravely, "You believe that our actions will be guided aright, if we seek help?"

"Oh, yes—yes—"

"And that if we do not, we shall stumble in our ignorance?"

"I don't know. I never thought of that."

"Never thought of it—"

"We never did it in our family. Father always said that if we really wanted to do right we could find the way." Gregory looked daunted, and then he frowned darkly. "Are you provoked with me? Do you think what I have said is wrong?"

"No, no! You must say what you believe. It would be double hypocrisy in me if I prevented you."

"But I would do it, if you wanted me to," she said.

"Oh, for me, for ME!" he protested. "I will try to tell you what I mean, and why you must not, for that very reason." But he had to speak of himself, of the miracle of finding her again by the means which should have lost her to him forever; and of the significance of this. Then it appeared to him that he could not reject such a leading without error, without sin. "Such a thing could not have merely happened."

It seemed so to Clementina, too; she eagerly consented that this was something they must think of, as well. But the light waned, the dark thickened in the room before he left her to do so. Then he said fervently, "We must not doubt that everything will come right," and his words seemed an effect of inspiration to them both.

XXVII

After Gregory was gone a misgiving began in Clementina's mind, which grew more distinct, through all the difficulties of accounting to Mrs. Lander for his long stay, The girl could see that it was with an obscure jealousy that she pushed her questions, and said at last, "That Mr. Hinkle is about the best of the lot. He's the only one that's eva had the mannas to ask after me, except that lo'd. He did."

Clementina could not pretend that Gregory had asked, but she could not blame him for a forgetfulness of Mrs. Lander which she had shared with him. This helped somehow to deepen the misgiving which followed her from Mrs. Lander's bed to her own, and haunted her far into the night. She could escape from it only by promising herself to deal with it the first thing in the morning. She did this in terms much briefer than she thought she could have commanded. She supposed she would have to write a very long letter, but she came to the end of all she need say, in a very few lines.

DEAR MR. GREGORY:

"I have been thinking about what you said yesterday, and I have to

tell you something. Then you can do what is right for both of us;

you will know better than I can. But I want you to understand that

if I go with you in your missionary life, I shall do it for you, and

not for anything else. I would go anywhere and live anyhow for you,

but it would be for you; I do not believe that I am religious, and I

know that I should not do it for religion.

"That is all; but I could not get any peace till I let you know just how I felt.

"CLEMENTINA CLAXON."

The letter went early in the morning, though not so early but it was put in Gregory's hand as he was leaving his hotel to go to Mrs. Lander's. He tore it open, and read it on the way, and for the first moment it seemed as if it were Providence leading him that he might lighten Clementina's heart of its doubts with the least delay. He had reasoned that if she would share for his sake the life that he should live for righteousness' sake they would be equally blest in it, and it would be equally consecrated in both. But this luminous conclusion faded in his thought as he hurried on, and he found himself in her presence with something like a hope that she would be inspired to help him.

His soul lifted at the sound of the gay voice in which she asked, "Did you get my letta?" and it seemed for the instant as if there could be no trouble that their love could not overcome.

"Yes," he said, and he put his arms around her, but with a provisionality in his embrace which she subtly perceived.

"And what did you think of it?" she asked. "Did you think I was silly?"

He was aware that she had trusted him to do away her misgiving. "No, no," he answered, guiltily. "Wiser than I am, always. I—I want to talk with you about it, Clementina. I want you to advise me."

He felt her shrink from him, and with a pang he opened his arms to free her. But it was right; he must. She had been expecting him to say that there was nothing in her misgiving, and he could not say it.

"Clementina," he entreated, "why do you think you are not religious?"

"Why, I have never belonged to chu'ch," she answered simply. He looked so daunted, that she tried to soften the blow after she had dealt it. "Of course, I always went to chu'ch, though father and motha didn't. I went to the Episcopal —to Mr. Richling's. But I neva was confirmed."

"But-you believe in God?"

"Why, certainly!"

"And in the Bible?"

"Why, of cou'se!"

"And that it is our duty to bear the truth to those who have never heard of it?"

"I know that is the way you feel about it; but I am not certain that I should feel so myself if you didn't want me to. That's what I got to thinking about last night." She added hopefully, "But perhaps it isn't so great a thing as I—"

"It's a very great thing," he said, and from standing in front of her, he now sat down beyond a little table before her sofa. "How can I ask you to share my life if you don't share my faith?"

"Why, I should try to believe everything that you do, of cou'se."

"Because I do?"

"Well-yes."

"You wring my heart! Are you willing to study—to look into these questions —to—to"—It all seemed very hopeless, very absurd, but she answered seriously:

"Yes, but I believe it would all come back to just where it is, now."

"What you say, Clementina, makes me so happy; but it ought to make me— miserable! And you would do all this, be all this for me, a wretched and erring creature of the dust, and yet not do it for—God?"

Clementina could only say, "Perhaps if He meant me to do it for Him, He would have made me want to. He made you."

"Yes," said Gregory, and for a long time he could not say any more. He sat with his elbow on the table, and his head against his lifted hand.

"You see," she began, gently, "I got to thinking that even if I eva came to believe what you wanted me to, I should be doing it after all, because you wanted me to—"

"Yes, yes," he answered, desolately. "There is no way out of it. If you only hated me, Clementina, despised me—I don't mean that. But if you were not so good, I could have a more hope for you—for myself. It's because you are so good that I can't make myself wish to change you, and yet I know—I am afraid that if you told me my life and objects were wrong, I should turn from them, and be whatever you said. Do you tell me that?"

"No, indeed!" cried Clementina, with abhorrence. "Then I should despise you."

He seemed not to heed her. He moved his lips as if he were talking to himself, and he pleaded, "What shall we do?"

"We must try to think it out, and if we can't—if you can't let me give up to you unless I do it for the same reason that you do; and if I can't let you give up for me, and I know I could neva do that; then—we mustn't!"

"Do you mean, we must part? Not see each other again?"

"What use would it be?"

"None," he owned. She had risen, and he stood up perforce. "May I—may I come back to tell you?"

"Tell me what?" she asked.

"You are right! If I can't make it right, I won't come. But I won't say good bye. I—can't."

She let him go, and Maddalena came in at the door. "Signorina," she said, "the signora is not well. Shall I send for the doctor?"

"Yes, yes, Maddalena. Run!" cried Clementina, distractedly. She hurried to Mrs. Lander's room, where she found her too sick for reproaches, for anything but appeals for help and pity. The girl had not to wait for Doctor Welwright's coming to understand that the attack was severer than any before.

It lasted through the day, and she could see that he was troubled. It had not followed upon any imprudeuce, as Mrs. Lander pathetically called Clementina to witness when her pain had been so far quelled that she could talk of her seizure.

He found her greatly weakened by it the next day, and he sat looking thoughtfully at her before he said that she needed toning up. She caught at the notion. "Yes, yes! That's what I need, docta! Toning up! That's what I need."

He suggested, "How would you like to try the sea air, and the baths—at Venice?"

"Oh, anything, anywhere, to get out of this dreadful hole! I ha'n't had a well minute since I came. And Clementina," the sick woman whimpered, "is so taken up all the time, he'a, that I can't get the right attention."

The doctor looked compassionately away from the girl, and said, "Well, we must arrange about getting you off, then."

"But I want you should go with me, doctor, and see me settled all right. You can, can't you? I sha'n't ca'e how much it costs?"

The doctor said gravely he thought he could manage it and he ignored the long unconscious sigh of relief that Clementina drew.

In all her confusing anxieties for Mrs. Lander, Gregory remained at the bottom of her heart a dumb ache. When the pressure of her fears was taken from her she began to suffer for him consciously; then a letter came from him:

"I cannot make it right. It is where it was, and I feel that I must

not see you again. I am trying to do right, but with the fear that

I am wrong. Send some word to help me before I go away to-morrow.

F. G."

It was what she had expected, she knew now, but it was none the less to be borne because of her expectation. She wrote back:

"I believe you are doing the best you can, and I shall always

believe that."

Her note brought back a long letter from him. He said that whatever he did, or wherever he went, he should try to be true to her ideal of him. If they renounced their love now for the sake of what seemed higher than their love, they might suffer, but they could not choose but do as they were doing.

Clementina was trying to make what she could of this when Miss Milray's name came up, and Miss Milray followed it.

"I wanted to ask after Mrs. Lander, and I want you to tell her I did. Will you? Dr. Welwright says he's going to take her to Venice. Well, I'm sorry—sorry for your going, Clementina, and I'm truly sorry for the cause of it. I shall miss you, my dear, I shall indeed. You know I always wanted to steal you, but you'll do me the justice to say I never did, and I won't try, now."

"Perhaps I wasn't worth stealing," Clementina suggested, with a ruefulness in her smile that went to Miss Milray's heart.

She put her arms round her and kissed her. "I wasn't very kind to you, the other day, Clementina, was I?"

"I don't know," Clementina faltered, with half-averted face.

"Yes, you do! I was trying to make-believe that I didn't want to meddle with your affairs; but I was really vexed that you hadn't told me your story before.

It hasn't taken me all this time to reflect that you couldn't, but it has to make myself come and confess that I had been dry and cold with you." She hesitated. "It's come out all right, hasn't it, Clementina?" she asked, tenderly. "You see I want to meddle, now."

"We ah' trying to think so," sighed the girl.

"Tell me about it!" Miss Milray pulled her down on the sofa with her, and modified her embrace to a clasp of Clementina's bands.

"Why, there isn't much to tell," she began, but she told what there was, and Miss Milray kept her countenance concerning the scruple that had parted Clementina and her lover. "Perhaps he wouldn't have thought of it," she said, in a final self-reproach, "if I hadn't put it into his head."

"Well, then, I'm not sorry you put it into his head," cried Miss Milray. "Clementina, may I say what I think of Mr. Gregory's performance?"

"Why, certainly, Miss Milray!"

I think he's not merely a gloomy little bigot, but a very hard-hearted little wretch, and I'm glad you're rid of him. No, stop! Let me go on! You said I might! she persisted, at a protest which imparted itself from Clementina's restive hands. "It was selfish and cruel of him to let you believe that he had forgotten you. It doesn't make it right now, when an accident has forced him to tell you that he cared for you all along."

"Why, do you look at it that way, Miss Milray? If he was doing it on my account?"

"He may think he was doing it on your account, but I think he was doing it on his own. In such a thing as that, a man is bound by his mistakes, if he has made any. He can't go back of them by simply ignoring them. It didn't make it the same for you when he decided for your sake that he would act as if he had never spoken to you."

"I presume he thought that it would come right, sometime," Clementina urged. "I did."

"Yes, that was very well for you, but it wasn't at all well for him. He behaved cruelly; there's no other word for it."

"I don't believe he meant to be cruel, Miss Milray," said Clementina.

"You're not sorry you've broken with him?" demanded Miss Milray, severely, and she let go of Clementina's hands.

"I shouldn't want him to think I hadn't been fai'a."

"I don't understand what you mean by not being fair," said Miss Milray, after a study of the girl's eyes.

"I mean," Clementina explained, "that if I let him think the religion was all the'e was, it wouldn't have been fai'a."

"Why, weren't you sincere about that?"

"Of cou'se I was!" returned the girl, almost indignantly. "But if the'e was anything else, I ought to have told him that, too; and I couldn't."

"Then you can't tell me, of course?" Miss Milray rose in a little pique.

"Perhaps some day I will," the girl entreated. "And perhaps that was all."

Miss Milray laughed. "Well, if that was enough to end it, I'm satisfied, and I'll let you keep your mystery—if it is one—till we meet in Venice; I shall be there early in June. Good bye, dear, and say good bye to Mrs. Lander for me."

XXVIII.

Dr. Welwright got his patient a lodging on the Grand Canal in Venice, and decided to stay long enough to note the first effect of the air and the baths, and to look up a doctor to leave her with.

This took something more than a week, which could not all be spent in Mrs. Lander's company, much as she wished it. There were hours which he gave to going about in a gondola with Clementina, whom he forbade to be always at the invalid's side. He tried to reassure her as to Mrs. Lander's health, when he found her rather mute and absent, while they drifted in the silvery sun of the late April weather, just beginning to be warm, but not warm enough yet for the tent of the open gondola. He asked her about Mrs. Lander's family, and Clementina could only tell him that she had always said she had none. She told him the story of her own relation to her, and he said, "Yes, I heard something of that from Miss Milray." After a moment of silence, during which he looked curiously into the girl's eyes, "Do you think you can bear a little more care, Miss Claxon?"

"I think I can," said Clementina, not very courageously, but patiently.

"It's only this, and I wouldn't tell you if I hadn't thought you equal to it. Mrs. Lander's case puzzles me: But I shall leave Dr. Tradonico watching it, and if it takes the turn that there's a chance it may take, he will tell you, and you'd better find out about her friends, and—let them know. That's all."

"Yes," said Clementina, as if it were not quite enough. Perhaps she did not fully realize all that the doctor had intended; life alone is credible to the young; life and the expectation of it.

The night before he was to return to Florence there was a full moon; and when he had got Mrs. Lander to sleep he asked Clementina if she would not go out on the lagoon with him. He assigned no peculiar virtue to the moonlight, and he had no new charge to give her concerning his patient when they were embarked. He seemed to wish her to talk about herself, and when she strayed from the topic, he prompted her return. Then he wished to know how she liked Florence, as compared with Venice, and all the other cities she had seen, and when she said she had not seen any but Boston and New York, and London for one night, he wished to know whether she liked Florence as well. She said she liked it best of all, and he told her he was very glad, for he liked it himself better than any place he had ever seen. He spoke of his family in America, which was formed of grownup brothers and sisters, so that he had none of the closest and tenderest ties obliging him to return; there was no reason why he should not spend all his days in Florence, except for some brief visits home. It would be another thing with such a place as Venice; he could never have the same settled feeling there: it was beautiful, but it was unreal; it would be like spending one's life at the opera. Did not she think so?

She thought so, oh, yes; she never could have the home-feeling at Venice that she had at Florence.

"Exactly; that's what I meant—a home-feeling; I'm glad you had it." He let the gondola dip and slide forward almost a minute before he added, with an effect of pulling a voice up out of his throat somewhere, "How would you like to live there—with me—as my wife?"

"Why, what do you mean, Dr. Welwright?" asked Clementina, with a vague laugh.

Dr. Welwright laughed, too; but not vaguely; there was a mounting cheerfulness in his laugh. "What I say. I hope it isn't very surprising."

"No; but I never thought of such a thing."

"Perhaps you will think of it now."

"But you're not in ea'nest!"

"I'm thoroughly in earnest," said the doctor, and he seemed very much amused at her incredulity.

"Then; I'm sorry," she answered. "I couldn't."

"No?" he said, still with amusement, or with a courage that took that form. "Why not?"

"Because I am—not free."

For an interval they were so silent that they could hear each other breathe: Then, after he had quietly bidden the gondolier go back to their hotel, he asked, "If you had been free you might have answered me differently?"

"I don't know," said Clementina, candidly. "I never thought of it."

"It isn't because you disliked me?"

"Oh, no!"

"Then I must get what comfort I can out of that. I hope, with all my heart, that you may be happy."

"Why, Dr. Welwright!" said Clementina. "Don't you suppose that I should be glad to do it, if I could? Any one would!"

"It doesn't seem very probable, just now," he answered, humbly. "But I'll believe it if you say so."

"I do say so, and I always shall."

"Thank you."

Dr. Welwright professed himself ready for his departure, at breakfast next morning and he must have made his preparations very late or very early. He was explicit in his charges to Clementina concerning Mrs. Lander, and at the end of them, he said, "She will not know when she is asking too much of you, but you will, and you must act upon your knowledge. And remember, if you are in need of help, of any kind, you're to let me know. Will you?"

"Yes, I will, Dr. Welwright."

"People will be going away soon, and I shall not be so busy. I can come back if Dr. Tradonico thinks it necessary."

He left Mrs. Lander full of resolutions to look after her own welfare in every way, and she went out in her gondola the same morning. She was not only to take the air as much as possible, but she was to amuse herself, and she decided that she would have her second breakfast at the Caffe Florian. Venice was beginning to fill up with arrivals from the south, and it need not have been so surprising to find Mr. Hinkle there over a cup of coffee. He said he had just that moment been thinking of her, and meaning to look her up at the hotel. He said that he had stopped at Venice because it was such a splendid place to introduce his gleaner; he invited Mrs. Lander to become a partner in the enterprise; he promised her a return of fifty per cent. on her investment. If he could once introduce his gleaner in Venice, he should be a made man. He asked Mrs. Lander, with real feeling, how she was; as for Miss Clementina, he need not ask.

"Oh, indeed, the docta thinks she wants a little lookin' after, too," said Mrs. Lander.

"Well, about as much as you do, Mrs. Lander," Hinkle allowed, tolerantly. "I don't know how it affects you, ma'am, such a meeting of friends in these strange waters, but it's building me right up. It's made another man of me, already, and I've got the other man's appetite, too. Mind my letting him have his breakfast here with me at your table?" He bade the waiter just fetch his plate. He attached himself to them; he spent the day with them. Mrs. Lander asked him to dinner at her lodgings, and left him to Clementina over the coffee.

"She's looking fine, doesn't the doctor think? This air will do everything for her."

"Oh, yes; she's a great deal betta than she was befo'e we came."

"That's right. Well, now, you've got me here, you must let me make myself useful any way I can. I've got a spare month that I can put in here in Venice, just as well as not; I sha'n't want to push north till the frost's out of the ground. They wouldn't have a chance to try my gleaner, on the other side of the Alps much before September, anyway. Now, in Ohio, the part I come from, we cut our wheat in June. When is your wheat harvest at Middlemount?"

Clementina laughed. "I don't believe we've got any. I guess it's all grass."

"I wish you could see our country out there, once."

"Is it nice?"

"Nice? We're right in the centre of the state, measuring from north to south, on the old National Road." Clementina had never heard of this road, but she did not say so. "About five miles back from the Ohio River, where the coal comes up out of the ground, because there's so much of it there's no room for it below. Our farm's in a valley, along a creek bottom, what you Yankees call an intervals; we've got three hundred acres. My grandfather took up the land, and then he went back to Pennsylvania to get the girl he'd left there—we were Pennsylvania Dutch; that's where I got my romantic name—they drove all the way out to Ohio again in his buggy, and when he came in sight of our valley with his bride, he stood up in his buggy and pointed with his whip. 'There! As far as the sky is blue, it's all ours!'"

Clementina owned the charm of his story as he seemed to expect, but when he said, "Yes, I want you to see that country, some day," she answered cautiously.

"It must be lovely. But I don't expect to go West, eva."

"I like your Eastern way of saying everr," said Hinkle, and he said it in his Western way. "I like New England folks."

Clementina smiled discreetly. "They have their faults like everybody else, I presume."

"Ah, that's a regular Yankee word: presume," said Hinkle. "Our teacher, my first one, always said presume. She was from your State, too."

XXIX.

In the time of provisional quiet that followed for Clementina, she was held from the remorses and misgivings that had troubled her before Hinkle came. She still thought that she had let Dr. Welwright go away believing that she had not cared enough for the offer which had surprised her so much, and she blamed herself for not telling him how doubly bound she was to Gregory; though when she tried to put her sense of this in words to herself she could not make out that she was any more bound to him than she had been before they met in Florence, unless she wished to be so. Yet somehow in this time of respite, neither the regret for Dr. Welwright nor the question of Gregory persisted very strongly, and there were whole days when she realized before she slept that she had not thought of either.

She was in full favor again with Mrs. Lander, whom there was no one to embitter in her jealous affection. Hinkle formed their whole social world, and Mrs. Lander made the most of him. She was always having him to the dinners which her landlord served her from a restaurant in her apartment, and taking him out with Clementina in her gondola. He came into a kind of authority with them both which was as involuntary with him as with them, and was like an effect of his constant wish to be doing something for them.

One morning when they were all going out in Mrs. Lander's gondola, she sent Clementina back three times to their rooms for outer garments of differing density. When she brought the last Mrs. Lander frowned.

"This won't do. I've got to have something else—something lighter and warma."

"I can't go back any moa, Mrs. Landa," cried the girl, from the exasperation of her own nerves.

"Then I will go back myself," said Mrs. Lander with dignity, "and we sha'n't need the gondoler any more this mo'ning," she added, "unless you and Mr. Hinkle wants to ride."

She got ponderously out of the boat with the help of the gondolier's elbow, and marched into the house again, while Clementina followed her. She did not offer to help her up the stairs; Hinkle had to do it, and he met the girl slowly coming up as he returned from delivering Mrs. Lander over to Maddalena.

"She's all right, now," he ventured to say, tentatively.

"Is she?" Clementina coldly answered.

In spite of her repellent air, he persisted, "She's a pretty sick woman, isn't she?"

"The docta doesn't say."

"Well, I think it would be safe to act on that supposition. Miss Clementina—I think she wants to see you."

"I'm going to her directly."

Hinkle paused, rather daunted. "She wants me to go for the doctor."

"She's always wanting the docta." Clementina lifted her eyes and looked very coldly at him.

"If I were you I'd go up right away," he said, boldly.

She felt that she ought to resent his interference, but the mild entreaty of his pale blue eyes, or the elder-brotherly injunction of his smile, forbade her. "Did she ask for me?"

"No."

"I'll go to her," she said, and she kept herself from smiling at the long sigh of relief he gave as she passed him on the stairs.

Mrs. Lander began as soon as she entered her room, "Well, I was just wonderin' if you was goin' to leave me here all day alone, while you staid down the'e, carryin' on with that simpleton. I don't know what's got into the men."

"Mr. Hinkle has gone for the docta," said Clementina, trying to get into her voice the kindness she was trying to feel.

"Well, if I have one of my attacks, now, you'll have yourself to thank for it."

By the time Dr. Tradonico appeared Mrs. Lander was so much better that in her revulsion of feeling she was all day rather tryingly affectionate in her indirect appeals for Clementina's sympathy.

"I don't want you should mind what I say, when I a'n't feelin' just right," she began that evening, after she had gone to bed, and Clementina sat looking out of the open window, on the moonlit lagoon.

"Oh, no," the girl answered, wearily.

Mrs. Lander humbled herself farther. "I'm real sorry I plagued you so, to-day, and I know Mr. Hinkle thought I was dreadful, but I couldn't help it. I should like to talk with you, Clementina, about something that's worryin' me, if you a'n't busy."

"I'm not busy, now, Mrs. Lander," said Clementina, a little coldly, and relaxing the clasp of her hands; to knit her fingers together had been her sole business, and she put even this away.

She did not come nearer the bed, and Mrs. Lander was obliged to speak without the advantage of noting the effect of her words upon her in her face. "It's like this: What am I agoin' to do for them relations of Mr. Landa's out in Michigan?"

"I don't know. What relations?"

"I told you about 'em: the only ones he's got: his half-sista's children. He neva saw 'em, and he neva wanted to; but they're his kin, and it was his money. It don't seem right to pass 'em ova. Do you think it would yourself, Clementina?"

"Why, of cou'se not, Mrs. Lander. It wouldn't be right at all."

Mrs. Lander looked relieved, and she said, as if a little surprised, "I'm glad you feel that way; I should feel just so, myself. I mean to do by you just what I always said I should. I sha'n't forget you, but whe'e the'e's so much I got to thinkin' the'e'd ought to some of it go to his folks, whetha he ca'ed for 'em or not. It's worried me some, and I guess if anything it's that that's made me wo'se lately."

"Why by Mrs. Landa," said the girl, "Why don't you give it all to them?"

"You don't know what you'a talkin' about," said Mrs. Lander, severely. "I guess if I give 'em five thousand or so amongst'em, it's full moa than they eve' thought of havin', and it's moa than they got any right to. Well, that's all right, then; and we don't need to talk about it any moa. Yes," she resumed, after a moment, "that's what I shall do. I hu'n't eva felt just satisfied with that last will I got made, and I guess I shall tear it up, and get the fust American lawyer that comes along to make me a new one. The prop'ty's all goin' to you, but I guess I shall leave five thousand apiece to the two families out the'e. You won't miss it, any, and I presume it's what Mr. Landa would expect I should do; though why he didn't do it himself, I can't undastand, unless it was to show his confidence in me."

She began to ask Clementina how she felt about staying in Venice all summer; she said she had got so much better there already that she believed she should be well by fall if she stayed on. She was certain that it would put her all back if she were to travel now, and in Europe, where it was so hard to know how to get to places, she did not see how they could pick out any that would suit them as well as Venice did.

Clementina agreed to it all, more or less absentmindedly, as she sat looking into the moonlight, and the day that had begun so stormily ended in kindness between them.

The next morning Mrs. Lander did not wish to go out, and she sent Clementina and Hinkle together as a proof that they were all on good terms again. She did not spare the girl this explanation in his presence, and when they were in the gondola he felt that he had to say, "I was afraid you might think I was rather meddlesome yesterday."

"Oh, no," she answered. "I was glad you did."

"Yes," he returned, "I thought you would be afterwards." He looked at her wistfully with his slanted eyes and his odd twisted smile and they both gave way in the same conscious laugh. "What I like," he explained further, "is to be understood when I've said something that doesn't mean anything, don't you? You know anybody can understand you if you really mean something; but most of the time you don't, and that's when a friend is useful. I wish you'd call on me if you're ever in that fix."

"Oh, I will, Mr. Hinkle," Clementina promised, gayly.

"Thank you," he said, and her gayety seemed to turn him graver. "Miss Clementina, might I go a little further in this direction, without danger?"

"What direction?" she added, with a flush of sudden alarm.

"Mrs. Lander."

"Why, suttainly!" she answered, in quick relief.

"I wish you'd let me do some of the worrying about her for you, while I'm here. You know I haven't got anything else to do!"

"Why, I don't believe I worry much. I'm afraid I fo'get about her when I'm not with her. That's the wo'st of it."

"No, no," he entreated, "that's the best of it. But I want to do the worrying for you even when you're with her. Will you let me?"

"Why, if you want to so very much."

"Then it's settled," he said, dismissing the subject.

But she recurred to it with a lingering compunction.

"I presume that I don't remember how sick she is because I've neva been sick at all, myself."

"Well," he returned, "You needn't be sorry for that altogether. There are worse things than being well, though sick people don't always think so. I've wasted a good deal of time the other way, though I've reformed, now."

They went on to talk about themselves; sometimes they talked about others, in excursions which were more or less perfunctory, and were merely in the way of illustration or instance. She got so far in one of these as to speak of her family, and he seemed to understand them. He asked about them all, and he said he believed in her father's unworldly theory of life. He asked her if they thought at home that she was like her father, and he added, as if it followed, "I'm the worldling of my family. I was the youngest child, and the only boy in a flock of girls. That always spoils a boy."

"Are you spoiled?" she asked.

"Well, I'm afraid they'd be surprised if I didn't come to grief somehow—all but —mother; she expects I'll be kept from harm."

"Is she religious?"

"Yes, she's a Moravian. Did you ever hear of them?" Clementina shook her head. "They're something, like the Quakers, and something like the Methodists. They don't believe in war; but they have bishops."

"And do you belong to her church?"

"No," said the young man. "I wish I did, for her sake. I don't belong to any. Do you?"

"No, I go to the Episcopal, at home. Perhaps I shall belong sometime. But I think that is something everyone must do for themselves." He looked a little alarmed at the note of severity in her voice, and she explained. "I mean that if you try to be religious for anything besides religion, it isn't being religious;— and no one else has any right to ask you to be."

"Oh, that's what I believe, too," he said, with comic relief. "I didn't know but I'd been trying to convert you without knowing it." They both laughed, and were then rather seriously silent.

He asked, after a moment, in a fresh beginning, "Have you heard from Miss Milray since you left Florence?"

"Oh, yes, didn't I tell you? She's coming here in June."

"Well, she won't have the pleasure of seeing me, then. I'm going the last of May."

"I thought you were going to stay a month!" she protested.

"That will be a month; and more, too."

"So it will," she owned.

"I'm glad it doesn't seem any longer-say a year—Miss Clementina!"

"Oh, not at all," she returned. "Miss Milray's brother and his wife are coming with her. They've been in Egypt."

"I never saw them," said Hinkle. He paused, before he added, "Well, it would seem rather crowded after they get here, I suppose," and he laughed, while Clementina said nothing.

XXX

Hinkle came every morning now, to smoothe out the doubts and difficulties that had accumulated in Mrs. Lander's mind over night, and incidentally to propose some pleasure for Clementina, who could feel that he was pitying her in her slavery to the sick woman's whims, and yet somehow entreating her to bear them. He saw them together in what Mrs. Lander called her well days; but there were other days when he saw Clementina alone, and then she brought him word from Mrs. Lander, and reported his talk to her after he went away. On one of these she sent him a cheerfuller message than usual, and charged the girl to explain that she was ever so much better, but had not got up because she felt that every minute in bed was doing her good. Clementina carried back his regrets and congratulation, and then told Mrs. Lander that he had asked her to go out with him to see a church, which he was sorry Mrs. Lander could not see too. He professed to be very particular about his churches, for he said he had noticed that they neither of them had any great gift for sights, and he had it on his conscience to get the best for them. He told Clementina that the church he had for them now could not be better if it had been built expressly for them, instead of having been used as a place of worship for eight or ten generations of Venetians before they came. She gave his invitation to Mrs. Lander, who could not always be trusted with his jokes, and she received it in the best part.

"Well, you go!" she said. "Maddalena can look after me, I guess. He's the only one of the fellas, except that lo'd, that I'd give a cent for." She added, with a sudden lapse from her pleasure in Hinkle to her severity with Clementina, "But you want to be ca'eful what you' doin'."

"Ca'eful?"

"Yes!—About Mr. Hinkle. I a'n't agoin' to have you lead him on, and then say you didn't know where he was goin'. I can't keep runnin' away everywhe'e, fo' you, the way I done at Woodlake."

Clementina's heart gave a leap, whether joyful or woeful; but she answered indignantly, "How can you say such a thing to me, Mrs. Lander. I'm not leading him on!"

"I don't know what you call it. You're round with him in the gondoler, night and day, and when he's he'e, you'a settin' with him half the time on the balcony, and it's talk, talk, the whole while." Clementina took in the fact with silent recognition, and Mrs. Lander went on. "I ain't sayin' anything against it. He's the only one I don't believe is afta the money he thinks you'a goin' to have; but if you don't want him, you want to look what you're about."

The girl returned to Hinkle in the embarrassment which she was helpless to hide, and without the excuse which she could not invent for refusing to go with him. "Is Mrs. Lander worse—or anything?" he asked.

"Oh, no. She's quite well," said Clementina; but she left it for him to break the constraint in which they set out. He tried to do so at different points, but it seemed to close upon them—the more inflexibly. At last he asked, as they were drawing near the church, "Have you ever seen anything of Mr. Belsky since you left Florence?"

"No," she said, with a nervous start. "What makes you ask?"

"I don't know. But you see nearly everybody again that you meet in your travels. That friend of his—that Mr. Gregory—he seems to have dropped out, too. I believe you told me you used to know him in America."

"Yes," she answered, briefly; she could not say more; and Hinkle went on. "It seemed to me, that as far as I could make him out, he was about as much of a crank in his way as the Russian. It's curious, but when you were talking about religion, the other day, you made me think of him!" The blood went to Clementina's heart. "I don't suppose you had him in mind, but what you said fitted him more than anyone I know of. I could have almost believed that he had been trying to convert you!" She stared at him, and he laughed. "He tackled me one day there in Florence all of a sudden, and I didn't know what to say, exactly. Of course, I respected his earnestness; but I couldn't accept his view of things and I tried to tell him so. I had to say just where I stood, and why, and I mentioned some books that helped to get me there. He said he never read anything that went counter to his faith; and I saw that he didn't want to save me, so much as he wanted to convince me. He didn't know it, and I didn't tell him that I knew it, but I got him to let me drop the subject. He seems to have been left over from a time when people didn't reason about their beliefs, but only argued. I didn't think there was a man like that to be found so late in the century, especially a young man. But that was just where I was mistaken. If there was to be a man of that kind at all, it would have to be a young one. He'll be a good deal opener-minded when he's older. He was conscientious; I could see that; and he did take the Russian's death to heart as long as he was dead. But I'd like to talk with him ten years from now; he wouldn't be where he is."

Clementina was still silent, and she walked up the church steps from the gondola without the power to speak. She made no show of interest in the pictures and statues; she never had really cared much for such things, and now his attempts to make her look at them failed miserably. When they got back again into the boat he began, "Miss Clementina, I'm afraid I oughtn't to have spoken as I did of that Mr. Gregory. If he is a friend of yours—"

"He is," she made herself answer.

"I didn't mean anything against him. I hope you don't think I wanted to be unfair?"

"You were not unfair. But I oughtn't to have let you say it, Mr. Hinkle. I want to tell you something—I mean, I must"—She found herself panting and breathless. "You ought to know it—Mr. Gregory is—I mean we are—"

She stopped and she saw that she need not say more.

In the days that followed before the time that Hinkle had fixed to leave Venice, he tried to come as he had been coming, to see Mrs. Lander, but he evaded her when she wished to send him out with Clementina. His quaintness had a heartache in it for her; and he was boyishly simple in his failure to hide his suffering. He had no explicit right to suffer, for he had asked nothing and been denied nothing, but perhaps for this reason she suffered the more keenly for him.

A senseless resentment against Gregory for spoiling their happiness crept into her heart; and she wished to show Hinkle how much she valued his friendship at any risk and any cost. When this led her too far she took herself to task with a severity which hurt him too. In the midst of the impulses on which she acted, there were times when she had a confused longing to appeal to him for counsel as to how she ought to behave toward him.

There was no one else whom she could appeal to. Mrs. Lander, after her first warning, had not spoken of him again, though Clementina could feel in the grimness with which she regarded her variable treatment of him that she was silently hoarding up a sum of inculpation which would crush her under its weight when it should fall upon her. She seemed to be growing constantly better, now, and as the interval since her last attack widened behind her, she began to indulge her appetite with a recklessness which Clementina, in a sense of her own unworthiness, was helpless to deal with. When she ventured to ask her once whether she ought to eat of something that was very unwholesome for her, Mrs. Lander answered that she had taken her case into her own hands, now, for she knew more about it than all the doctors. She would thank Clementina not to bother about her; she added that she was at least not hurting anybody but herself, and she hoped Clementina would always be able to say as much.

Clementina wished that Hinkle would go away, but not before she had righted herself with him, and he lingered his month out, and seemed as little able to go as she to let him. She had often to be cheerful for both, when she found it too much to be cheerful for herself. In his absence she feigned free and open talks with him, and explained everything, and experienced a kind of ghostly comfort in his imagined approval and forgiveness, but in his presence, nothing really happened except the alternation of her kindness and unkindness, in which she was too kind and then too unkind.

The morning of the' day he was at last to leave Venice, he came to say good bye. He did not ask for Mrs. Lander, when the girl received him, and he did not give himself time to lose courage before he began, "Miss Clementina, I don't know whether I ought to speak to you after what I understood you to mean about Mr. Gregory." He looked steadfastly at her but she did not answer, and he went on. "There's just one chance in a million, though, that I didn't understand you rightly, and I've made up my mind that I want to take that chance. May I?" She tried to speak, but she could not. "If I was wrong—if there was nothing between you and him—could there ever be anything between you and me?"

His pleading looks entreated her even more than his words.

"There was something," she answered, "with him."

"And I mustn't know what," the young man said patiently.

"Yes—yes!" she returned eagerly. "Oh, yes! I want you to know—I want to tell you. I was only sixteen yea's old, and he said that he oughtn't to have spoken; we were both too young. But last winta he spoke again. He said that he had always felt bound"—She stopped, and he got infirmly to his feet. "I wanted to tell you from the fust, but—"

"How could you? You couldn't. I haven't anything more to say, if you are bound to him."

"He is going to be a missionary and he wanted me to say that I would believe just as he did; and I couldn't. But I thought that it would come right; and—yes, I felt bound to him, too. That is all—I can't explain it!"

"Oh, I understand!" he returned, listlessly.

"And do you blame me for not telling before?" She made an involuntary movement toward him, a pathetic gesture which both entreated and compassionated.

"There's nobody to blame. You have tried to do just right by me, as well as him. Well, I've got my answer. Mrs. Lander—can I—"

"Why, she isn't up yet, Mr. Hinkle." Clementina put all her pain for him into the expression of their regret.

"Then I'll have to leave my good-bye for her with you. I don't believe I can come back again." He looked round as if he were dizzy. "Good-bye," he said, and offered his hand. It was cold as clay.

When he was gone, Clementina went into Mrs. Lander's room, and gave her his message.

"Couldn't he have come back this aftanoon to see me, if he ain't goin' till five?" she demanded jealously.

"He said he couldn't come back," Clementina answered sadly.

The woman turned her head on her pillow and looked at the girl's face. "Oh!" she said for all comment.

XXXI.

The Milrays came a month later, to seek a milder sun than they had left burning in Florence. The husband and wife had been sojourning there since their arrival from Egypt, but they had not been his sister's guests, and she did not now pretend to be of their party, though the same train, even the same carriage, had brought her to Venice with them. They went to a hotel, and Miss Milray took lodgings where she always spent her Junes, before going to the Tyrol for the summer.

"You are wonderfully improved, every way," Mrs. Milray said to Clementina when they met. "I knew you would be, if Miss Milray took you in hand; and I can see she has. What she doesn't know about the world isn't worth knowing! I hope she hasn't made you too worldly? But if she has, she's taught you how to keep from showing it; you're just as innocent-looking as ever, and that's the main thing; you oughtn't to lose that. You wouldn't dance a skirt dance now before a ship's company, but if you did, no one would suspect that you knew any better. Have you forgiven me, yet? Well, I didn't use you very well, Clementina, and I never pretended I did. I've eaten a lot of humble pie for that, my dear. Did Miss Milray tell you that I wrote to her about it? Of course you won't say how she told you; but she ought to have done me the justice to say that I tried to be a friend at court with her for you. If she didn't, she wasn't fair."

"She neva said anything against you, Mrs. Milray," Clementina answered.

"Discreet as ever, my dear! I understand! And I hope you understand about that old affair, too, by this time. It was a complication. I had to get back at Lioncourt somehow; and I don't honestly think now that his admiration for a young girl was a very wholesome thing for her. But never mind. You had that Boston goose in Florence, too, last winter, and I suppose he gobbled up what little Miss Milray had left of me. But she's charming. I could go down on my knees to her art when she really tries to finish any one."

Clementina noticed that Mrs. Milray had got a new way of talking. She had a chirpiness, and a lift in her inflections, which if it was not exactly English was no longer Western American. Clementina herself in her association with Hinkle had worn off her English rhythm, and in her long confinement to the conversation of Mrs. Lander, she had reverted to her clipped Yankee accent. Mrs. Milray professed to like it, and said it brought back so delightfully those pleasant days at Middlemount, when Clementina really was a child. "I met somebody at Cairo, who seemed very glad to hear about you, though he tried to seem not. Can you guess who it was? I see that you never could, in the world! We got quite chummy one day, when we were going out to the pyramids together, and he gave himself away, finely. He's a simple soul! But when they're in love they're all so! It was a little queer, colloguing with the ex-headwaiter on society terms; but the head-waitership was merely an episode, and the main thing is that he is very talented, and is going to be a minister. It's a pity he's so devoted to his crazy missionary scheme. Some one ought to get hold of him, and point him in the direction of a rich New York congregation. He'd find heathen enough among them, and he could do the greatest amount of good with their money; I tried to talk it into him. I suppose you saw him in Florence, this spring?" she suddenly asked.

"Yes," Clementina answered briefly.

"And you didn't make it up together. I got that much out of Miss Milray. Well, if he were here, I should find out why. But I don't suppose you would tell me." She waited a moment to see if Clementina would, and then she said, "It's a pity, for I've a notion I could help you, and I think I owe you a good turn, for the way I behaved about your dance. But if you don't want my help, you don't."

"I would say so if I did, Mrs. Milray," said Clementina. "I was hu't, at the time; but I don't care anything for it, now. I hope you won't think about it any more!"

"Thank you," said Mrs. Milray, "I'll try not to," and she laughed. "But I should like to do something to prove my repentance."

Clementina perceived that for some reason she would rather have more than less cause for regret; and that she was mocking her; but she was without the wish or the power to retaliate, and she did not try to fathom Mrs. Milray's motives. Most motives in life, even bad motives, lie nearer the surface than most people commonly pretend, and she might not have had to dig deeper into Mrs. Milray's nature for hers than that layer of her consciousness where she was aware that Clementina was a pet of her sister-in-law. For no better reason she herself made a pet of Mrs. Lander, whose dislike of Miss Milray was not hard to divine, and whose willingness to punish her through Clementina was akin to her own. The sick woman was easily flattered back into her first belief in Mrs. Milray and accepted her large civilities and small services as proof of her virtues. She began to talk them into Clementina, and to contrast them with the wicked principles and actions of Miss Milray.

The girl had forgiven Mrs. Milray, but she could not go back to any trust in her; and she could only passively assent to her praise. When Mrs. Lander pressed her for anything more explicit she said what she thought, and then Mrs. Lander accused her of hating Mrs. Milray, who was more her friend than some that flattered her up for everything, and tried to make a fool of her.

"I undastand now," she said one day, "what that recta meant by wantin' me to make life ba'd for you; he saw how easy you was to spoil. Miss Milray is one to praise you to your face, and disgrace you be hind your back, and so I tell you. When Mrs. Milray thought you done wrong she come and said so; and you can't forgive her."

Clementina did not answer. She had mastered the art of reticence in her relations with Mrs. Lander, and even when Miss Milray tempted her one day to give way, she still had strength to resist. But she could not deny that Mrs. Lander did things at times to worry her, though she ended compassionately with the reflection: "She's sick."

"I don't think she's very sick, now," retorted her friend.

"No; that's the reason she's so worrying. When she's really sick, she's betta."

"Because she's frightened, I suppose. And how long do you propose to stand it?

"I don't know," Clementina listlessly answered.

"She couldn't get along without me. I guess I can stand it till we go home; she says she is going home in the fall."

Miss Milray sat looking at the girl a moment.

"Shall you be glad to go home?"

"Oh yes, indeed!"

"To that place in the woods?"

"Why, yes! What makes you ask?"

"Nothing. But Clementina, sometimes I think you don't quite understand yourself. Don't you know that you are very pretty and very charming? I've told you that often enough! But shouldn't you like to be a great success in the world? Haven't you ever thought of that? Don't you care for society?"

The girl sighed. "Yes, I think that's all very nice I did ca'e, one while, there in Florence, last winter!"

"My dear, you don't know how much you were admired. I used to tell you, because I saw there was no spoiling you; but I never told you half. If you had only had the time for it you could have been the greatest sort of success; you were formed for it. It wasn't your beauty alone; lots of pretty girls don't make anything of their beauty; it was your temperament. You took things easily and naturally, and that's what the world likes. It doesn't like your being afraid of it, and you were not afraid, and you were not bold; you were just right." Miss Milray grew more and more exhaustive in her analysis, and enjoyed refining upon it. "All that you needed was a little hard-heartedness, and that would have come in time; you would have learned how to hold your own, but the chance was snatched from you by that old cat! I could weep over you when I think how you have been wasted on her, and now you're actually willing to go back and lose yourself in the woods!"

"I shouldn't call it being lost, Miss Milray."

"I don't mean that, and you must excuse me, my dear. But surely your people —your father and mother—would want to have you get on in the world—to make a brilliant match—"

Clementina smiled to think how far such a thing was from their imaginations. "I don't believe they would ca'e. You don't undastand about them, and I couldn't make you. Fatha neva liked the notion of my being with such a rich woman as Mrs. Lander, because it would look as if we wanted her money."

"I never could have imagined that of you, Clementina!"

"I didn't think you could," said the girl gratefully. "But now, if I left her when she was sick and depended on me, it would look wohse, yet—as if I did it because she was going to give her money to Mr. Landa's family. She wants to do that, and I told her to; I think that would be right; don't you?"

"It would be right for you, Clementina, if you preferred it—and—I should prefer it. But it wouldn't be right for her. She has given you hopes—she has made promises—she has talked to everybody."

"I don't ca'e for that. I shouldn't like to feel beholden to any one, and I think it really belongs to his relations; it was HIS."

Miss Milray did not say anything to this. She asked, "And if you went back, what would you do there? Labor in the fields, as poor little Belsky advised?"

Clementina laughed. "No; but I expect you'll think it's almost as crazy. You know how much I like dancing? Well, I think I could give dancing lessons at the Middlemount. There are always a good many children, and girls that have not grown up, and I guess I could get pupils enough, as long as the summa lasted; and come winter, I'm not afraid but what I could get them among the young folks at the Center. I used to teach them before I left home."

Miss Milray sat looking at her. "I don't know about such things; but it sounds sensible—like everything about you, my dear. It sounds queer, perhaps because you're talking of such a White Mountain scheme here in Venice."

"Yes, don't it?" said Clementina, sympathetically. "I was thinking of that, myself. But I know I could do it. I could go round to different hotels, different days. Yes, I should like to go home, and they would be glad to have me. You can't think how pleasantly we live; and we're company enough for each other. I presume I should miss the things I've got used to ova here, at fust; but I don't believe I should care a great while. I don't deny but what the wo'ld is nice; but you have to pay for it; I don't mean that you would make me—"

"No, no! We understand each other. Go on!"

Miss Milray leaned towards her and pressed the girl's arm reassuringly.

As often happens with people when they are told to go on, Clementina found that she had not much more to say. "I think I could get along in the wo'ld, well enough. Yes, I believe I could do it. But I wasn't bohn to it, and it would be a great deal of trouble—a great deal moa than if I had been bohn to it. I think it would be too much trouble. I would rather give it up and go home, when Mrs. Landa wants to go back."

Miss Milray did not speak for a time. "I know that you are serious, Clementina; and you're wise always, and good—"

"It isn't that, exactly," said Clementina. "But is it—I don't know how to express it very well—is it wo'th while?"

Miss Milray looked at her as if she doubted the girl's sincerity. Even when the world, in return for our making it our whole life, disappoints and defeats us with its prizes, we still question the truth of those who question the value of these prizes; we think they must be hopeless of them, or must be governed by some interest momentarily superior.

Clementina pursued, "I know that you have had all you wanted of the wo'ld—"

"Oh, no!" the woman broke out, almost in anguish. "Not what I wanted! What I tried for. It never gave me what I wanted. It—couldn't!"

"Well?"

"It isn't worth while in that sense. But if you can't have what you want,—if there's been a hollow left in your life—why the world goes a great way towards filling up the aching void." The tone of the last words was lighter than their meaning, but Clementina weighed them aright.

"Miss Milray," she said, pinching the edge of the table by which she sat, a little nervously, and banging her head a little, "I think I can have what I want."

"Then, give the whole world for it, child!"

"There is something I should like to tell you."

"Yes!"

"For you to advise me about."

"I will, my dear, gladly and truly!"

"He was here before you came. He asked me—"

Miss Milray gave a start of alarm. She said, to gain time: "How did he get here? I supposed he was in Germany with his—"

"No; he was here the whole of May."

"Mr. Gregory!"

"Mr. Gregory?" Clementina's face flushed and drooped Still lower. "I meant Mr. Hinkle. But if you think I oughtn't—"

"I don't think anything; I'm so glad! I supposed from what you said about the world, that it must be—But if it isn't, all the better. If it's Mr. Hinkle that you can have—"

"I'm not sure I can. I should like to tell you just how it is, and then you will know." It needed fewer words for this than she expected, and then Clementina took a letter from her pocket, and gave it to Miss Milray. "He wrote it on the train, going away, and it's not very plain; but I guess you can make it out."

Miss Milray received the penciled leaves, which seemed to be pages torn out of a note-book. They were dated the day Hinkle left Venice, and the envelope bore the postmark of Verona. They were not addressed, but began abruptly: "I believe I have made a mistake; I ought not to have given you up till I knew something that no one but you can tell me. You are not bound to any body unless you wish to be so. That is what I see now, and I will not give you up if I can help it. Even if you had made a promise, and then changed your mind, you would not be bound in such a thing as this. I say this, and I know you will not believe I say it because I want you. I do want you, but I would not urge you to break your faith. I only ask you to realize that if you kept your word when your heart had gone out of it, you would be breaking your faith; and if you broke your word you would be keeping your faith. But if your heart is still in your word, I have no more to say. Nobody knows but you. I would get out and take the first train back to Venice if it were not for two things. I know it would be hard on me; and I am afraid it might be hard on you. But if you will write me a line at Milan, when you get this, or if you will write to me at London before July; or at New York at any time—for I expect to wait as long as I live —"

The letter ended here in the local addresses which the writer gave.

Miss Milray handed the leaves back to Clementina, who put them into her pocket, and apparently waited for her questions.

"And have you written?"

"No," said the girl, slowly and thoughtfully, "I haven't. I wanted to, at fust; and then, I thought that if he truly meant what he said he would be willing to wait."

"And why did you want to wait?"

Clementina replied with a question of her own. "Miss Milray, what do you think about Mr. Gregory?"

"Oh, you mustn't ask me that, my dear! I was afraid I had told you too plainly, the last time."

"I don't mean about his letting me think he didn't ca'e for me, so long. But don't you think he wants to do what is right! Mr. Gregory, I mean."

"Well, if you put me on my honor, I'm afraid I do."

"You see," Clementina resumed. "He was the fust one, and I did ca'e for him a great deal; and I might have gone on caring for him, if—When I found out that I didn't care any longer, or so much, it seemed to me as if it must be wrong. Do you think it was?"

"No-no."

"When I got to thinking about some one else at fust it was only not thinking about him—I was ashamed. Then I tried to make out that I was too young in the fust place, to know whether I really ca'ed for any one in the right way; but after I made out that I was, I couldn't feel exactly easy—and I've been wanting to ask you, Miss Milray—"

"Ask me anything you like, my dear!"

"Why, it's only whether a person ought eva to change."

"We change whether we ought, or not. It isn't a matter of duty, one way or another."

"Yes, but ought we to stop caring for somebody, when perhaps we shouldn't if somebody else hadn't come between? That is the question."

"No," Miss Milray retorted, "that isn't at all the question. The question is which you want and whether you could get him. Whichever you want most it is right for you to have."

"Do you truly think so?"

"I do, indeed. This is the one thing in life where one may choose safest what one likes best; I mean if there is nothing bad in the man himself."

"I was afraid it would be wrong! That was what I meant by wanting to be fai'a with Mr. Gregory when I told you about him there in Florence. I don't believe but what it had begun then."

"What had begun?"

"About Mr. Hinkle."

Miss Milray burst into a laugh. "Clementina, you're delicious!" The girl looked hurt, and Miss Milray asked seriously, "Why do you like Mr. Hinkle best—if you do?"

Clementina sighed. "Oh, I don't know. He's so resting."

"Then that settles it. From first to last, what we poor women want is rest. It would be a wicked thing for you to throw your life away on some one who would worry you out of it. I don't wish to say any thing against Mr. Gregory. I dare say he is good—and conscientious; but life is a struggle, at the best, and it's your duty to take the best chance for resting."

Clementina did not look altogether convinced, whether it was Miss Milray's logic or her morality that failed to convince her. She said, after a moment, "I should like to see Mr. Gregory again."

"What good would that do?"

"Why, then I should know."

"Know what?"

"Whether I didn't really ca'e for him any more—or so much."

"Clementina," said Miss Milray, "you mustn't make me lose patience with you —"

"No. But I thought you said that it was my duty to do what I wished."

"Well, yes. That is what I said," Miss Milray consented. "But I supposed that you knew already."

"No," said Clementina, candidly, "I don't believe I do."

"And what if you don't see him?"

"I guess I shall have to wait till I do. The'e will be time enough."

Miss Milray sighed, and then she laughed. "You ARE young!"

XXXII.

Miss Milray went from Clementina to call upon her sister-in-law, and found her brother, which was perhaps what she hoped might happen.

"Do you know," she said, "that that old wretch is going to defraud that poor thing, after all, and leave her money to her husband's half-sister's children?"

"You wish me to infer the Mrs. Lander—Clementina situation?" Milray returned.

"Yes!"

"I'm glad you put it in terms that are not actionable, then; for your words are decidedly libellous."

"What do you mean?"

"I've just been writing Mrs. Lander's will for her, and she's left all her property to Clementina, except five thousand apiece to the half-sister's three children."

"I can't believe it!"

"Well," said Milray, with his gentle smile, "I think that's safe ground for you. Mrs. Lander will probably have time enough to change her will as well as her mind several times yet before she dies. The half-sister's children may get their rights yet."

"I wish they might!" said Miss Milray, with an impassioned sigh. "Then perhaps I should get Clementina—for a while."

Her brother laughed. "Isn't there somebody else wants Clementina?

"Oh, plenty. But she's not sure she wants anybody else."

"Does she want you?"

"No, I can't say she does. She wants to go home."

"That's not a bad scheme. I should like to go home myself if I had one. What would you have done with Clementina if you had got her, Jenny?"

"What would any one have done with her? Married her brilliantly, of course."

"But you say she isn't sure she wishes to be married at all?"

Miss Milray stated the case of Clementina's divided mind, and her belief that she would take Hinkle in the end, together with the fear that she might take Gregory. "She's very odd," Miss Milray concluded. "She puzzles me. Why did you ever send her to me?"

Milray laughed. "I don't know. I thought she would amuse you, and I thought it would be a pleasure to her."

They began to talk of some affairs of their own, from which Miss Milray returned to Clementina with the ache of an imperfectly satisfied intention. If she had meant to urge her brother to seek justice for the girl from Mrs. Lander, she was not so well pleased to have found justice done already. But the will had been duly signed and witnessed before the American vice-consul, and she must get what good she could out of an accomplished fact. It was at least a consolation to know that it put an end to her sister-in-law's patronage of the girl, and it would be interesting to see Mrs. Milray adapt her behavior to Clementina's fortunes. She did not really dislike her sister-in-law enough to do her a wrong; she was only willing that she should do herself a wrong. But one of the most disappointing things in all hostile operations is that you never can know what the enemy would be at; and Mrs. Milray's manoeuvres were sometimes dictated by such impulses that her strategy was peculiarly baffling. The thought of her past unkindness to Clementina may still have rankled in her, or she may simply have felt the need of outdoing Miss Milray by an unapproachable benefaction. It is certain that when Baron Belsky came to Venice a few weeks after her own arrival, they began to pose at each other with reference to Clementina; she with a measure of consciousness, he with the singleness of a nature that was all pose. In his forbearance to win Clementina from Gregory he had enjoyed the distinction of an unique suffering; and in allowing the fact to impart itself to Mrs. Milray, he bathed in the warmth of her flattering sympathy. Before she withdrew this, as she must when she got tired of him, she learned from him where Gregory was; for it seemed that Gregory had so far forgiven the past that they had again written to each other.

During the fortnight of Belsky's stay in Venice Mrs. Lander was much worse, and Clementina met him only once, very briefly—She felt that he had behaved like a very silly person, but that was all over now, and she had no wish to punish him for it. At the end of his fortnight he went northward into the Austrian Tyrol, and a few days later Gregory came down from the Dolomites to Venice.

It was in his favor with Clementina that he yielded to the impulse he had to come directly to her; and that he let her know with the first words that he had acted upon hopes given him through Belsky from Mrs. Milray. He owned that he doubted the authority of either to give him these hopes, but he said he could not abandon them without a last effort to see her, and learn from her whether they were true or false.

If she recognized the design of a magnificent reparation in what Mrs. Milray had done, she did not give it much thought. Her mind was upon distant things as she followed Gregory's explanation of his presence, and in the muse in which she listened she seemed hardly to know when he ceased speaking.

"I know it must seem to take something for granted which I've no right to take for granted. I don't believe you could think that I cared for anything but you, or at all for what Mrs. Lander has done for you."

"Do you mean her leaving me her money?" asked Clementina, with that boldness her sex enjoys concerning matters of finance and affection.

"Yes," said Gregory, blushing for her. "As far as I should ever have a right to care, I could wish there were no money. It could bring no blessing to our life. We could do no good with it; nothing but the sacrifice of ourselves in poverty could be blessed to us."

"That is what I thought, too," Clementina replied.

"Oh, then you did think—"

"But afterwards, I changed my Mind. If she wants to give me her money I shall take it."

Gregory was blankly silent again.

"I shouldn't know how to refuse, and I don't know as I should have any right to." Gregory shrank a little from her reyankeefied English, as well as from the apparent cynicism of her speech; but he shrank in silence still. She startled him by asking with a kindness that was almost tenderness, "Mr. Gregory, how do you think anything has changed?"

"Changed?"

"You know how it was when you went away from Florence. Do you think differently now? I don't. I don't think I ought to do something for you, and pretend that I was doing it for religion. I don't believe the way you do; and I know I neva shall. Do you want me in spite of my saying that I can neva help you in your work because I believe in it?"

"But if you believe in me—"

She shook her bead compassionately. "You know we ahgued that out before. We are just whe'e we were. I am sorry. Nobody had any right to tell you to come he'e. But I am glad you came—" She saw the hope that lighted up his face, but she went on unrelentingly—"I think we had betta be free."

"Free?"

"Yes, from each other. I don't know how you have felt, but I have not felt free. It has seemed to me that I promised you something. If I did, I want to take my promise back and be free."

Her frankness appealed to his own. "You are free. I never held you bound to me in my fondest hopes. You have always done right."

"I have tried to. And I am not going to let you go away thinking that the reason I said is the only reason. It isn't. I wish to be free because—there is some one else, now." It was hard to tell him this, but she knew that she must not do less; and the train that carried him from Venice that night bore a letter from her to Hinkle.

XXXIII

Clementina told Miss Milray what had happened, but with Mrs. Milray the girl left the sudden departure of Gregory to account for itself.

They all went a week later, and Mrs. Milray having now done her whole duty to Clementina had the easiest mind concerning her. Miss Milray felt that she was leaving her to greater trials than ever with Mrs. Lander; but since there was nothing else, she submitted, as people always do with the trials of others, and when she was once away she began to forget her.

By this time, however, it was really better for her. With no one to suspect of tampering with her allegiance, Mrs. Lander returned to her former fondness for the girl, and they were more peaceful if not happier together again. They had long talks, such as they used to have, and in the first of these Clementina told her how and why she had written to Mr. Hinkle. Mrs. Lander said that it suited her exactly.

"There ha'n't but just two men in Europe behaved like gentlemen to me, and one is Mr. Hinkle, and the other is that lo'd; and between the two I ratha you'd have Mr. Hinkle; I don't know as I believe much in American guls marryin' lo'ds, the best of 'em."

Clementina laughed. "Why, Mrs. Landa, Lo'd Lioncou't never thought of me in the wo'ld!"

"You can't eva know. Mrs. Milray was tellin' that he's what they call a pooa lo'd, and that he was carryin' on with the American girls like everything down there in Egypt last winta. I guess if it comes to money you'd have enough to buy him and sell him again."

The mention of money cast a chill upon their talk; and Mrs. Lander said gloomily, "I don't know as I ca'e so much for that will Mr. Milray made for me, after all. I did want to say ten thousand apiece for Mr. Landa's relations; but I hated to befo'e him; I'd told the whole kit of 'em so much about you, and I knew what they would think."

She looked at Clementina with recurring grudge, and the girl could not bear it.

"Then why don't you tear it up, and make another? I don't want anything, unless you want me to have it; and I'd ratha not have anything."

"Yes, and what would folks say, afta youa taken' care of me?"

"Do you think I do it fo' that?"

"What do you do it fo'?"

"What did you want me to come with you fo'?"

"That's true." Mrs. Lander brightened and warmed again. "I guess it's all right. I guess I done right, and I got to be satisfied. I presume I could get the consul to make me a will any time."

Clementina did not relent so easily. "Mrs. Landa, whateva you do I don't ca'e to know it; and if you talk to me again about this I shall go home. I would stay with you as long as you needed me, but I can't if you keep bringing this up."

"I suppose you think you don't need me any moa! Betta not be too su'a."

The girl jumped to her feet, and Mrs. Lander interposed. "Well, the'a! I didn't mean anything, and I won't pesta you about it any moa. But I think it's pretty ha'd. Who am I going to talk it ova with, then?"

"You can talk it ova with the vice-consul," paid Clementina, at random.

"Well, that's so." Mrs. Lander let Clementina get her ready for the night, in sign of returning amity; when she was angry with her she always refused her help, and made her send Maddalena.

The summer heat increased, and the sick woman suffered from it, but she could not be persuaded that she had strength to get away, though the vice-consul, whom she advised with, used all his logic with her. He was a gaunt and weary widower, who described himself as being officially between hay and grass; the consul who appointed him had resigned after going home, and a new consul had not yet been sent out to remove him. On what she called her well days Mrs. Lander went to visit him, and she did not mind his being in his shirt-sleeves, in the bit of garden where she commonly found him, with his collar and cravat off, and clouded in his own smoke; when she was sick she sent for him, to visit her. He made excuses as often as she could, and if he saw Mrs. Lander's gondola coming down the Grand Canal to his house he hurried on his cast clothing, and escaped to the Piazza, at whatever discomfort and risk from the heat.

"I don't know how you stand it, Miss Claxon," he complained to Clementina, as soon as he learned that she was not a blood relation of Mrs. Lander's, and divined that she had her own reservations concerning her. "But that woman will be the death of me if she keeps this up. What does she think I'm here for? If this goes on much longer I'll resign. The salary won't begin to pay for it. What am I going to do? I don't want to hurt her feelings, or not to help her; but I know ten times as much about Mrs. Lander's liver as I do about my own, now."

He treated Clementina as a person of mature judgment and a sage discretion, and he accepted what comfort she could offer him when she explained that it was everything for Mrs. Lander to have him to talk with. "She gets tied of talking to me," she urged, "and there's nobody else, now."

"Why don't she hire a valet de place, and talk to him? I'd hire one myself for her. It would be a good deal cheaper for me. It's as much as I can do to stand this weather as it is."

The vice-consul laughed forlornly in his exasperation, but he agreed with Clementina when she said, in further excuse, that Mrs. Lander was really very sick. He pushed back his hat, and scratched his head with a grimace.

"Of course, we've got to remember she's sick, and I shall need a little sympathy myself if she keeps on at me this way. I believe I'll tell her about my liver next time, and see how she likes it. Look here, Miss Claxon! Couldn't we get her off to some of those German watering places that are good for her complaints? I believe it would be the best thing for her—not to mention me."

Mrs. Lander was moved by the suggestion which he made in person afterwards; it appealed to her old nomadic instinct; but when the consul was gone she gave it up. "We couldn't git the'e, Clementina. I got to stay he'e till I git up my stren'th. I suppose you'd be glad enough to have me sta't, now the'e's nobody he'e but me," she added, suspiciously. "You git this scheme up, or him?"

Clementina did not defend herself, and Mrs. Lander presently came to her defence. "I don't believe but what he meant it fo' the best—or you, whichever it was, and I appreciate it; but all is I couldn't git off. I guess this aia will do me as much good as anything, come to have it a little coola."

They went every afternoon to the Lido, where a wheeled chair met them, and Mrs. Lander was trundled across the narrow island to the beach. In the evenings they went to the Piazza, where their faces and figures had become known, and the Venetians gossipped them down to the last fact of their relation with an accuracy creditable to their ingenuity in the affairs of others. To them Mrs. Lander was the sick American, very rich, and Clementina was her adoptive daughter, who would have her millions after her. Neither knew the character they bore to the amiable and inquisitive public of the Piazza, or cared for the fine eyes that aimed their steadfast gaze at them along the tubes of straw-barreled Virginia cigars, or across little cups of coffee. Mrs. Lander merely remarked that the Venetians seemed great for gaping, and Clementina was for the most part innocent of their stare.

She rested in the choice she had made in a content which was qualified by no misgiving. She was sorry for Gregory, when she remembered him; but her thought was filled with some one else, and she waited in faith and patience for the answer which should come to the letter she had written. She did not know where her letter would find him, or when she should hear from him; she believed that she should hear, and that was enough. She said to herself that she would not lose hope if no answer came for months; but in her heart she fixed a date for the answer by letter, and an earlier date for some word by cable; but she feigned that she did not depend upon this; and when no word came she convinced herself that she had not expected any.

It was nearing the end of the term which she had tacitly given her lover to make the first sign by letter, when one morning Mrs. Lander woke her. She wished to say that she had got the strength to leave Venice at last, and she was going as soon as their trunks could be packed. She had dressed herself, and she moved about restless and excited. Clementina tried to reason her out of her haste; but she irritated her, and fixed her in her determination. "I want to get away, I tell you; I want to get away," she answered all persuasion, and there seemed something in her like the wish to escape from more than the oppressive environment, though she spoke of nothing but the heat and the smell of the canal. "I believe it's that, moa than any one thing, that's kept me sick he'e," she said. "I tell you it's the malariar, and you'll be down, too, if you stay."

She made Clementina go to the banker's, and get money to pay their landlord's bill, and she gave him notice that they were going that afternoon. Clementina wished to delay till they had seen the vice-consul and the doctor; but Mrs. Lander broke out, "I don't want to see 'em, either of 'em. The docta wants to keep me he'e and make money out of me; I undastand him; and I don't believe that consul's a bit too good to take a pussentage. Now, don't you say a wo'd to either of 'em. If you don't do exactly what I tell you I'll go away and leave you he'e. Now, will you?"

Clementina promised, and broke her word. She went to the vice-consul and told him she had broken it, and she agreed with him that he had better not come unless Mrs. Lander sent for him. The doctor promptly imagined the situation and said he would come in casually during the morning, so as not to alarm the invalid's suspicions. He owned that Mrs. Lander was getting no good from remaining in Venice, and if it were possible for her to go, he said she had better go somewhere into cooler and higher air.

His opinion restored him to Mrs. Lander's esteem, when it was expressed to her, and as she was left to fix the sum of her debt to him, she made it handsomer than anything he had dreamed of. She held out against seeing the vice-consul till the landlord sent in his account. This was for the whole month which she had just entered upon, and it included fantastic charges for things hitherto included in the rent, not only for the current month, but for the months past when, the landlord explained, he had forgotten to note them. Mrs. Lander refused to pay these demands, for they touched her in some of those economies which the gross rich practice amidst their profusion. The landlord replied that she could not leave his house, either with or without her effects, until she had paid. He declared Clementina his prisoner, too, and he would not send for the vice-consul at Mrs. Lander's bidding. How far he was within his rights in all this they could not know, but he was perhaps himself doubtful, and he consented to let them send for the doctor, who, when he came, behaved like anything but the steadfast friend that Mrs. Lander supposed she had bought in him. He advised paying the account without regard to its justice, as the shortest and simplest way out of the trouble; but Mrs. Lander, who saw him talking amicably and even respectfully with the landlord, when he ought to have treated him as an extortionate scamp, returned to her former ill opinion of him; and the vice-consul now appeared the friend that Doctor Tradonico had falsely seemed. The doctor consented, in leaving her to her contempt of him, to carry a message to the vice-consul, though he came back, with his finger at the side of his nose, to charge her by no means to betray his bold championship to the landlord.

The vice-consul made none of those shows of authority which Mrs. Lander had expected of him. She saw him even exchanging the common decencies with the landlord, when they met; but in fact it was not hard to treat the smiling and courteous rogue well. In all their disagreement he had looked as constantly to the comfort of his captives as if they had been his chosen guests. He sent Mrs. Lander a much needed refreshment at the stormiest moment of her indignation, and he deprecated without retort the denunciations aimed at him in Italian which did not perhaps carry so far as his conscience. The consul talked with him in a calm scarcely less shameful than that of Dr. Tradonico; and at the end of their parley which she had insisted upon witnessing, he said:

"Well, Mrs. Lander, you've got to stand this gouge or you've got to stand a law suit. I think the gouge would be cheaper in the end. You see, he's got a right to his month's rent."

"It ain't the rent I ca'e for: it's the candles, and the suvvice, and the things he says we broke. It was undastood that everything was to be in the rent, and his two old chaias went to pieces of themselves when we tried to pull 'em out from the wall; and I'll neva pay for 'em in the wo'ld."

"Why," the vice-consul pleaded, "it's only about forty francs for the whole thing—"

"I don't care if it's only fotty cents. And I must say, Mr. Bennam, you're about the strangest vice-consul, to want me to do it, that I eva saw."

The vice-consul laughed unresentfully. "Well, shall I send you a lawyer?"

"No!" Mrs. Lander retorted; and after a moment's reflection she added, "I'm goin' to stay my month, and so you may tell him, and then I'll see whetha he can make me pay for that breakage and the candles and suvvice. I'm all wore out, as it is, and I ain't fit to travel, now, and I don't know when I shall be. Clementina, you can go and tell Maddalena to stop packin'. Or, no! I'll do it."

She left the room without further notice of the consul, who said ruefully to Clementina, "Well, I've missed my chance, Miss Claxon, but I guess she's done the wisest thing for herself."

"Oh, yes, she's not fit to go. She must stay, now, till it's coola. Will you tell the landlo'd, or shall—"

"I'll tell him," said the vice-consul, and he had in the landlord. He received her message with the pleasure of a host whose cherished guests have consented to remain a while longer, and in the rush of his good feeling he offered, if the charge for breakage seemed unjust to the vice-consul, to abate it; and since the signora had not understood that she was to pay extra for the other things, he would allow the vice-consul to adjust the differences between them; it was a trifle, and he wished above all things to content the signora, for whom he professed a cordial esteem both on his own part and the part of all his family.

"Then that lets me out for the present," said the vice-consul, when Clementina repeated Mrs. Lander's acquiescence in the landlord's proposals, and he took his straw hat, and called a gondola from the nearest 'traghetto', and bargained at an expense consistent with his salary, to have himself rowed back to his own garden-gate.

The rest of the day was an era of better feeling between Mrs. Lander and her host than they had ever known, and at dinner he brought in with his own hand a dish which he said he had caused to be specially made for her. It was so tempting in odor and complexion that Mrs. Lander declared she must taste it, though as she justly said, she had eaten too much already; when it had once tasted it she ate it all, against Clementina's protestations; she announced at the end that every bite had done her good, and that she never felt better in her life. She passed a happy evening, with renewed faith in the air of the lagoon; her sole regret now was that Mr. Lander had not lived to try it with her, for if he had she was sure he would have been alive at that moment.

She allowed herself to be got to bed rather earlier than usual; before Clementina dropped asleep she heard her breathing with long, easy, quiet respirations, and she lost the fear of the landlord's dish which had haunted her through the evening. She was awakened in the morning by a touch on her shoulder. Maddalena hung over her with a frightened face, and implored her to come and look at the signora, who seemed not at all well. Clementina ran into her room, and found her dead. She must have died some hours before without a struggle, for the face was that of sleep, and it had a dignity and beauty which it had not worn in her life of self-indulgent wilfulness for so many years that the girl had never seen it look so before.

XXXIV

The vice-consul was not sure how far his powers went in the situation with which Mrs. Lander had finally embarrassed him. But he met the new difficulties with patience, and he agreed with Clementina that they ought to see if Mrs. Lander had left any written expression of her wishes concerning the event. She had never spoken of such a chance, but had always looked forward to getting well and going home, so far as the girl knew, and the most careful search now brought to light nothing that bore upon it. In the absence of instructions to the contrary, they did what they must, and the body, emptied of its life of senseless worry and greedy care, was laid to rest in the island cemetery of Venice.

When all was over, the vice-consul ventured an observation which he had hitherto delicately withheld. The question of Mrs. Lander's kindred had already been discussed between him and Clementina, and he now felt that another question had duly presented itself. "You didn't notice," he suggested, "anything like a will when we went over the papers?" He had looked carefully for it, expecting that there might have been some expression of Mrs. Lander's wishes in it. "Because," he added, "I happen to know that Mr. Milray drew one up for her; I witnessed it."

"No," said Clementina, "I didn't see anything of it. She told me she had made a will; but she didn't quite like it, and sometimes she thought she would change it. She spoke of getting you to do it; I didn't know but she had."

The vice-consul shook his head. "No. And these relations of her husband's up in Michigan; you don't know where they live, exactly?"

"No. She neva told me; she wouldn't; she didn't like to talk about them; I don't even know their names."

The vice-consul thoughtfully scratched a corner of his chin through his beard. "If there isn't any will, they're the heirs. I used to be a sort of wild-cat lawyer, and I know that much law."

"Yes," said Clementina. "She left them five thousand dollas apiece. She said she wished she had made it ten."

"I guess she's made it a good deal more, if she's made it anything. Miss Claxon, don't you understand that if no will turns up, they come in for all her money.

"Well, that's what I thought they ought to do," said Clementina.

"And do you understand that if that's so, you don't come in for anything? You must excuse me for mentioning it; but she has told everybody that you were to have it, and if there is no will—"

He stopped and bent an eye of lack-lustre compassion on the girl, who replied, "Oh, yes. I know that; it's what I always told her to do. I didn't want it."

"You didn't want it?"

"No."

"Well!" The vice-consul stared at her, but he forbore the comment that her indifference inspired. He said after a pause, "Then what we've got to do is to advertise for the Michigan relations, and let 'em take any action they want to."

"That's the only thing we could do, I presume."

This gave the vice-consul another pause. At the end of it he got to his feet. "Is there anything I can do for you, Miss Claxon?"

She went to her portfolio and produced Mrs. Lander's letter of credit. It had been made out for three thousand pounds, in Clementina's name as well as her own; but she had lived wastefully since she had come abroad, and little money remained to be taken up. With the letter Clementina handed the vice-consul the roll of Italian and Austrian bank-notes which she had drawn when Mrs. Lander decided to leave Venice; they were to the amount of several thousand lire and golden. She offered them with the insensibility to the quality of money which so many women have, and which is always so astonishing to men. "What must I do with these?" she asked.

"Why, keep them! returned the vice-consul on the spur of his surprise.

"I don't know as I should have any right to," said Clementina. "They were hers."

"Why, but"—The vice-consul began his protest, but he could not end it logically, and he did not end it at all. He insisted with Clementina that she had a right to some money which Mrs. Lander had given her during her life; he took charge of the bank-notes in the interest of the possible heirs, and gave her his receipt for them. In the meantime he felt that he ought to ask her what she expected to do.

"I think," she said, "I will stay in Venice awhile."

The vice-consul suppressed any surprise he might have felt at a decision given with mystifying cheerfulness. He answered, Well, that was right; and for the second time he asked her if there was anything he could do for her.

"Why, yes," she returned. "I should like to stay on in the house here, if you could speak for me to the padrone."

"I don't see why you shouldn't, if we can make the padrone understand it's different."

"You mean about the price?" The vice-consul nodded. "That's what I want you should speak to him about, Mr. Bennam, if you would. Tell him that I haven't got but a little money now, and he would have to make it very reasonable. That is, if you think it would be right for me to stay, afta the way he tried to treat Mrs. Lander."

The vice-consul gave the point some thought, and decided that the attempted extortion need not make any difference with Clementina, if she could get the right terms. He said he did not believe the padrone was a bad fellow, but he liked to take advantage of a stranger when he could; we all did. When he came to talk with him he found him a man of heart if not of conscience. He entered into the case with the prompt intelligence and vivid sympathy of his race, and he made it easy for Clementina to stay till she had heard from her friends in America. For himself and for his wife, he professed that she could not stay too long, and they proposed that if it would content the signorina still further they would employ Maddalena as chambermaid till she wished to return to Florence; she had offered to remain if the signorina stayed.

"Then that is settled," said Clementina with a sigh of relief; and she thanked the vice-consul for his offer to write to the Milrays for her, and said that she would rather write herself.

She meant to write as soon as she heard from Mr. Hinkle, which could not be long now, for then she could be independent of the offers of help which she dreaded from Miss Milray, even more than from Mrs. Milray; it would be harder to refuse them; and she entered upon a passage of her life which a nature less simple would have found much more trying. But she had the power of taking everything as if it were as much to be expected as anything else. If nothing at all happened she accepted the situation with implicit resignation, and with a gayety of heart which availed her long, and never wholly left her.

While the suspense lasted she could not write home as frankly as before, and she sent off letters to Middlemount which treated of her delay in Venice with helpless reticence. They would have set another sort of household intolerably wondering and suspecting, but she had the comfort of knowing that her father would probably settle the whole matter by saying that she would tell what she meant when she got round to it; and apart from this she had mainly the comfort of the vice-consul's society. He had little to do besides looking after her, and he employed himself about this in daily visits which the padrone and his wife regarded as official, and promoted with a serious respect for the vice-consular dignity. If the visits ended, as they often did, in a turn on the Grand Canal, and an ice in the Piazza, they appealed to the imagination of more sophisticated witnesses, who decided that the young American girl had inherited the millions of the sick lady, and become the betrothed of the vice-consul, and that they were thus passing the days of their engagement in conformity to the American custom, however much at variance with that of other civilizations.

This view of the affair was known to Maddalena, but not to Clementina, who in those days went back in many things to the tradition of her life at Middlemount. The vice-consul was of a tradition almost as simple, and his longer experience set no very wide interval between them. It quickly came to his telling her all about his dead wife and his married daughters, and how, after his home was broken up, he thought he would travel a little and see what that would do for him. He confessed that it had not done much; he was always homesick, and he was ready to go as soon as the President sent out a consul to take his job off his hands. He said that he had not enjoyed himself so much since he came to Venice as he was doing now, and that he did not know what he should do if Clementina first got her call home. He betrayed no curiosity as to the peculiar circumstances of her stay, but affected to regard it as something quite normal, and he watched over her in every way with a fatherly as well as an official vigilance which never degenerated into the semblance of any other feeling. Clementina rested in his care in entire security. The world had quite fallen from her, or so much of it as she had seen at Florence, and in her indifference she lapsed into life as it was in the time before that with a tender renewal of her allegiance to it. There was nothing in the conversation of the vice-consul to distract her from this; and she said and did the things at Venice that she used to do at Middlemount, as nearly as she could; to make the days of waiting pass more quickly, she tried to serve herself in ways that scandalized the proud affection of Maddalena. It was not fit for the signorina to make her bed or sweep her room; she might sew and knit if she would; but these other things were for servants like herself. She continued in the faith of Clementina's gentility, and saw her always as she had seen her first in the brief hour of her social splendor in Florence. Clementina tried to make her understand how she lived at Middlemount, but she only brought before Maddalena the humiliating image of a contadina, which she rejected not only in Clementina's behalf, but that of Miss Milray. She told her that she was laughing at her, and she was fixed in her belief when the girl laughed at that notion. Her poverty she easily conceived of; plenty of signorine in Italy were poor; and she protected her in it with the duty she did not divide quite evenly between her and the padrone.

The date which Clementina had fixed for hearing from Hinkle by cable had long passed, and the time when she first hoped to hear from him by letter had come and gone. Her address was with the vice-consul as Mrs. Lander's had been, and he could not be ignorant of her disappointment when he brought her letters which she said were from home. On the surface of things it could only be from home that she wished to hear, but beneath the surface he read an anxiety which mounted with each gratification of this wish. He had not seen much of the girl while Hinkle was in Venice; Mrs. Lander had not begun to make such constant use of him until Hinkle had gone; Mrs. Milray had told him of Clementina's earlier romance, and it was to Gregory that the vice-consul related the anxiety which he knew as little in its nature as in its object.

Clementina never doubted the good faith or constancy of her lover; but her heart misgave her as to his well-being when it sank at each failure of the vice-consul to bring her a letter from him. Something must have happened to him, and it must have been something very serious to keep him from writing; or there was some mistake of the post-office. The vice-consul indulged himself in personal inquiries to make sure that the mistake was not in the Venetian post-office; but he saw that he brought her greater distress in ascertaining the fact. He got to dreading a look of resolute cheerfulness that came into her face, when he shook his head in sign that there were no letters, and he suffered from the covert eagerness with which she glanced at the superscriptions of those he brought and failed to find the hoped-for letter among them. Ordeal for ordeal, he was beginning to regret his trials under Mrs. Lander. In them he could at least demand Clementina's sympathy, but against herself this was impossible. Once she noted his mute distress at hers, and broke into a little laugh that he found very harrowing.

"I guess you hate it almost as much as I do, Mr. Bennam."

"I guess I do. I've half a mind to write the letter you want, myself."

"I've half a mind to let you—or the letter I'd like to write."

It had come to her thinking she would write again to Hinkle; but she could not bring herself to do it. She often imagined doing it; she had every word of such a letter in her mind; and she dramatized every fact concerning it from the time she should put pen to paper, to the time when she should get back the answer that cleared the mystery of his silence away. The fond reveries helped her to bear her suspense; they helped to make the days go by, to ease the doubt with which she lay down at night, and the heartsick hope with which she rose up in the morning.

One day, at the hour of his wonted visit, she say the vice-consul from her balcony coming, as it seemed to her, with another figure in his gondola, and a thousand conjectures whirled through her mind, and then centred upon one idea. After the first glance she kept her eyes down, and would not look again while she told herself incessantly that it could not be, and that she was a fool and a goose and a perfect coot, to think of such a thing for a single moment. When she allowed herself, or forced herself, to look a second time; as the boat drew near, she had to cling to the balcony parapet for support, in her disappointment.

The person whom the vice-consul helped out of the gondola was an elderly man like himself, and she took a last refuge in the chance that he might be Hinkle's father, sent to bring her to him because he could not come to her; or to soften some terrible news to her. Then her fancy fluttered and fell, and she waited patiently for the fact to reveal itself. There was something countrified in the figure of the man, and something clerical in his face, though there was nothing in his uncouth best clothes that confirmed this impression. In both face and figure there was a vague resemblance to some one she had seen before, when the vice-consul said:

"Miss Claxon, I want to introduce the Rev. Mr. James B. Orson, of Michigan." Mr. Orson took Clementina's hand into a dry, rough grasp, while he peered into her face with small, shy eyes. The vice-consul added with a kind of official formality, "Mr. Orson is the half-nephew of Mr. Lander," and then Clementina now knew whom it was that he resembled. "He has come to Venice," continued the vice-consul, "at the request of Mrs. Lander; and he did not know of her death until I informed him of the fact. I should have said that Mr. Orson is the son of Mr. Lander's half-sister. He can tell you the balance himself." The vice-consul pronounced the concluding word with a certain distaste, and the effect of gladly retiring into the background.

"Won't you sit down?" said Clementina, and she added with one of the remnants of her Middlemount breeding, "Won't you let me take your hat?"

Mr. Orson in trying to comply with both her invitations, knocked his well worn silk hat from the hand that held it, and sent it rolling across the room, where Clementina pursued it and put it on the table.

"I may as well say at once," he began in a flat irresonant voice, "that I am the representative of Mrs. Lander's heirs, and that I have a letter from her enclosing her last will and testament, which I have shown to the consul here —"

"Vice-consul," the dignitary interrupted with an effect of rejecting any part in the affair.

"Vice-consul, I should say,—and I wish to lay them both before you, in order that—"

"Oh, that is all right," said Clementina sweetly. "I'm glad there is a will. I was afraid there wasn't any at all. Mr. Bennam and I looked for it everywhe'e." She smiled upon the Rev. Mr. Orson, who silently handed her a paper. It was the will which Milray had written for Mrs. Lander, and which, with whatever crazy motive, she had sent to her husband's kindred. It provided that each of them should be given five thousand dollars out of the estate, and that then all should go to Clementina. It was the will Mrs. Lander told her she had made, but she had never seen the paper before, and the legal forms hid the meaning from her so that she was glad to have the vice-consul make it clear. Then she said tranquilly, "Yes, that is the way I supposed it was."

Mr. Orson by no means shared her calm. He did not lift his voice, but on the level it had taken it became agitated. "Mrs. Lander gave me the address of her lawyer in Boston when she sent me the will, and I made a point of calling on him when I went East, to sail. I don't know why she wished me to come out to her, but being sick, I presume she naturally wished to see some of her own family."

He looked at Clementina as if he thought she might dispute this, but she consented at her sweetest, "Oh, yes, indeed," and he went on:

"I found her affairs in a very different condition from what she seemed to think. The estate was mostly in securities which had not been properly looked after, and they had depreciated until they were some of them not worth the paper they were printed on. The house in Boston is mortgaged up to its full value, I should say; and I should say that Mrs. Lander did not know where she stood. She seemed to think that she was a very rich woman, but she lived high, and her lawyer said he never could make her understand how the money was going. Mr. Lander seemed to lose his grip, the year he died, and engaged in some very unfortunate speculations; I don't know whether he told her. I might enter into details—"

"Oh, that is not necessary," said Clementina, politely, witless of the disastrous quality of the facts which Mr. Orson was imparting.

"But the sum and substance of it all is that there will not be more than enough to pay the bequests to her own family, if there is that."

Clementina looked with smiling innocence at the vice-consul.

"That is to say," he explained, "there won't be anything at all for you, Miss Claxon."

"Well, that's what I always told Mrs. Lander I ratha, when she brought it up. I told her she ought to give it to his family," said Clementina, with a satisfaction in the event which the vice-consul seemed unable to share, for he remained gloomily silent. "There is that last money I drew on the letter of credit, you can give that to Mr. Orson."

"I have told him about that money," said the vice-consul, dryly. "It will be handed over to him when the estate is settled, if there isn't enough to pay the bequests without it."

"And the money which Mrs. Landa gave me before that," she pursued, eagerly. Mr. Orson had the effect of pricking up his ears, though it was in fact merely a gleam of light that came into his eyes.

"That's yours," said the vice-consul, sourly, almost savagely. "She didn't give it to you without she wanted you to have it, and she didn't expect you to pay her bequests with it. In my opinion," he burst out, in a wrathful recollection of his own sufferings from Mrs. Lander, "she didn't give you a millionth part of your due for all the trouble she made you; and I want Mr. Orson to understand that, right here."

Clementina turned her impartial gaze upon Mr. Orson as if to verify the impression of this extreme opinion upon him; he looked as if he neither accepted nor rejected it, and she concluded the sentence which the vice-consul had interrupted. "Because I ratha not keep it, if there isn't enough without it."

The vice-consul gave way to violence. "It's none of your business whether there's enough or not. What you've got to do is to keep what belongs to you, and I'm going to see that you do. That's what I'm here for." If this assumption of official authority did not awe Clementina, at least it put a check upon her headlong self-sacrifice. The vice-consul strengthened his hold upon her by asking, "What would you do. I should like to know, if you gave that up?"

"Oh, I should get along," she returned, Light-heartedly, but upon questioning herself whether she should turn to Miss Milray for help, or appeal to the vice-consul himself, she was daunted a little, and she added, "But just as you say, Mr. Bennam."

"I say, keep what fairly belongs to you. It's only two or three hundred dollars at the outside," he explained to Mr. Orson's hungry eyes; but perhaps the sum did not affect the country minister's imagination as trifling; his yearly salary must sometimes have been little more.

The whole interview left the vice-consul out of humor with both parties to the affair; and as to Clementina, between the ideals of a perfect little saint, and a perfect little simpleton he remained for the present unable to class her.

XXXV

Clementina and the Vice-Consul afterwards agreed that Mrs. Lander must have sent the will to Mr. Orson in one of those moments of suspicion when she distrusted everyone about her, or in that trouble concerning her husband's kindred which had grown upon her more and more, as a means of assuring them that they were provided for.

"But even then," the vice-consul concluded, "I don't see why she wanted this man to come out here. The only explanation is that she was a little off her base towards the last. That's the charitable supposition."

"I don't think she was herself, some of the time," Clementina assented in acceptance of the kindly construction.

The vice-consul modified his good will toward Mrs. Lander's memory so far as to say, "Well, if she'd been somebody else most of the time, it would have been an improvement."

The talk turned upon Mr. Orson, and what he would probably do. The vice-consul had found him a cheap lodging, at his request, and he seemed to have settled down at Venice either without the will or without the power to go home, but the vice-consul did not know where he ate, or what he did with himself except at the times when he came for letters. Once or twice when he looked him up he found him writing, and then the minister explained that he had promised to "correspond" for an organ of his sect in the Northwest; but he owned that there was no money in it. He was otherwise reticent and even furtive in his manner. He did not seem to go much about the city, but kept to his own room; and if he was writing of Venice it must have been chiefly from his acquaintance with the little court into which his windows looked. He affected the vice-consul as forlorn and helpless, and he pitied him and rather liked him as a fellow-victim of Mrs. Lander.

One morning Mr. Orson came to see Clementina, and after a brief passage of opinion upon the weather, he fell into an embarrassed silence from which he pulled himself at last with a visible effort. "I hardly know how to lay before you what I have to say, Miss Claxon," he began, "and I must ask you to put the best construction upon it. I have never been reduced to a similar distress before. You would naturally think that I would turn to the vice-consul, on such an occasion; but I feel, through our relation to the—to Mrs. Lander—ah— somewhat more at home with you."

He stopped, as if he wished to be asked his business, and she entreated him, "Why, what is it, Mr. Osson? Is there something I can do? There isn't anything I wouldn't!"

A gleam, watery and faint, which still could not be quite winked away, came into his small eyes. "Why, the fact is, could you—ah—advance me about five dollars?"

"Why, Mr. Orson!" she began, and he seemed to think she wished to withdraw her offer of help, for he interposed.

"I will repay it as soon as I get an expected remittance from home. I came out on the invitation of Mrs. Lander, and as her guest, and I supposed—"

"Oh, don't say a wo'd!" cried Clementina, but now that he had begun he was powerless to stop.

"I would not ask, but my landlady has pressed me for her rent—I suppose she needs it—and I have been reduced to the last copper—"

The girl whose eyes the tears of self pity so rarely visited, broke into a sob that seemed to surprise her visitor. But she checked herself as with a quick inspiration: "Have you been to breakfast?"

"Well—ah—not this morning," Mr. Orson admitted, as if to imply that having breakfasted some other morning might be supposed to serve the purpose.

She left him and ran to the door. "Maddalena, Maddalena!" she called; and Maddalena responded with a frightened voice from the direction of the kitchen:

"Vengo subito!"

She hurried out with the coffee-pot in her hand, as if she had just taken it up when Clementina called; and she halted for the whispered colloquy between them which took place before she set it down on the table already laid for breakfast; then she hurried out of the room again. She came back with a cantaloupe and grapes, and cold ham, and put them before Clementina and her guest, who both ignored the hunger with which he swept everything before him. When his famine had left nothing, he said, in decorous compliment:

"That is very good coffee, I should think the genuine berry, though I am told that they adulterate coffee a great deal in Europe."

"Do they?" asked Clementina. "I didn't know it."

She left him still sitting before the table, and came back with some bank-notes in her hand. "Are you sure you hadn't betta take moa?" she asked.

"I think that five dollars will be all that I shall require," he answered, with dignity. "I should be unwilling to accept more. I shall undoubtedly receive some remittances soon."

"Oh, I know you will," Clementina returned, and she added, "I am waiting for lettas myself; I don't think any one ought to give up."

The preacher ignored the appeal which was in her tone rather than her words, and went on to explain at length the circumstances of his having come to Europe so unprovided against chances. When he wished to excuse his imprudence, she cried out, "Oh, don't say a wo'd! It's just like my own fatha," and she told him some things of her home which apparently did not interest him very much. He had a kind of dull, cold self-absorption in which he was indeed so little like her father that only her kindness for the lonely man could have justified her in thinking there was any resemblance.

She did not see him again for a week, and meantime she did not tell the vice-consul of what had happened. But an anxiety for the minister began to mingle with her anxieties for herself; she constantly wondered why she did not hear from her lover, and she occasionally wondered whether Mr. Orson were not falling into want again. She had decided to betray his condition to the vice-consul, when he came, bringing the money she had lent him. He had received a remittance from an unexpected source; and he hoped she would excuse his delay in repaying her loan. She wished not to take the money, at least till he was quite sure he should not want it, but he insisted.

"I have enough to keep me, now, till I hear from other sources, with the means for returning home. I see no object in continuing here, under the circumstances."

In the relief which she felt for him Clementina's heart throbbed with a pain which was all for herself. Why should she wait any longer either? For that instant she abandoned the hope which had kept her up so long; a wave of homesickness overwhelmed her.

"I should like to go back, too," she said. "I don't see why I'm staying."

"Mr. Osson, why can't you let me"—she was going to say—"go home with you?" But she really said what was also in her heart, "Why can't you let me give you the money to go home? It is all Mrs. Landa's money, anyway."

"There is certainly that view of the matter," he assented with a promptness that might have suggested a lurking grudge for the vice-consul's decision that she ought to keep the money Mrs. Lander had given her.

But Clementina urged unsuspiciously: "Oh, yes, indeed! And I shall feel better if you take it. I only wish I could go home, too!"

The minister was silent while he was revolving, with whatever scruple or reluctance, a compromise suitable to the occasion. Then he said, "Why should we not return together?"

"Would you take me?" she entreated.

"That should be as you wished. I am not much acquainted with the usages in such matters, but I presume that it would be entirely practicable. We could ask the vice-consul."

"Yes—"

"He must have had considerable experience in cases of the kind. Would your friends meet you in New York, or—"

"I don't know," said Clementina with a pang for the thought of a meeting she had sometimes fancied there, when her lover had come out for her, and her father had been told to come and receive them. "No," she sighed, "the'e wouldn't be time to let them know. But it wouldn't make any difference. I could get home from New Yo'k alone," she added, listlessly. Her spirits had fallen again. She saw that she could not leave Venice till she had heard in some sort from the letter she had written. "Perhaps it couldn't be done, after all. But I will see Mr. Bennam about it, Mr. Osson; and I know he will want you to have that much of the money. He will be coming he'e, soon."

He rose upon what he must have thought her hint, and said, "I should not wish to have him swayed against his judgment."

The vice-consul came not long after the minister had left her, and she began upon what she wished to do for him.

The vice-consul was against it. "I would rather lend him the money out of my own pocket. How are you going to get along yourself, if you let him have so much?"

She did not answer at once. Then she said, hopelessly, "I've a great mind to go home with him. I don't believe there's any use waiting here any longa." The vice-consul could not say anything to this. She added, "Yes, I believe I will go home. We we'e talking about it, the other day, and he is willing to let me go with him."

"I should think he would be," the vice-consul retorted in his indignation for her. "Did you offer to pay for his passage?"

"Yes," she owned, "I did," and again the vice-consul could say nothing. "If I went, it wouldn't make any difference whether it took it all or not. I should have plenty to get home from New York with."

"Well," the vice-consul assented, dryly, "it's for you to say."

"I know you don't want me to do it!"

"Well, I shall miss you," he answered, evasively.

"And I shall miss you, too, Mr. Bennam. Don't you believe it? But if I don't take this chance to get home, I don't know when I shall eva have anotha. And there isn't any use waiting—no, there isn't!"

The vice-consul laughed at the sort of imperative despair in her tone. "How are you going? Which way, I mean."

They counted up Clementina's debts and assets, and they found that if she took the next steamer from Genoa, which was to sail in four days, she would have enough to pay her own way and Mr. Orson's to New York, and still have some thirty dollars over, for her expenses home to Middlemount. They allowed for a second cabin-passage, which the vice-consul said was perfectly good on the Genoa steamers. He rather urged the gentility and comfort of the second cabin-passage, but his reasons in favor of it were wasted upon Clementina's indifference; she wished to get home, now, and she did not care how. She asked the vice-consul to see the minister for her, and if he were ready and willing, to telegraph for their tickets. He transacted the business so promptly that he was able to tell her when he came in the evening that everything was in train. He excused his coming; he said that now she was going so soon, he wanted to see all he could of her. He offered no excuse when he came the next morning; but he said he had got a letter for her and thought she might want to have it at once.

He took it out of his hat and gave it to her. It was addressed in Hinkle's writing; her answer had come at last; she stood trembling with it in her hand.

The vice-consul smiled. "Is that the one?"

"Yes," she whispered back.

"All right." He took his hat, and set it on the back of his head before he left her without other salutation.

Then Clementina opened her letter. It was in a woman's hand, and the writer made haste to explain at the beginning that she was George W. Hinkle's sister, and that she was writing for him; for though he was now out of danger, he was still very weak, and they had all been anxious about him. A month before, he had been hurt in a railroad collision, and had come home from the West, where the accident happened, suffering mainly from shock, as his doctor thought; he had taken to his bed at once, and had not risen from it since. He had been out of his head a great part of the time, and had been forbidden everything that could distress or excite him. His sister said that she was writing for him now as soon as he had seen Clementina's letter; it had been forwarded from one address to another, and had at last found him there at his home in Ohio. He wished to say that he would come out for Clementina as soon as he was allowed to undertake the journey, and in the meantime she must let him know constantly where she was. The letter closed with a few words of love in his own handwriting.

Clementina rose from reading it, and put on her hat in a bewildered impulse to go to him at once; she knew, in spite of all the cautions and reserves of the letter that he must still be very sick. When she came out of her daze she found that she could only go to the vice-consul. She put the letter in his hands to let it explain itself. "You'll undastand, now," she said. "What shall I do?"

When he had read it, he smiled and answered, "I guess I understood pretty well before, though I wasn't posted on names. Well, I suppose you'll want to layout most of your capital on cables, now?"

"Yes," she laughed, and then she suddenly lamented, "Why didn't they telegraph?"

"Well, I guess he hadn't the head for it," said the vice-consul, "and the rest wouldn't think of it. They wouldn't, in the country."

Clementina laughed again; in joyous recognition of the fact, "No, my fatha wouldn't, eitha!"

The vice-consul reached for his hat, and he led the way to Clementina's gondola at his garden gate, in greater haste than she. At the telegraph office he framed a dispatch which for expansive fullness and precision was apparently unexampled in the experience of the clerk who took it and spelt over its English with them. It asked an answer in the vice-consul's care, and, "I'll tell you what, Miss Claxon," he said with a husky weakness in his voice, "I wish you'd let this be my treat."

She understood. "Do you really, Mr. Bennam?"

"I do indeed."

"Well, then, I will," she said, but when he wished to include in his treat the dispatch she sent home to her father announcing her coming, she would not let him.

He looked at his watch, as they rowed away. "It's eight o'clock here, now, and it will reach Ohio about six hours earlier; but you can't expect an answer tonight, you know."

"No"—She had expected it though, he could see that.

"But whenever it comes, I'll bring it right round to you. Now it's all going to be straight, don't you be afraid, and you're going home the quickest way you can get there. I've been looking up the sailings, and this Genoa boat will get you to New York about as soon as any could from Liverpool. Besides there's always a chance of missing connections and losing time between here and England. I should stick to the Genoa boat."

"Oh I shall," said Clementina, far less fidgetted than he. She was, in fact, resting securely again in the faith which had never really deserted her, and had only seemed for a little time to waver from her when her hope went. Now that she had telegraphed, her heart was at peace, and she even laughed as she answered the anxious vice-consul.

XXXVI

The next morning Clementina watched for the vice-consul from her balcony. She knew he would not send; she knew he would come; but it, was nearly noon before she saw him coming. They caught sight of each other almost at the same moment, and he stood up in his boat, and waved something white in his hand, which must be a dispatch for her.

It acknowledged her telegram and reported George still improving; his father would meet her steamer in New York. It was very reassuring, it was every thing hopeful; but when she had read it she gave it to the vice-consul for encouragement.

"It's all right, Miss Claxon," he said, stoutly. "Don't you be troubled about Mr. Hinkle's not coming to meet you himself. He can't keep too quiet for a while yet."

"Oh, yes," said Clementina, patiently.

"If you really want somebody to worry about, you can help Mr. Orson to worry about himself!" the vice-consul went on, with the grimness he had formerly used in speaking of Mrs. Lander. "He's sick, or he thinks he's going to be. He sent round for me this morning, and I found him in bed. You may have to go home alone. But I guess he's more scared than hurt."

Her heart sank, and then rose in revolt against the mere idea of delay. "I wonder if I ought to go and see him," she said.

"Well, it would be a kindness," returned the vice-consul, with a promptness that unmasked the apprehension he felt for the sick man.

He did not offer to go with her, and she took Maddalena. She found the minister seated in his chair beside his bed. A three days' beard heightened the gauntness of his face; he did not move when his padrona announced her.

"I am not any better," he answered when she said that she was glad to see him up. "I am merely resting; the bed is hard. I regret to say," he added, with a sort of formal impersonality, "that I shall be unable to accompany you home, Miss Claxon. That is, if you still think of taking the steamer this week."

Her whole being had set homeward in a tide that already seemed to drift the vessel from its moorings. "What—what do you mean?" she gasped.

"I didn't know," he returned, "but that in view of the circumstances—all the circumstances—you might be intending to defer your departure to some later steamer."

"No, no, no! I must go, now. I couldn't wait a day, an hour, a minute after the first chance of going. You don't know what you are saying! He might die if I told him I was not coming; and then what should I do?" This was what Clementina said to herself; but what she said to Mr. Orson, with an inspiration from her terror at his suggestion was, "Don't you think a little chicken broth would do you good, Mr. Osson? I don't believe but what it would."

A wistful gleam came into the preacher's eyes. "It might," he admitted, and then she knew what must be his malady. She sent Maddalena to a trattoria for the soup, and she did not leave him, even after she had seen its effect upon him. It was not hard to persuade him that he had better come home with her; and she had him there, tucked away with his few poor belongings, in the most comfortable room the padrone could imagine, when the vice-consul came in the evening.

"He says he thinks he can go, now," she ended, when she had told the vice-consul. "And I know he can. It wasn't anything but poor living."

"It looks more like no living," said the vice-consul. "Why didn't the old fool let some one know that he was short of money?" He went on with a partial transfer of his contempt of the preacher to her, "I suppose if he'd been sick instead of hungry, you'd have waited over till the next steamer for him."

She cast down her eyes. "I don't know what you'll think of me. I should have been sorry for him, and I should have wanted to stay." She lifted her eyes and looked the vice-consul defiantly in the face. "But he hadn't the fust claim on me, and I should have gone—I couldn't, have helped it!—I should have gone, if he had been dying!"

"Well, you've got more horse-sense," said the vice-consul, "than any ten men I ever saw," and he testified his admiration of her by putting his arms round her, where she stood before him, and kissing her. "Don't you mind," he explained. "If my youngest girl had lived, she would have been about your age."

"Oh, it's all right, Mr. Bennam," said Clementina.

When the time came for them to leave Venice, Mr. Orson was even eager to go. The vice-consul would have gone with them in contempt of the official responsibilities which he felt to be such a thankless burden, but there was really no need of his going, and he and Clementina treated the question with the matter-of-fact impartiality which they liked in each other. He saw her off at the station where Maddalena had come to take the train for Florence in token of her devotion to the signorina, whom she would not outstay in Venice. She wept long and loud upon Clementina's neck, so that even Clementina was once moved to put her handkerchief to her tearless eyes.

At the last moment she had a question which she referred to the vice consul. "Should you tell him?" she asked.

"Tell who what?" he retorted.

"Mr. Osson-that I wouldn't have stayed for him."

"Do you think it would make you feel any better?" asked the consul, upon reflection.

"I believe he ought to know."

"Well, then, I guess I should do it."

The time did not come for her confession till they had nearly reached the end of their voyage. It followed upon something like a confession from the minister himself, which he made the day he struggled on deck with her help, after spending a week in his berth.

"Here is something," he said, "which appears to be for you, Miss Claxon. I found it among some letters for Mrs. Lander which Mr. Bennam gave me after my arrival, and I only observed the address in looking over the papers in my valise this morning." He handed her a telegram. "I trust that it is nothing requiring immediate attention."

Clementina read it at a glance. "No," she answered, and for a while she could not say anything more; it was a cable message which Hinkle's sister must have sent her after writing. No evil had come of its failure to reach her, and she recalled without bitterness the suffering which would have been spared her if she had got it before. It was when she thought of the suffering of her lover from the silence which must have made him doubt her, that she could not speak. As soon as she governed herself against her first resentment she said, with a little sigh, "It is all right, now, Mr. Osson," and her stress upon the word seemed to trouble him with no misgiving. "Besides, if you're to blame for not noticing, so is Mr. Bennam, and I don't want to blame any one." She hesitated a moment before she added: "I have got to tell you something, now, because I think you ought to know it. I am going home to be married, Mr. Osson, and this message is from the gentleman I am going to be married to. He has been very sick, and I don't know yet as he'll be able to meet me in New Yo'k; but his fatha will."

Mr. Orson showed no interest in these facts beyond a silent attention to her words, which might have passed for an open indifference. At his time of life all such questions, which are of permanent importance to women, affect men hardly more than the angels who neither marry nor are given in marriage. Besides, as a minister he must have had a surfeit of all possible qualities in the love affairs of people intending matrimony. As a casuist he was more reasonably concerned in the next fact which Clementina laid before him.

"And the otha day, there in Venice when you we'e sick, and you seemed to think that I might put off stahting home till the next steamer, I don't know but I let you believe I would."

"I supposed that the delay of a week or two could make no material difference to you."

"But now you see that it would. And I feel as if I ought to tell you—I spoke to Mr. Bennam about it, and he didn't tell me not to—that I shouldn't have staid, no not for anything in the wo'ld. I had to do what I did at the time, but eva since it has seemed as if I had deceived you, and I don't want to have it seem so any longer. It isn't because I don't hate to tell you; I do; but I guess if it was to happen over again I couldn't feel any different. Do you want I should tell the deck-stewahd to bring you some beef-tea?"

"I think I could relish a small portion," said Mr. Orson, cautiously, and he said nothing more.

Clementina left him with her nerves in a flutter, and she did not come back to him until she decided that it was time to help him down to his cabin. He suffered her to do this in silence, but at the door he cleared his throat and began:

"I have reflected upon what you told me, and I have tried to regard the case from all points. I believe that I have done so, without personal feeling, and I think it my duty to say, fully and freely, that I believe you would have done perfectly right not to remain."

"Yes," said Clementina, "I thought you would think so."

They parted emotionlessly to all outward effect, and when they met again it was without a sign of having passed through a crisis of sentiment. Neither referred to the matter again, but from that time the minister treated Clementina with a deference not without some shadows of tenderness such as her helplessness in Venice had apparently never inspired. She had cast out of her mind all lingering hardness toward him in telling him the hard truth, and she met his faint relentings with a grateful gladness which showed itself in her constant care of him.

This helped her a little to forget the strain of the anxiety that increased upon her as the time shortened between the last news of her lover and the next; and there was perhaps no more exaggeration in the import than in the terms of the formal acknowledgment which Mr. Orson made her as their steamer sighted Fire Island Light, and they both knew that their voyage had ended: "I may not be able to say to you in the hurry of our arrival in New York that I am obliged to you for a good many little attentions, which I should be pleased to reciprocate if opportunity offered. I do not think I am going too far in saying that they are such as a daughter might offer a parent."

"Oh, don't speak of it, Mr. Osson!" she protested. "I haven't done anything that any one wouldn't have done."

"I presume," said the minister, thoughtfully, as if retiring from an extreme position, "that they are such as others similarly circumstanced, might have done, but it will always be a source of satisfaction for you to reflect that you have not neglected them."

XXXVII

In the crowd which thronged the steamer's dock at Hoboken, Clementina strained her eyes to make out some one who looked enough like her lover to be his father, and she began to be afraid that they might miss each other when she failed. She walked slowly down the gangway, with the people that thronged it, glad to be hidden by them from her failure, but at the last step she was caught aside by a small blackeyed, black-haired woman, who called out "Isn't this Miss Claxon? I'm Georrge's sisterr. Oh, you'rre just like what he said! I knew it! I knew it!" and then hugged her and kissed her, and passed her to the little lean dark old man next her. "This is fatherr. I knew you couldn't tell us, because I take afterr him, and Georrge is exactly like motherr."

George's father took her hand timidly, but found courage to say to his daughter, "Hadn't you betterr let her own fatherr have a chance at herr?" and amidst a tempest of apologies and self blame from the sister, Claxon showed himself over the shoulders of the little man.

"Why, there wa'n't no hurry, as long as she's he'a," he said, in prompt enjoyment of the joke, and he and Clementina sparely kissed each other.

"Why, fatha!" she said. "I didn't expect you to come to New Yo'k to meet me."

"Well, I didn't ha'dly expect it myself; but I'd neva been to Yo'k, and I thought I might as well come. Things ah' ratha slack at home, just now, anyway."

She did not heed his explanation. "We'e you sca'ed when you got my dispatch?"

"No, we kind of expected you'd come any time, the way you wrote afta Mrs. Landa died. We thought something must be up."

"Yes," she said, absently. Then, "Whe'e's motha?" she asked.

"Well, I guess she thought she couldn't get round to it, exactly," said the father. "She's all right. Needn't ask you!"

"No, I'm fust-rate," Clementina returned, with a silent joy in her father's face and voice. She went back in it to the girl of a year ago, and the world which had come between them since their parting rolled away as if it had never been there.

Neither of them said anything about that. She named over her brothers and sisters, and he answered, "Yes, yes," in assurance of their well-being, and then he explained, as if that were the only point of real interest, "I see your folks waitin' he'e fo' somebody, and I thought I'd see if it wa'n't the same one, and we kind of struck up an acquaintance on your account befo'e you got he'e, Clem."

"Your folks!" she silently repeated to herself. "Yes, they ah' mine!" and she stood trying to realize the strange fact, while George's sister poured out a voluminous comment upon Claxon's spare statement, and George's father admired her volubility with the shut smile of toothless age. She spoke with the burr which the Scotch-Irish settlers have imparted to the whole middle West, but it was music to Clementina, who heard now and then a tone of her lover in his sister's voice. In the midst of it all she caught sight of a mute unfriended figure just without their circle, his traveling shawl hanging loose upon his shoulders, and the valise which had formed his sole baggage in the voyage to and from Europe pulling his long hand out of his coat sleeve.

"Oh, yes," she said, "here is Mr. Osson that came ova with me, fatha; he's a relation of Mr. Landa's," and she presented him to them all.

He shifted his valise to the left hand, and shook hands with each, asking, "What name?" and then fell motionless again.

"Well," said her father, "I guess this is the end of this paht of the ceremony, and I'm goin' to see your baggage through the custom-house, Clementina; I've read about it, and I want to know how it's done. I want to see what you ah' tryin' to smuggle in."

"I guess you won't find much," she said. "But you'll want the keys, won't you?" She called to him, as he was stalking away.

"Well, I guess that would be a good idea. Want to help, Miss Hinkle?"

"I guess we might as well all help," said Clementina, and Mr. Orson included himself in the invitation. He seemed unable to separate himself from them, though the passage of Clementina's baggage through the customs, and its delivery to an expressman for the hotel where the Hinkles said they were staying might well have severed the last tie between them.

"Ah' you going straight home, Mr. Osson?" she asked, to rescue him from the forgetfulness into which they were all letting him fall.

"I think I will remain over a day," he answered. "I may go on to Boston before starting West."

"Well, that's right," said Clementina's father with the wish to approve everything native to him, and an instinctive sense of Clementina's wish to befriend the minister. "Betta come to oua hotel. We're all goin' to the same one."

"I presume it is a good one?" Mr. Orson assented.

"Well," said Claxon, "you must make Miss Hinkle, he'a, stand it if it ain't. She's got me to go to it."

Mr. Orson apparently could not enter into the joke; but he accompanied the party, which again began to forget him, across the ferry and up the elevated road to the street car that formed the last stage of their progress to the hotel. At this point George's sister fell silent, and Clementina's father burst out, "Look he'a! I guess we betty not keep this up any Tonga; I don't believe much in surprises, and I guess she betta know it now!"

He looked at George's sister as if for authority to speak further, and Clementina looked at her, too, while George's father nervously moistened his smiling lips with the tip of his tongue, and let his twinkling eyes rest upon Clementina's face.

"Is he at the hotel?" she asked.

"Yes," said his sister, monosyllabic for once.

"I knew it," said Clementina, and she was only half aware of the fullness with which his sister now explained how he wanted to come so much that the doctor thought he had better, but that they had made him promise he would not try to meet her at the steamer, lest it should be too great a trial of his strength.

"Yes," Clementina assented, when the story came to an end and was beginning over again.

She had an inexplicable moment when she stood before her lover in the room where they left her to meet him alone. She faltered and he waited constrained by her constraint.

"Is it all a mistake, Clementina?" he asked, with a piteous smile.

"No, no!"

"Am I so much changed?"

"No; you are looking better than I expected."

"And you are not sorry-for anything?"

"No, I am—Perhaps I have thought of you too much! It seems so strange."

"I understand," he answered. "We have been like spirits to each other, and now we find that we are alive and on the earth like other people; and we are not used to it."

"It must be something like that."

"But if it's something else—if you have the least regret,—if you would rather"—He stopped, and they remained looking at each other a moment. Then she turned her head, and glanced out of the window, as if something there had caught her sight.

"It's a very pleasant view, isn't it?" she said; and she lifted her hands to her head, and took off her hat, with an effect of having got home after absence, to stay.

XXXVIII

It was possibly through some sense finer than any cognition that Clementina felt in meeting her lover that she had taken up a new burden rather than laid down an old one. Afterwards, when they once recurred to that meeting, and she tried to explain for him the hesitation which she had not been able to hide, she could only say, "I presume I didn't want to begin unless I was sure I could carry out. It would have been silly."

Her confession, if it was a confession, was made when one of his returns to health, or rather one of the arrests of his unhealth, flushed them with hope and courage; but before that first meeting was ended she knew that he had overtasked his strength, in coming to New York, and he must not try it further. "Fatha," she said to Claxon, with the authority of a woman doing her duty, "I'm not going to let Geo'ge go up to Middlemount, with all the excitement. It will be as much as he can do to get home. You can tell mother about it; and the rest. I did suppose it would be Mr. Richling that would marry us, and I always wanted him to, but I guess somebody else can do it as well."

"Just as you say, Clem," her father assented. "Why not Brother Osson, he'a?" he suggested with a pleasure in the joke, whatever it was, that the minister's relation to Clementina involved. "I guess he can put off his visit to Boston long enough."

"Well, I was thinking of him," said Clementina. "Will you ask him?"

"Yes. I'll get round to it, in the mohning."

"No-now; right away. I've been talking with Geo'ge about it; and the'e's no sense in putting it off. I ought to begin taking care of him at once."

"Well, I guess when I tell your motha how you're layin' hold, she won't think it's the same pusson," said her father, proudly.

"But it is; I haven't changed a bit."

"You ha'n't changed for the wohse, anyway."

"Didn't I always try to do what I had to?"

"I guess you did, Clem."

"Well, then!"

Mr. Orson, after a decent hesitation, consented to perform the ceremony. It took place in a parlor of the hotel, according to the law of New York, which facilitates marriage so greatly in all respects that it is strange any one in the State should remain single. He had then a luxury of choice between attaching himself to the bridal couple as far as Ohio on his journey home to Michigan, or to Claxon who was going to take the boat for Boston the next day on his way to Middlemount. He decided for Claxon, since he could then see Mrs. Lander's lawyer at once, and arrange with him for getting out of the vice-consul's hands the money which he was holding for an authoritative demand. He accepted without open reproach the handsome fee which the elder Hinkle gave him for his services, and even went so far as to say, "If your son should ever be blest with a return to health, he has got a helpmeet such as there are very few of." He then admonished the young couple, in whatever trials life should have in store for them, to be resigned, and always to be prepared for the worst. When he came later to take leave of them, he was apparently not equal to the task of fitly acknowledging the return which Hinkle made him of all the money remaining to Clementina out of the sum last given her by Mrs. Lander, but he hid any disappointment he might have suffered, and with a brief, "Thank you," put it in his pocket.

Hinkle told Clementina of the apathetic behavior of Mr. Orson; he added with a laugh like his old self, "It's the best that he doesn't seem prepared for."

"Yes," she assented. "He wasn't very chee'ful. But I presume that he meant well. It must be a trial for him to find out that Mrs. Landa wasn't rich, after all."

It was apparently never a trial to her. She went to Ohio with her husband and took up her life on the farm, where it was wisely judged that he had the best chance of working out of the wreck of his health and strength. There was often the promise and always the hope of this, and their love knew no doubt of the future. Her sisters-in-law delighted in all her strangeness and difference, while they petted her as something not to be separated from him in their petting of their brother; to his mother she was the darling which her youngest had never ceased to be; Clementina once went so far as to say to him that if she was ever anything she would like to be a Moravian.

The question of religion was always related in their minds to the question of Gregory, to whom they did justice in their trust of each other. It was Hinkle himself who reasoned out that if Gregory was narrow, his narrowness was of his conscience and not of his heart or his mind. She respected the memory of her first lover; but it was as if he were dead, now, as well as her young dream of him, and she read with a curious sense of remoteness, a paragraph which her husband found in the religious intelligence of his Sunday paper, announcing the marriage of the Rev. Frank Gregory to a lady described as having been a frequent and bountiful contributor to the foreign missions. She was apparently a widow, and they conjectured that she was older than he. His departure for his chosen field of missionary labor in China formed part of the news communicated by the rather exulting paragraph.

"Well, that is all right," said Clementina's husband. "He is a good man, and he is where he can do nothing but good. I am glad I needn't feel sorry for him, any more."

Clementina's father must have given such a report of Hinkle and his family, that they felt easy at home in leaving her to the lot she had chosen. When Claxon parted from her, he talked of coming out with her mother to see her that fall; but it was more than a year before they got round to it. They did not come till after the birth of her little girl, and her father then humorously allowed that perhaps they would not have got round to it at all if something of the kind had not happened. The Hinkles and her father and mother liked one another, so much that in the first glow of his enthusiasm Claxon talked of settling down in Ohio, and the older Hinkle drove him about to look at some places that were for sale. But it ended in his saying one day that he missed the hills, and he did not believe that he would know enough to come in when it rained if he did not see old Middlemount with his nightcap on first. His wife and he started home with the impatience of their years, rather earlier than they had meant to go, and they were silent for a little while after they left the flag-station where Hinkle and Clementina had put them aboard their train.

"Well?" said Claxon, at last.

"Well?" echoed his wife, and then she did not speak for a little while longer. At last she asked,

"D'he look that way when you fust see him in New Yo'k?"

Claxon gave his honesty time to get the better of his optimism. Even then he answered evasively, "He doos look pootty slim."

"The way I cypher it out," said his wife, "he no business to let her marry him, if he wa'n't goin' to get well. It was throwin' of herself away, as you may say."

"I don't know about that," said Claxon, as if the point had occurred to him, too, and had been already argued in his mind. "I guess they must 'a' had it out, there in New York before they got married—or she had. I don't believe but what he expected to get well, right away. It's the kind of a thing that lingas along, and lingas along. As fah fo'th as Clem went, I guess there wa'n't any let about it. I guess she'd made up her mind from the staht, and she was goin' to have him if she had to hold him on his feet to do it. Look he'a! W hat would you done?"

"Oh, I presume we're all fools!" said Mrs. Claxon, impatient of a sex not always so frank with itself. "But that don't excuse him."

"I don't say it doos," her husband admitted. "But I presume he was expectin' to get well right away, then. And I don't believe," he added, energetically, "but what he will, yet. As I undastand, there ain't anything ogganic about him. It's just this he'e nuvvous prostration, resultin' from shock, his docta tells me; and he'll wo'k out of that all right."

They said no more, and Mrs. Claxon did not recur to any phase of the situation till she undid the lunch which the Hinkles had put up for them, and laid out on the napkin in her lap the portions of cold ham and cold chicken, the buttered biscuit, and the little pot of apple-butter, with the large bottle of cold coffee. Then she sighed, "They live well."

"Yes," said her husband, glad of any concession, "and they ah' good folks. And Clem's as happy as a bud with 'em, you can see that."

"Oh, she was always happy enough, if that's all you want. I presume she was happy with that hectorin' old thing that fooled her out of her money."

"I ha'n't ever regretted that money, Rebecca," said Claxon, stiffly, almost sternly, "and I guess you a'n't, eitha."

"I don't say I have," retorted Mrs. Claxon. "But I don't like to be made a fool of. I presume," she added, remotely, but not so irrelevantly, "Clem could ha' got 'most anybody, ova the'a."

"Well," said Claxon, taking refuge in the joke, "I shouldn't want her to marry a crowned head, myself."

It was Clementina who drove the clay-bank colt away from the station after the train had passed out of sight. Her husband sat beside her, and let her take the reins from his nerveless grasp; and when they got into the shelter of the piece of woods that the road passed through he put up his hands to his face, and broke into sobs. She allowed him to weep on, though she kept saying, "Geo'ge, Geo'ge," softly, and stroking his knee with the hand next him. When his sobbing stopped, she said, "I guess they've had a pleasant visit; but I'm glad we'a together again." He took up her hand and kissed the back of it, and then clutched it hard, but did not speak. "It's strange," she went on, "how I used to be home-sick for father and motha"—she had sometimes lost her Yankee accent in her association with his people, and spoke with their Western burr, but she found it in moments of deeper feeling—"when I was there in Europe, and now I'm glad to have them go. I don't want anybody to be between us; and I want to go back to just the way we we'e befo'e they came. It's been a strain on you, and now you must throw it all off and rest, and get up your strength. One thing, I could see that fatha noticed the gain you had made since he saw you in New Yo'k. He spoke about it to me the fust thing, and he feels just the way I do about it. He don't want you to hurry and get well, but take it slowly, and not excite yourself. He believes in your gleaner, and he knows all about machinery. He says the patent makes it puffectly safe, and you can take your own time about pushing it; it's su'a to go. And motha liked you. She's not one to talk a great deal—she always leaves that to father and me— but she's got deep feelings, and she just worshipped the baby! I neva saw her take a child in her ahms before; but she seemed to want to hold the baby all the time." She stopped, and then added, tenderly, "Now, I know what you ah' thinking about, Geo'ge, and I don't want you to think about it any more. If you do, I shall give up."

They had come to a bad piece of road where a Slough of thick mud forced the wagon-way over the stumps of a turnout in the woods. "You had better let me have the reins, Clementina," he said. He drove home over the yellow leaves of the hickories and the crimson leaves of the maples, that heavy with the morning dew, fell slanting through the still air; and on the way he began to sing; his singing made her heart ache. His father came out to put up the colt for him; and Hinkle would not have his help.

He unhitched the colt himself, while his father trembled by with bent knees; he clapped the colt on the haunch and started him through the pasture-bars with a gay shout, and then put his arm round Clementina's waist, and walked her into the kitchen amidst the grins of his mother and sisters, who said he ought to be ashamed.

The winter passed, and in the spring he was not so well as he had been in the fall. It was the out-door life which was best for him, and he picked up again in the summer. When another autumn came, it was thought best for him not to risk the confinement of another winter in the North. The prolongation of the summer in the South would complete his cure, and Clementina took her baby and went with him to Florida. He was very well, there, and courageous letters came to Middlemount and Ohio, boasting of the gains he had made. One day toward spring he came in languid from the damp, unnatural heat, and the next day he had a fever, which the doctor would not, in a resort absolutely free from malaria, pronounce malarial. After it had once declared itself, in compliance with this reluctance, a simple fever, Hinkle was delirious, and he never knew Clementina again for the mother of his child. They were once more at Venice in his ravings, and he was reasoning with her that Belsky was not drowned.

The mystery of his malady deepened into the mystery of his death. With that his look of health and youth came back, and as she gazed upon his gentle face, it wore to her the smile of quaint sweetness that she had seen it wear the first night it won her fancy at Miss Milray's horse in Florence.

XXXIX

Six years after Miss Milray parted with Clementina in Venice she found herself, towards the close of the summer, at Middlemount. She had definitely ceased to live in Florence, where she had meant to die, and had come home to close her eyes. She was in no haste to do this, and in the meantime she was now at Middlemount with her brother, who had expressed a wish to revisit the place in memory of Mrs. Milray. It was the second anniversary of her divorce, which had remained, after a married life of many vicissitudes, almost the only experience untried in that relation, and which had been happily accomplished in the courts of Dacotah, upon grounds that satisfied the facile justice of that State. Milray had dealt handsomely with his widow, as he unresentfully called her, and the money he assigned her was of a destiny perhaps as honored as its origin. She employed it in the negotiation of a second marriage, in which she redressed the balance of her first by taking a husband somewhat younger than herself.

Both Milray and his sister had a wish which was much more than a curiosity to know what had become of Clementina; they had heard that her husband was dead, and that she had come back to Middlemount; and Miss Milray was going to the office, the afternoon following their arrival, to ask the landlord about her, when she was arrested at the door of the ball-room by a sight that she thought very pretty. At the bottom of the room, clearly defined against the long windows behind her, stood the figure of a lady in the middle of the floor. In rows on either side sat little girls and little boys who left their places one after another, and turned at the door to make their manners to her. In response to each obeisance the lady dropped a curtsey, now to this side, now to that, taking her skirt between her finger tips on either hand and spreading it delicately, with a certain elegance of movement, and a grace that was full of poetry, and to Miss Milray, somehow, full of pathos. There remained to the end a small mite of a girl, who was the last to leave her place and bow to the lady. She did not quit the room then, like the others, but advanced toward the lady who came to meet her, and lifted her and clasped her to her breast with a kind of passion. She walked down toward the door where Miss Milray stood, gently drifting over the polished floor, as if still moved by the music that had ceased, and as she drew near, Miss Milray gave a cry of joy, and ran upon her. "Why, Clementina!" she screamed, and caught her and the child both in her arms.

She began to weep, but Clementina smiled instead of weeping, as she always used to do. She returned Miss Milray's affectionate greeting with a tenderness as great as her own, but with a sort of authority, such as sometimes comes to those who have suffered. She quieted the older woman with her own serenity, and met the torrent of her questions with as many answers as their rush permitted, when they were both presently in Miss Milray's room talking in their old way. From time to time Miss Milray broke from the talk to kiss the little girl, whom she declared to be Clementina all over again, and then returned to her better behavior with an effect of shame for her want of self-control, as if Clementina's mood had abashed her. Sometimes this was almost severe in its quiet; that was her mother coming to her share in her; but again she was like her father, full of the sunny gayety of self-forgetfulness, and then Miss Milray said, "Now you are the old Clementina!"

Upon the whole she listened with few interruptions to the story which she exacted. It was mainly what we know. After her husband's death Clementina had gone back to his family for a time, and each year since she had spent part of the winter with them; but it was very lonesome for her, and she began to be home-sick for Middlemount. They saw it and considered it. "They ah' the best people, Miss Milray!" she said, and her voice, which was firm when she spoke of her husband, broke in the words of minor feeling. Besides being a little homesick, she ended, she was not willing to live on there, doing nothing for herself, and so she had come back.

"And you are here, doing just what you planned when you talked your life over with me in Venice!"

"Yes, but life isn't eva just what we plan it to be, Miss Milray."

"Ah, don't I know it!"

Clementina surprised Miss Milray by adding, "In a great many things—I don't know but in most—it's better. I don't complain of mine—"

"You poor child! You never complained of anything—not even of Mrs. Lander!"

"But it's different from what I expected; and it's—strange."

"Yes; life is very strange."

"I don't mean-losing him. That had to be. I can see, now, that it had to be almost from the beginning. It seems to me that I knew it had to be from the fust minute I saw him in New Yo'k; but he didn't, and I am glad of that. Except when he was getting wohse, he always believed he should get well; and he was getting well, when he—"

Miss Milray did not violate the pause she made with any question, though it was apparent that Clementina had something on her mind that she wished to say, and could hardly say of herself.

She began again, "I was glad through everything that I could live with him so long. If there is nothing moa, here or anywhe'a, that was something. But it is strange. Sometimes it doesn't seem as if it had happened."

"I think I can understand, Clementina."

"I feel sometimes as if I hadn't happened myself." She stopped, with a patient little sigh, and passed her hand across the child's forehead, in a mother's fashion, and smoothed her hair from it, bending over to look down into her face. "We think she has her fatha's eyes," she said.

"Yes, she has," Miss Milray assented, noting the upward slant of the child's eyes, which gave his quaintness to her beauty. "He had fascinating eyes."

After a moment Clementina asked, "Do you believe that the looks are all that ah' left?"

Miss Milray reflected. "I know what you mean. I should say character was left, and personality—somewhere."

"I used to feel as if it we'e left here, at fust—as if he must come back. But that had to go."

"Yes."

"Everything seems to go. After a while even the loss of him seemed to go."

"Yes, losses go with the rest."

"That's what I mean by its seeming as if it never any of it happened. Some things before it are a great deal more real."

"Little things?"

"Not exactly. But things when I was very young." Miss Milray did not know quite what she intended, but she knew that Clementina was feeling her way to something she wanted to say, and she let her alone. "When it was all over, and I knew that as long as I lived he would be somewhere else, I tried to be paht of the wo'ld I was left in. Do you think that was right?"

"It was wise; and, yes, it was best," said Miss Milray, and for relief from the tension which was beginning to tell upon her own nerves, she asked, "I suppose you know about my poor brother? I'd better tell you to keep you from asking for Mrs. Milray, though I don't know that it's so very painful with him. There isn't any Mrs. Milray now," she added, and she explained why.

Neither of them cared for Mrs. Milray, and they did not pretend to be concerned about her, but Clementina said, vaguely, as if in recognition of Mrs. Milray's latest experiment, "Do you believe in second marriages?"

Miss Milray laughed, "Well, not that kind exactly."

"No," Clementina assented, and she colored a little.

Miss Milray was moved to add, "But if you mean another kind, I don't see why not. My own mother was married twice."

"Was she?" Clementina looked relieved and encouraged, but she did not say any more at once. Then she asked, "Do you know what ever became of Mr. Belsky?"

"Yes. He's taken his title again, and gone back to live in Russia; he's made peace with the Czar; I believe."

"That's nice," said Clementina; and Miss Milray made bold to ask:

"And what has become of Mr. Gregory?"

Clementina answered, as Miss Milray thought, tentatively and obliquely: "You know his wife died."

"No, I never knew that she lived."

"Yes. They went out to China, and she died the'a."

"And is he there yet? But of course! He could never have given up being a missionary."

"Well," said Clementina, "he isn't in China. His health gave out, and he had to come home. He's in Middlemount Centa."

Miss Milray suppressed the "Oh!" that all but broke from her lips. "Preaching to the heathen, there?" she temporized.

"To the summa folks," Clementina explained, innocent of satire. "They have got a Union Chapel the'a, now, and Mr. Gregory has been preaching all summa." There seemed nothing more that Miss Milray could prompt her to say, but it was not quite with surprise that she heard Clementina continue, as if it were part of the explanation, and followed from the fact she had stated, "He wants me to marry him."

Miss Milray tried to emulate her calm in asking, "And shall you?"

"I don't know. I told him I would see; he only asked me last night. It would be kind of natural. He was the fust. You may think it is strange—"

Miss Milray, in the superstition of her old-maidenhood concerning love, really thought it cold-blooded and shocking; but she said, "Oh, no."

Clementina resumed: "And he says that if it was right for me to stop caring for him when I did, it is right now for me to ca'e for him again, where the'e's no one to be hu't by it. Do you think it is?"

"Yes; why not?" Miss Milray was forced to the admission against what she believed the finer feelings 'of her nature.

Clementina sighed, "I suppose he's right. I always thought he was good. Women don't seem to belong very much to themselves in this wo'ld, do they?"

"No, they seem to belong to the men, either because they want the men, or the men want them; it comes to the same thing. I suppose you don't wish me to advise you, my dear?"

"No. I presume it's something I've got to think out for myself."

"But I think he's good, too. I ought to say that much, for I didn't always stand his friend with you. If Mr. Gregory has any fault it's being too scrupulous."

"You mean, about that old trouble—our not believing just the same?" Miss Milray meant something much more temperamental than that, but she allowed Clementina to limit her meaning, and Clementina went on. "He's changed all round now. He thinks it's all in the life. He says that in China they couldn't understand what he believed, but they could what he lived. And he knows I neva could be very religious."

It was in Miss Milray's heart to protest, "Clementina, I think you are one of the most religious persons I ever knew," but she forebore, because the praise seemed to her an invasion of Clementina's dignity. She merely said, "Well, I am glad he is one of those who grow more liberal as they grow older. That is a good sign for your happiness. But I dare say it's more of his happiness you think."

"Oh, I should like to be happy, too. There would be no sense in it if I wasn't."

"No, certainly not."

"Miss Milray," said Clementina, with a kind of abruptness, "do you eva hear anything from Dr. Welwright?"

"No! Why?" Miss Milray fastened her gaze vividly upon her.

"Oh, nothing. He wanted me to promise him, there in Venice, too."

"I didn't know it."

"Yes. But—I couldn't, then. And now—he's written to me. He wants me to let him come ova, and see me."

"And—and will you?" asked Miss Milray, rather breathlessly.

"I don't know. I don't know as I'd ought. I should like to see him, so as to be puffectly su'a. But if I let him come, and then didn't—It wouldn't be right! I always felt as if I'd ought to have seen then that he ca'ed for me, and stopped him; but I didn't. No, I didn't," she repeated, nervously. "I respected him, and I liked him; but I neva"—She stopped, and then she asked, "What do you think I'd ought to do, Miss Milray?"

Miss Milray hesitated. She was thinking superficially that she had never heard Clementina say had ought, so much, if ever before. Interiorly she was recurring to a sense of something like all this before, and to the feeling which she had then that Clementina was really cold-blooded and self-seeking. But she remembered that in her former decision, Clementina had finally acted from her heart and her conscience, and she rose from her suspicion with a rebound. She dismissed as unworthy of Clementina any theory which did not account for an ideal of scrupulous and unselfish justice in her.

"That is something that nobody can say but yourself, Clementina," she answered, gravely.

"Yes," sighed Clementina, "I presume that is so."

She rose, and took her little girl from Miss Milray's knee. "Say good-bye," she bade, looking tenderly down at her.

Miss Milray expected the child to put up her lips to be kissed. But she let go her mother's hand, took her tiny skirts between her finger-tips, and dropped a curtsey.

"You little witch!" cried Miss Milray. "I want a hug," and she crushed her to her breast, while the child twisted her face round and anxiously questioned her mother's for her approval. "Tell her it's all right, Clementina!" cried Miss Milray. "When she's as old as you were in Florence, I'm going to make you give her to me."

"Ah' you going back to Florence?" asked Clementina, provisionally.

"Oh, no! You can't go back to anything. That's what makes New York so impossible. I think we shall go to Los Angeles."

XL

On her way home Clementina met a man walking swiftly forward. A sort of impassioned abstraction expressed itself in his gait and bearing. They had both entered the shadow of the deep pine woods that flanked the way on either side, and the fallen needles helped with the velvety summer dust of the roadway to hush their steps from each other. She saw him far off, but he was not aware of her till she was quite near him.

"Oh!" he said, with a start. "You filled my mind so full that I couldn't have believed you were anywhere outside of it. I was coming to get you—I was coming to get my answer."

Gregory had grown distinctly older. Sickness and hardship had left traces in his wasted face, but the full beard he wore helped to give him an undue look of age.

"I don't know," said Clementina, slowly, "as I've got an answa fo' you, Mr. Gregory—yet."

"No answer is better that the one I am afraid of!"

"Oh, I'm not so sure of that," she said, with gentle perplexity, as she stood, holding the hand of her little girl, who stared shyly at the intense face of the man before her.

"I am," he retorted. "I have been thinking it all ever, Clementina. I've tried not to think selfishly about it, but I can't pretend that my wish isn't selfish. It is! I want you for myself, and because I've always wanted you, and not for any other reason. I never cared for any one but you in the way I cared for you, and —"

"Oh!" she grieved. "I never ca'ed at all for you after I saw him."

"I know it must be shocking to you; I haven't told you with any wretched hope that it would commend me to you!"

"I don't say it was so very bad," said Clementina, reflectively, "if it was something you couldn't help."

"It was something I couldn't help. Perhaps I didn't try."

"Did-she know it?"

"She knew it from the first; I told her before we were married."

Clementina drew back a little, insensibly pulling her child with her. "I don't believe I exactly like it."

"I knew you wouldn't! If I could have thought you would, I hope I shouldn't have wished—and feared—so much to tell you."

"Oh, I know you always wanted to do what you believed was right, Mr. Gregory," she answered. "But I haven't quite thought it out yet. You mustn't hurry me."

"No, no! Heaven forbid." He stood aside to let her pass.

"I was just going home," she added.

"May I go with you?"

"Yes, if you want to. I don't know but you betta; we might as well; I want to talk with you. Don't you think it's something we ought to talk about-sensibly?"

"Why, of course! And I shall try to be guided by you; I should always submit to be ruled by you, if—"

"That's not what I mean, exactly. I don't want to do the ruling. You don't undastand me."

"I'm afraid I don't," he assented, humbly.

"If you did, you wouldn't say that—so." He did not venture to make any answer, and they walked on without speaking, till she asked, "Did you know that Miss Milray was at the Middlemount?"

"Miss Milray! Of Florence?"

"With her brother. I didn't see him; Mrs. Milray is not he'a; they ah' divo'ced. Miss Milray used to be very nice to me in Florence. She isn't going back there any moa. She says you can't go back to anything. Do you think we can?"

She had left moments between her incoherent sentences where he might interrupt her if he would, but he waited for her question. "I hoped we might; but perhaps—"

"No, no. We couldn't. We couldn't go back to that night when you threw the slippas into the riva, no' to that time in Florence when we gave up, no' to that day in Venice when I had to tell you that I ca'ed moa fo' some one else. Don't you see?"

"Yes, I see," he said, in quick revulsion from the hope he had expressed. "The past is full of the pain and shame of my errors!"

"I don't want to go back to what's past, eitha," she reasoned, without gainsaying him.

She stopped again, as if that were all, and he asked, "Then is that my answer?"

"I don't believe that even in the otha wo'ld we shall want to go back to the past, much, do you?" she pursued, thoughtfully.

Once Gregory would have answered confidently; he even now checked an impulse to do so. "I don't know," he owned, meekly.

"I do like you, Mr. Gregory!" she relented, as if touched by his meekness, to the confession. "You know I do—moa than I ever expected to like anybody again. But it's not because I used to like you, or because I think you always acted nicely. I think it was cruel of you, if you ca'ed for me, to let me believe you didn't, afta that fust time. I can't eva think it wasn't, no matta why you did it."

"It was atrocious. I can see that now."

"I say it, because I shouldn't eva wish to say it again. I know that all the time you we'e betta than what you did, and I blame myself a good deal moa fo' not knowing when you came to Florence that I had begun to ca'e fo'some one else. But I did wait till I could see you again, so as to be su'a which I ca'ed for the most. I tried to be fai'a, before I told you that I wanted to be free. That is all," she said, gently, and Gregory perceived that the word was left definitely to him.

He could not take it till he had disciplined himself to accept unmurmuringly his sentence as he understood it. "At any rate," he began, "I can thank you for rating my motive above my conduct."

"Oh," she said. "I don't think either of us acted very well. I didn't know till aftawa'ds that I was glad to have you give up, the way you did in Florence. I was—bewild'ed. But I ought to have known, and I want you to undastand everything, now. I don't ca'e for you because I used to when I was almost a child, and I shouldn't want you to ca'e for me eitha, because you did then. That's why I wish you had neva felt that you had always ca'ed fo' me."

"Yes," said Gregory. He let fall his head in despair.

"That is what I mean," said Clementina. "If we ah' going to begin togetha, now, it's got to be as if we had neva begun before. And you mustn't think, or say, or look as if the'e had been anything in oua lives but ouaselves. Will you? Do you promise?" She stopped, and put her hand on his breast, and pushed against it with a nervous vehemence.

"No!" he said. "I don't promise, for I couldn't keep my promise. What you ask is impossible. The past is part of us; it can't be ignored any more than it can be destroyed. If we take each other, it must be for all that we have been as well as all that we are. If we haven't the courage for that we must part."

He dropped the little one's hand which he had been holding, and moved a few steps aside. "Don't!" she said. "They'll think I've made you," and he took the child's hand again.

They had emerged from the shadow of the woods, and come in sight of her father's house. Claxon was standing coatless before the door in full enjoyment of the late afternoon air; his wife beside him, at sight of Gregory, quelled a natural impulse to run round the corner of the house from the presence of strangers.

"I wonda what they'a sayin'," she fretted.

"It looks some as if she was sayin' yes," said Claxon, with an impersonal enjoyment of his conjecture. "I guess she saw he was bound not to take no for an answa."

"I don't know as I should like it very much," his wife relucted. "Clem's doin' very well, as it is. She no need to marry again."

"Oh, I guess it a'n't that altogetha. He's a good man." Claxon mused a moment upon the figures which had begun to advance again, with the little one between them, and then gave way in a burst of paternal pride, "And I don't know as I should blame him so very much for wantin' Clem. She always did want to be of moa use—But I guess she likes him too."